MW01518315

Lessons in *Letting Go*

CARA McKENNA

ELLORA'S CAVE
EXOTIKA™
www.EllorasCave.com

WILLING VICTIM

For the past couple years Laurel's been coasting, hiding in the backseat while her life drifts off course. Then one summer afternoon a tall, built bruiser named Flynn strides in and steers her straight into an infatuation she never saw coming.

Flynn introduces Laurel to things she's never imagined — to the violent but exciting realm of the underground boxing circuit, to rough sex and even rougher role-playing, and to an attraction she craves even as it intimidates her. As Flynn invites her deeper into his world and his life, Laurel has to make a choice — let fear keep her holed up where it's safe, or take a chance and fight for the man who makes her feel more alive than she'd dreamed possible.

CURIO

Caroly Evardt never expected to find herself patronizing a male prostitute. Then again, she never expected to be weeks from her thirtieth birthday and still a virgin.

When a friend mentions that a gorgeous male model in Paris sells his body as well as his image, Caroly's intrigued. Finally, a chance to sample the gifts of a beautiful man — no strings, no stakes, no fear of rejection.

But she soon discovers that Didier Pedra amounts to more than a striking face and talented body. He's a kind, charming, damaged man, and after a few evenings of pleasurable education, Caroly's interest blossoms into something far deeper than mere lust. Her simple arrangement is suddenly feeling downright dangerous...

An Ellora's Cave Publication

www.ellorascave.com

Lessons in Letting Go

ISBN 9781419965418
ALL RIGHTS RESERVED.
Willing Victim Copyright © 2010 Cara McKenna
Curio Copyright © 2011 Cara McKenna
Edited by Jaynie Ritchie and Kelli Collins.
Design and Photography by Syneca.
Model: Alex and Lisa.

Trade paperback publication 2011

LESSONS IN LETTING GO
Cara McKenna

ဆ

WILLING VICTIM
~9~

CURIO
~153~

WILING VICTIM

∽

Dedication

&⩩

For Editor-in-Chief Kelli Collins, who tactfully called me a "troublemaker" when I suspect she really meant "pain in the ass".

Author Note

&⩩

This story contains role-playing scenarios that may upset some readers. Although all of the sexual acts in this story are expressly 100-percent consensual, I strongly urge readers who are sensitive about rape — even in a simulated capacity — *not* to read this book.

Chapter One

ဆ

"Why you wanna lie to me?"

Laurel gritted her teeth, stared down at the book in her hands, the paragraph she'd been trying to read for the past five minutes. The afternoon had started out idyllic—a perfect July day in Boston, sunny with a cooling breeze, a prime, shaded bench all to herself off the waterfront's beaten tourist path. A pleasant escape from her un-air-conditioned apartment and the glares of her bar exam-obsessed roommate.

Then the couple had arrived.

They'd been arguing even before they'd taken up residence two benches down from Laurel. Young, probably early twenties, with accents that suggested both had grown up in the area. Every fifth word that left the man's mouth was a nasal "fuckin'". *Ya fuckin' mothah. Ya fuckin' sistah. My fuckin' douchebag boss.* Laurel sneaked a glance. The guy was white but dressed as though he'd prefer to be Puerto Rican like his girlfriend. That stereotyped look—baggy black jeans, pristine work boots, awful pencil-thin chinstrap facial hair and a white undershirt, which in this case looked as if it deserved the nasty nickname "wife beater". The girlfriend wore a similar top but her jeans were two sizes too small, the crazy-low-rise style girls constantly fussed with to keep their ass cracks from peeking.

Laurel tried her damnedest to block them out and focus on her book but it was like ignoring a wasp in her ear. The antagonism escalated.

"Don't you *call* me a liar," the girl shouted and stood, shouldering an elaborate gold purse.

The guy hopped theatrically to his feet. "Then don't lie to me."

The girl tried to argue back but he just kept chanting, "Don't lie to me. Don't lie to me. Don't lie to me," over and over, drowning her out. His tone was half threat, half jeer, and he came nearer with each repetition until their faces were frighteningly close.

"You need to back the fuck off," the girl said, holding her ground but looking rattled.

"An' you need to tell me the fuckin' truth."

Laurel's heart pounded. She wanted to find the balls to say something, to do the right thing, but she was afraid of the guy. He had a mean, dog-fight look about him and the fact he was posturing made him seem even more likely to snap. A walker entered her periphery and Laurel's cheeks burned, embarrassed to be here, acting as if she couldn't see what was going on. The walker, a middle-aged woman dressed for the office, gave them a wide berth, also pretending to ignore the fight.

The altercation paused until the woman had gone, then escalated.

"Why you foolin' with me?" the guy demanded, shaking his girlfriend by the shoulders.

Laurel's meekness dissolved. "Hey!"

The guy turned to give her a cursory study. "Mind your own fucking business."

"Don't touch her like that," Laurel said, hoping she sounded assertive, glad her voice wasn't as shaky as her hands.

The woman crossed her arms and cocked her head. "What d'you know about it, bitch?"

Oh awesome. Laurel gave them each a disgusted look and pretended to go back to her reading, praying she'd at least embarrassed or annoyed them enough to prompt a relocation. No such luck.

"I know you fucked him, so just admit to it."

"I didn't fuck nobody," the girl said.

Laurel's body buzzed, hot and chaotic. She felt powerless and pissed and worthless, probably just how this obnoxious girl felt.

"Fuckin' liar," the guy said.

Laurel heard the squeak of a sneaker and whipped her head around as the guy grasped his girlfriend by her fleshy upper arm, rough enough to bruise. Laurel grabbed her bag and fished for her phone, ready to announce her intentions to call the cops, but steps interrupted her—heavy, purposeful footfalls on the wooden walkway.

Laurel turned as a huge man passed in front of her, striding toward the fighting couple.

The girl said, "Holy shit," but her boyfriend had his back to the other man and didn't see it coming when a big hand closed around his neck, turned him and backed him up against the wall behind them.

The man dwarfed the young thug by a good six inches in height and fifty pounds of muscle. He was built and dressed like a construction worker—jeans, steel-toes, tee shirt, big arms smeared with gray dust. He held the guy against the bricks by the throat until the kid's face turned purple, ignoring the slaps and punches thrown at his arms.

"Let him go!" the girl said.

Laurel gaped.

The man gave the guy's neck one last squeeze, a motion that thumped the back of his head against the wall, then he released him and stepped away.

The guy doubled over a moment, coughing. His voice returned as a faint squeak. "What the fuck, dude?"

The construction worker took a few sideways steps in the direction he'd been heading, casting the kid and his girlfriend a warning squint. "Both of you, grow the fuck up and buy some pants that fit." With that, he turned and continued down the walkway.

Laurel shoved her book in her purse and went after him. At least fifty percent of the impulse was her desire to get the hell away from the couple.

She jogged to flank the man, having to crane her neck to meet his eyes. Six-three, she bet. "Hey."

"Can I help you?" His tone was tough to place— impatient or just no-nonsense. He had the accent and the look of textbook working-class Boston Irishness, as though he'd come from a long line of coal shovelers or bricklayers or cynics.

"No, I just thought that was awesome." Laurel offered a smile and took him in on a primitive level, registering a turn-on she'd never considered before—brutish, vigilante justice.

"Yeah, nothing more awesome than using violence to fight violence," the man said.

"He had it coming. And it was way more effective than when I tried to make them shut up."

His pace dropped to accommodate her shorter strides. His size gave Laurel a thrill, exacerbated by the leftover adrenaline of the fight. She glanced at his left hand—no ring and no pale strip of skin where a ring might live when he wasn't on the job.

"Are you on your lunch break?" Laurel asked, wondering who this bold woman was who'd taken over her mouth and body.

"Maybe." He glanced down at her again—hazel-blue eyes, wary in that standoffish New England way.

"Well," Laurel said, "can I buy you lunch?"

Eyebrows rose, brown like his short hair and sideburns and fresh stubble. "Why?"

"Why not?" She grinned at him, wondering if she looked warm and friendly or utterly psychotic.

"Good point. Yeah, okay." He turned them toward the financial district, up a set of steps and through the tidy alley beside the huge waterfront hotel.

There was something about him…not charisma. Energy. Laurel had hit an emotional wall in the last couple years and being so close to all that aliveness felt good. It felt magnetic, as if maybe she could siphon some of his fuel if she kept her body near enough to his. They strolled in silence a few blocks to a shabby but popular sandwich joint.

"Meatball sub," the man said, letting Laurel head to the back to order for them. She waited by the pick-up counter, stealing glances at the table her companion had snagged for them. He stared out the front window at the passing flow of pedestrians, looking sort of calm, sort of blank, big arms crossed over his chest. The clerk called their order and Laurel snapped out of her trance.

The restaurant was designed to feed people and get them back out the door—the tables were tall and there weren't any chairs, the idea being for customers to stand and for families with small children to find a different fucking place to eat. Laurel carried their sandwiches over, plus two coffees she'd ordered on impulse.

"Thanks," the man said but pushed his cup back across the table. "Don't drink caffeine."

"Oh. Here, mine's decaf." She slid him the other cup and he accepted it with a hesitant face. She'd regret the swap in a half hour when she felt edgy and restless, but she had an odd, ridiculous desire to please this man.

"I'm Laurel, by the way." She offered her hand. He shook it just how she knew he would, quick and firm. "That was awesome, what you did."

"So you said."

She swallowed and unwrapped her turkey sub, picking out the onions she'd specifically asked be left off. "Where are you working?"

"Congress Street. Other side," he added, waving a hand to mean across the bridge, probably in Fort Point, a hotbed of renovation and new construction. "Where do you work?" he asked.

"I have today off, but I work up the street. Near Faneuil." *In Faneuil,* she corrected to herself but didn't feel like telling such a manly spectacle of townie-ness that she pandered to tourists.

"Where're you from?" he asked through a mouthful of food.

Laurel found it charming. Having a man actively *not* try to hit on her was strangely alluring. "I grew up near Providence. I've been in and around Boston for…" She did the math. "God, eleven years. You must be from here."

"Oh?"

"Yup." She decided to flirt, even if it was doomed to be one-sided. "Say my name."

"What, Laurel?" *Larrul.*

She smiled.

He smiled back, tight but genuine. "Fine, busted."

"How can you work construction without any caffeine?" she asked, sipping her own watery coffee. "Don't you have to start work at like six a.m.?"

"Sometimes. But it makes me punchy."

The image of his hand around the other man's throat flashed across her mind. "I could see that."

He nodded, focused on his sandwich.

"Are you single?" Laurel nearly clapped a palm to her mouth, so shocked she'd asked that.

He raised his face to meet her eyes, chewed and swallowed before he spoke. "You asking me out?"

You'll never see him again in your life if he turns you down. Just say yes. "I don't know. How old are you?"

16

"Thirty-two," he said, one eyebrow raised.

"Yes, I'm asking you out then."

"Sorry, but I'll take a pass."

The reply stung her ego a moment but she shook it off. "Why not?"

"I'm not your type," he said and took another bite.

She smiled at him. "And how would you know my type?"

"I'm not any woman's type, practically. That's how I know."

"Are you gay? Wow, you had me fool—"

"Not gay. Just not a big hit with the ladies."

She squinted at him, intrigued. Either he was being serious or he subscribed to a complicated, psychological-warfare style of flirting. "Ex-con?"

He shook his head.

"Drug addict?"

He took a deep, demonstrative swallow of the decaf and Laurel figured a man who abstained from coffee was probably pretty clean.

"Asshole?" she guessed.

He nodded, brows rising again, false smile curling his lips.

"Well, I've gone out with plenty of assholes," Laurel said.

"Then I'm sure you've had your fill." He popped the last bite of his sub in his mouth and crumpled its wax paper, tossed it in a can by the door.

"Give me one good reason why not," she said.

"Redheads make me nervous."

Laurel ran a defensive hand over her ponytail. "It's not my natural—"

"Doesn't matter, and I'm just fuckin' with you... You don't like hearin' no, do you?" He smiled, genuine this time, and the gesture etched cracks all over his tough-guy veneer.

She smiled back.

"Fine." He tugged a napkin from the table's dispenser and Laurel dug a pen from her purse. He scribbled an address in South Boston. "Friday and Saturday nights, eight to one. Tell the guy working that Flynn invited you."

Laurel studied his slanted handwriting. "Okay," she said, wondering if all this newfound impulsivity would leave her by the weekend.

"If that doesn't scare you off," he said, "you can try askin' me out again."

"All right—"

"You take care now. Thanks for lunch." He forced another smile and turned away.

"Bye." He pushed the door open and she watched his broad back then grabbed her purse and hurried out. She kept a quarter block between them, trailing him back toward the waterfront. The businessmen who usually steamrolled everyone in their paths parted for him like fish avoiding a dolphin. Caffeine prickled in Laurel's blood and she decided she liked him, officially. She'd like to be seen with a tall, strong, self-proclaimed asshole, out at a bar. Or better yet, to be visited by him while she was working. She'd like all her coworkers to see him and maybe warn her that he was trouble. She entertained a teenagerish fantasy in which she was the only woman who understood him, the dewy-eyed lead in her own wrong-side-of-the-tracks, star-crossed-lovers musical. Which was idiotic given that she wasn't exactly an uptown princess.

She lost him as he crossed the street and she got stuck with a *don't walk* sign. He strode through the cavernous hotel archway, turning a corner on the other side and disappearing from sight. Laurel looked down at the napkin again, at her open invitation. She had to work Friday night, but Saturday she was off after four. Eight to one, he'd said, and she bet he was a bartender. Or else a very methodical drinker. Impatient pedestrians surged around her as the sign turned to *walk* and she joined the crush.

Flynn, she thought. She repeated the syllable a few times, guessing it was his last name. There were probably a thousand Flynns in South Boston. And by early Sunday morning she hoped to have a date with one of them.

Chapter Two

🙾

The nine bus rattled over the bridge as the sun disappeared beyond the buildings to the west. Laurel leaned against the window watching brick-lined blocks fly past between frequent stops. The robot voice announced Dorchester Street and she made her way to the front, thanked the driver and exited. Until the moment her feet hit the sidewalk, ushered her out of the dry, cold fridge of the bus and into the sticky July heat, she hadn't been nervous. Now everything changed. She was a short walk from that man, the one whose face she could only roughly conjure three days after their introduction. Her throat tightened and she knew if her nerves had kicked in before she boarded the bus she'd have never gotten this far.

Too close to pussy out now.

The city smelled tired and beat, as though it'd spent a long day toiling in the summer sun. Laurel walked a couple blocks and found the address Flynn had given her, a bar with absolutely no pretense. It was one of those one-story brick buildings that could've easily been a real estate office or a laundromat or the sort of law firm that advertised with an 888 number. The sign over the door simply said "Bar". The picture window showcased beer signs and the backsides of the drinkers who were leaning on the inside sill. Laurel took a deep breath and wrapped her fist around the door handle, not pulling yet. *Darts Night, Tuesdays, Nickel Wings from six to –*

She didn't get to finish reading the flier before the door swung open at her. She stepped back as two laughing men in Sox caps exited, oblivious or uncaring that they'd nearly knocked her down. They made a bee-line for the corner and dug packs of cigarettes from their back pockets. Laurel wasted a glare at them and yanked the door back open, greeted by near-deafening music.

The bar was steeped in a breed of nasty fragrance that'd gone unnoticed before the smoking ban drove its camouflage outdoors — restroom base with fry grease overtones. The dark space was filled close to capacity by bodies and loud, barking conversations. Laurel made her way around the venue, squeezing past a dozen sweatshirt-clad men, a few of whom gave her a cursory study. She didn't spot Flynn and bit her lip, feeling as if she'd made a mistake coming here. She threaded her way to the taps, dodging the gesticulations of beer-impassioned baseball enthusiasts.

The bar wasn't even made of real wood. Laurel leaned on the laminate and caught the eye of the bartender. He shouted over the music with all the charm of a carnie.

"Help you, Red?"

"I'm looking for Flynn," she shouted back.

He leaned over the counter and pointed into the chaos. "Unmarked door past the men's room. Make sure you close it behind you."

"Thanks." *Unmarked door?*

She stopped in the fluorescent-lit peace of the women's room to check her makeup and hair in the smoke-clouded mirror. None of the stall doors had working locks or toilet paper that wasn't trailing on the tile so she decided to skip a pit-stop until later, when she'd likely be drunk enough to lower her standards.

Beyond the restrooms was a short stretch of hallway with the promised plain door at the end. Laurel pushed it open, greeted by a new set of smells. She stepped onto a landing and pulled it shut, started down a flight of metal steps toward an open doorway. She left the piss and grease behind, slipping into a headier cocktail of perspiration and something else, something medicinal. The temperature rose even as she descended. The music faded, replaced by barking voices, weird sounds. Her mouth fell open as she turned a corner and entered an alternate reality.

What had been a basement at one point was a boxing arena now, its perimeter lit by dim red bulbs, bright white ones hanging above the ring. Far less crowded than the bar but still bustling with a few dozen people, mostly men. The fighters in the elevated square ring were carrying on a tired, shuffling dance, both looking exhausted, both dripping sweat. Laurel's fist tightened around her purse strap.

She jumped as a bell clanged. A pale, skinny teenager climbed up and over the ropes, grabbed one of the men's wrists and thrust it into the air. The victory was met by jeers, not claps, the crowd clearly thinking the performance had been subpar.

Laurel felt displaced beyond belief, the pheromones drifting through the heady atmosphere pricking up her senses and magnifying her nerves. She made a wide circle around the ring. Her heart thumped hard then froze.

The first thing she saw was Flynn's throat as he stretched his neck from side to side, tendons flashing, sweat slipping from his jaw to settle in the cradle at one end of his collarbone. He was bare to the waist, powerful muscles lit stark by the white light, sultry by the red. He looked both lean and heavy, raw and bruised and tattooed and feral. Muscles ticced and jumped in his arms as he stripped cotton bandaging off his wrists and tossed it in the trash basket behind him.

Laurel had no clue how to approach him but another girl beat her to it. Flynn looked up from rewrapping his hands as the woman stepped close, holding out a red plastic cup. He accepted it with a couple words and drank, Adam's apple bobbing with his swallows. He set it on the ground beside a towel and crossed his arms over his chest. The woman set her fingertips on his forearms, stroking his skin as she said something and smiled. He nodded and reached a hand out, cupping the back of the woman's head, leaning in and planting a gruff, possessive kiss on her mouth. She smiled and licked her lips as they separated, gave him a little wave and walked off.

Laurel's heart beat somewhere between hummingbird and jackhammer. She aimed a final look at Flynn, hating him and hating her body for wanting his so fiercely. She felt drunk from the atmosphere and her own chemical chaos as she strode to the corner where the woman was filling another red cup from a keg set on a folding table.

Laurel made a quick inventory of her clothes, carefully chosen that afternoon to appeal to the sort of man she'd guessed Flynn was. *Idiot.* But judging by this woman's similar ensemble, Laurel had gotten the dress code mainly right—jeans and ballet flats and a tank top, her rumpled hair strategically styled to look as though she'd rolled out of bed at noon. *Idiot, idiot, idiot.*

Laurel stepped forward, throat constricting anew. "Excuse me."

The woman straightened and smiled. "Hi. Beer?"

She blinked. "Um, sure."

The woman slid a cup off a tall stack beside the keg and filled it, handing it to Laurel.

"Thanks."

"This your first time here?" the woman asked, friendly, as though they were meeting at a mutual friend's baby shower. Her niceness made Laurel hate Flynn even more deeply.

"Do I look that out of place?"

The woman smiled again and nodded. "You do."

"I didn't know exactly what I was getting into when I agreed to come... What is this, exactly?" Laurel asked. "A fight club?"

"Yeah, I guess you'd say that. It's a gym by day, but it's definitely not in the phone book. Every weekend it's like open mic night for amateur fighters. And some not so amateur." The woman's eyes inventoried the room, hitting Flynn and a few other burly specimens.

"Do the people drinking upstairs know about it?" Laurel asked.

She shook her head. "Only the staff. I think that's why they keep the music so fucking loud, to cover up the sounds of ass-kicking. And I bet somebody gets wasted once in a while and wanders down here, looking for the can and getting a heck of a surprise."

Laurel nodded, swallowed the lump still lodged in her throat. She couldn't keep up the pretense of chit-chat any longer, not with this friendly woman. "Look, I'm sorry, this sort of isn't my business at all, but I thought you deserved to know…"

The woman's brows rose over the lip of the cup as she took a sip. "Know what?"

"I met him the other day." Laurel nodded to where Flynn leaned against the cinderblock wall, watching the match. "Flynn? He's the one who invited me… We sort of flirted a little and I asked him out. I'm sorry. I didn't know he had someone. He made it sound like he was single. I thought you should know."

The woman laughed, the skin beside her dark eyes crinkling and placing her age around thirty-five. "You're cute. Don't worry though, Flynn's not my boyfriend."

Laurel blinked, unsure what to do. So he wasn't a shady asshole…that was something. Not enough to salvage Laurel's hopes for the evening, but something.

"Flynn and I just sort of…scratch each other's kinky itches." She made a silly face. "Sorry if that's too much information. Anyhow, it's just casual."

Laurel smiled to hide her deepening discomfort. She drank her beer and both women turned to watch the fight.

At length, Laurel found the balls to ask, "What kind of itch?" The warm buzz of the alcohol and the intoxicating, masculine smell of the place made their conversation seem strangely appropriate. Or nearly. "Oh sorry. I'm Laurel, by the way."

The woman accepted the hand Laurel put out. "Pam. And Flynn's just willing to go places with me that other guys won't. Sort of rough places. Well, really rough places."

"I see."

"He's not afraid to be a bad person," Pam said. "In bed."

"I'll bet." Laurel watched him warming up, throwing punches at the air as his eyes followed the fight center stage. His abs and chest tightened with each invisible strike, making Laurel imagine him above her in bed, thrusting. She didn't hate him anymore, nor her body's craving for his, but knowing he had a lover and a set of sexual proclivities she didn't share weighed the attraction down. He'd warned her, so no harm no foul. Laurel decided if she wasn't destined to score a date tonight, she'd at least make the most of the trip and indulge in a little tourism, explore this strange, violent microcosm she'd stumbled into.

"Flynn looks like one of the bigger guys," Laurel said. "Is he good?"

"Yeah, he is. So good he's probably bored."

She and Pam wandered closer to the ring to make room for the queue forming by the keg.

"Why do you think he does it then?" Laurel asked. "Money?"

Pam shrugged. "No money, except maybe a few shady bets in the corners. You'd have to know Flynn to get it. He likes hitting. He likes getting hit too, I think. He's a bit of a thug," she added with a fond smile.

"In and out of bed, it sounds like," Laurel said. Not that it was necessarily a criticism.

Pam shrugged again. "What I told you, about him sexually…don't jump to condemn him or anything. He's actually really kind."

25

Laurel frowned, not sure she was looking to get pushed around under the sheets, supposed kindness aside. She let herself process a hunk of disappointment, sad that her ridiculous impulse to have a fling with the man wasn't going to pan out. So much for her brief foray into adventurousness.

"It doesn't make him a bad person," Pam said, seeming to study Laurel's expression. "He gets off on being rough and domineering and cruel, but it's not who he *is*." Her eyes moved to the ring. "Just like me wanting to pretend a man is forcing me once in a while doesn't mean I secretly think I deserve to get raped or that I'd ever in a million years *want* to be. It's all about control—having it or giving it up. It's really freeing, when it's your thing." Pam's therapist-office tone made it clear she'd had to explain this to a few skeptics in her time.

"I'm afraid it's not *my* thing." Laurel took a couple sips, studying the man who made her body so antsy with curiosity, sad she couldn't get on board with his kinks. Though thank goodness she hadn't found out the hard way.

Pam licked her lips, mischievous. "You sure? Anybody can see how you look at him. There might be some tiny sliver of your animal self that's just a little bit attracted to that. Our bodies can hone in on those things. You can't always choose who turns your crank."

"I don't think I'd ever want to pretend I was being…forced. No offense to you, I mean. It just sounds really creepy."

"It's not always that intense," Pam said. "Sometimes just being bossed around is enough."

A flare of collective noise filled the air as one of the boxers took a hard hook to the head.

"Think about it," Pam said.

Laurel jolted as the bell rang and fighters fell back, looking limp and exhausted. The ref called a winner and the crowd cheered and booed its agreement or dissent.

"Flynn's next," Pam said. "Watch him and try to let yourself relax and think about what it is you find so attractive about him."

Laurel's eyes took him in again. She swallowed. "I'm going to grab another beer. Do you want one?"

"Yeah, I'd love that."

Laurel returned with two fresh cups just as Flynn and another man climbed into the ring, donning their gloves and game faces, looking impossibly tall from where Laurel stood. Flynn wore low-slung track pants that showcased the sinful V of his hip muscles and tight expanse of his abdomen. Laurel wanted to tug them down an inch, enough to expose the dark hair she imagined must be hiding just behind the waistband. His eyes were at once calculating and wild, an image of his face in the throes of excitement flashed like a dirty movie across her mind—a meanness in that stare, a cruel sneer on his lips, a flare of his nostrils, a heaviness in his lids as he gave himself over to the dark things he craved. Her throat went dry as chalk.

Flynn's opponent was a black guy, nearly as tall as him and maybe a dozen pounds bulkier.

"Corners," the young ref said and the men tapped gloves before Flynn stepped to one side, facing away from Laurel. He had a fierce back, two strong muscles pinched together between his shoulder blades, his shoulders rounded swells above cut arms.

The bell sounded. Not men anymore. Animals. Circling, anticipating, sizing one another up and sniffing for weaknesses. Laurel's focus glazed over as she imagined those strong arms braced on either side of her ribs, tight, that powerful chest and stomach clenching with rough, selfish thrusts.

Pam nudged her softly with an elbow. "Still not curious?"

She kept her eyes on the fight, in awe of the cold look on Flynn's face. "There's something about it, I know. But it still scares me, the stuff you said he's into."

"I'm sure he'd let you watch."

"Watch what?" Laurel asked, glancing sideways.

Pam shrugged. "Us. Me and him. Tonight, after the matches are over. I'm going home with him. You're more than welcome to come and see what it's all about."

Dear God. Laurel studied Pam's face, so blasé considering what she'd just offered. "I don't know. That sounds, like, *intensely* private and...intense."

"You might be surprised how much easier it is to explore things with strangers."

Laurel took a deep drink. "I appreciate your insanely generous offer, but I don't think I'm looking to do any exploring. I'd feel like the weird, disapproving prude in the corner."

Pam shrugged. "We could ignore you. And you could leave anytime you needed to. I know it sounds counterintuitive, but it's a safe place to be. He knows what women need. He's sensitive that way. He can tell like *that*," she snapped her fingers, "when a woman's not into it anymore. He can with me, anyhow. He knows before I do if a line's about to get crossed."

Laurel didn't reply. Her attention was glued on the match, on Flynn. "Jesus," she muttered a minute later. "His body is fucking astounding."

"You want to *really* see that man working, think about what I offered."

A chance to watch that body, doing what it was surely designed to do...the temptation clenched Laurel's pussy and stopped her breath. Up in the ring, the violence escalated. Flynn and the black guy were trading jabs and blocks, seeming evenly matched. Laurel's curiosity landed a hit of its own, knocking her fear to the mat momentarily.

"What's it like?" she asked, keeping her voice low. "Are there handcuffs and ropes and that stuff? Like gags and blindfolds?"

"Sometimes he ties me down," Pam said, "but not always. Sometimes he just holds me with his hands or pins me with his body. I don't like blindfolds usually. I like watching him." She smiled, looking sheepish. "And he's not really into all the accessories and things. Like, his apartment looks like an apartment, not a torture chamber."

"How long have you two been lovers?"

"A few months."

"When you first started...hanging out, I guess...was it like instantly hot and mind-blowing?" Laurel asked. A scary-loud whack drew her eyes to the match. It looked as if Flynn had just taken a hit to the ear. She glanced back at Pam. "Did you know right away that role-playing that sort of stuff was like, your thing?"

"*He* knew, I think, like right away. But we didn't go nuts the very first time. When we started, it was mostly just rough sex. Then we moved to him holding me down, then him holding me and me struggling, and then, you know, further. It's like a pool. There's a shallow end. Or you can just sit by the side in a lounge chair and watch."

Laurel turned to the action just as the black guy caught Flynn hard in the jaw, stunned him a moment and pushed him back, the top rope dragging along Flynn's upper back. The ref shouted and the black guy eased off. Flynn got back to standing, a red stripe branded across his shoulders from the friction. Laurel sucked in an empathetic breath.

The fight broke up between rounds, the men heading to opposite corners where they were handed cups of water. Or possibly beer. Laurel guessed a person would have to be drunk to volunteer for this kind of punishing exhibitionism.

Flynn fought differently the next time the bell clanged. He blocked twice as many strikes as before and landed more of his own—sharp, taunting punches designed to infuriate, not incapacitate. By the end of the three-minute round Flynn had taken only a swing to the neck and a couple ineffective jabs. The round wrapped and Pam jogged over to be the one who handed him his water. Laurel saw her touching his knee as he drank and offering a few encouraging-looking words before she returned to Laurel.

"Still enjoying yourself?"

"It *is* sort of…freakishly manly," Laurel offered, swirling her beer in its cup. "I'll give you that."

The bell rang to start the final round and it went nothing like the first two. Flynn came out on the offensive and didn't let up. His punches were loud, gloves on skin making this sound like what it was—fists pounding meat. The black guy landed a couple decent shots but Flynn didn't seem to register them. He wailed on his opponent until a nasty right hook caught the guy in the jaw and landed him on the mat. He didn't get up fast enough and the bell sounded, ending the fight after only a minute's action.

The teenaged ref climbed up and over the ropes, one sneaker sliding on sweat. He righted himself as the black guy made it to kneeling. Flynn's face was blank as the kid thrust his fist into the air, announcing the match's obvious winner. He received somber applause, the sound of undeniable respect tempered by a dozen grudges. He stripped off his gloves and climbed out of the ring, headed to his spot by the wall. A couple men clapped him on the back as he passed but he didn't seem to notice. The black guy clamored over the ropes with some difficulty and a friend helped him to the concrete floor. He walked to the other side of the basement, rattling a body-sized punching bag with a vicious swing, pissed to high heaven.

Laurel looked back at Flynn just as he looked to her. His eyes held hers a long moment, too significant for her to pretend she didn't understand the invitation. She huffed out her fear and rounded the crowd to approach the victor. A nasty purple bruise ringed his eye and he was peppered with other little cuts and marks Laurel had missed in the dim lighting.

"Hey," she said.

"Hey yourself, sub shop girl. Took me a minute to remember why I recognized you." He stooped to grab a tube of ointment and squeezed a measure across his fingers, releasing a concentrated whiff of that medicinal smell that permeated the gym. Laurel watched his arm muscles twitch as he rubbed it into the long scrape along the backs of his shoulders. Her skin flushed as she remembered how those arms had thrilled and frightened her when he'd been fighting. Knowing she'd see that again soon.

"That was...something," Laurel said.

"Oh good." Flynn stretched his neck. "I always strive to be something."

"You okay?" she asked. "You've got blood on you."

"Mine or his?"

"I'm not sure. Plus this." She touched her fingers to the now greasy scrape along his back. His skin felt scalding hot and he didn't flinch.

"Just rope burn." He recapped the tube and tossed it to the ground.

"And a black eye."

"That's from yesterday. See you been talking to Pam. She scare you off yet?"

"No, she said only nice things about you. She...she invited me along. For after the fight."

His face was impassive. "Did she then?"

"Yeah."

"You looking for me to second that invite?" he asked, raising an eyebrow.

"I don't know. Are you okay with that, though? If I wanted to?"

He thought for a long moment, unfocused eyes staring past Laurel's face. "Up to her. But forgive me if I search you for hidden cameras if you decide to tag along."

Laurel wasn't sure if the remark was serious or not and chose to ignore it. "I don't know what I'll decide. It sounds really...personal."

"It's up to you girls," he said and wiped his hand on a rag then ran it over his sweat-matted hair. "I'm just a willing body."

"She made it sound like you're more than that," Laurel said, voice low.

"She makes me out like a saint sometimes. Patron-fucking-saint of the masochists. You can make up your own mind about it if you come along."

"What time are you guys leaving?"

"I got one more fight coming up. We'll probably head out in an hour, hour and a half."

"Can I get you a beer or something?" Laurel asked. "Or is drinking during a fight a no-no?"

"I don't drink, period," Flynn said, "but you can find me a glass of water if you're itching to be useful."

She nodded and wandered away, found a water cooler and filled a plastic cup for him. She handed it over, wanting to do more...wanting to press a towel to his sweaty skin and clean his cuts and ice his bruises. She felt a strange desire to *care* for him, to apply feminine affection and counteract all the masculine damage. She stared at the black and gray tattoo that spanned his chest, a design that might translate nicely into the leading for a stained-glass window—a medieval-looking scene with a winged man in robes skewering a pointy-tailed creature with some kind of sword. Latin words in calligraphic script arched above it. *Quis ut Deus.*

Flynn swallowed the last of the water and looked down at her. "What goes on between me and her, it's not pretty. If you can't stand lookin' at a little rope burn, you probably won't enjoy yourself."

"Do you hurt her?"

He made a gesture, something between a shrug and another neck stretch. "Neither me or her would say I do, but it's rough."

"From what she's explained about it, I'm curious." *And tipsy enough to admit it.*

"Curious is all well and good but I don't know you. And neither does she. If you freak out and go screaming about it all over town or the fucking internet, you could seriously fuck with the lives of two consenting adults. You follow?"

"I'm not a psycho," Laurel said.

"Good. I don't have much of an upstanding reputation to protect, but Pam's a decent girl. I'd be royally pissed if anybody ever messed her around."

Laurel pursed her lips. "Are you threatening me?"

"I never threaten a woman unless she begs me to." His smile came slow and sticky, dripping with put-on sweetness.

"Well I promise I have no intention of outing either of you. Asking to come along for the ride isn't something I'm all that eager to shout from the rooftops, you know."

"You asking to come along then?" That smile again, more dangerous than his arms or knuckles or threats.

She nodded and swallowed, wondering what the hell she'd just signed up for.

* * * * *

At a quarter to one, Laurel snapped to lucidity. Four hours of fighting and a steady infusion of beer had numbed her senses, though she snapped to attention when Flynn took to the ring. His final fight was much like the earlier one, starting out seemingly well-matched but ending in a near

33

knockout. She watched him pull on a tee shirt and toss a bunch of things into a gym bag.

Laurel balanced her plastic cup on top of an overflowing trash bin and approached where he stood, Pam by his side.

Flynn met Laurel's eyes as she neared. "Still here then, sub shop girl?"

"Looks like it."

Flynn nodded and Pam smiled and they headed for a door at the opposite end of the basement from where Laurel had entered. They walked down a couple poorly lit hallways and up a long set of stairs, emerging in an alley behind the bar. After hours in the heady, sultry sauna of the gym, the city's thick summer heat managed to feel refreshing.

They squeezed passed a Dumpster and a couple parked cars in the alley, out of the dark and onto the sidewalk. Flynn led the way, leading them down side streets for a few blocks.

They stopped at the entrance to a hulking brick building—one of the city's many repurposed factories, though this one wasn't ritzy like the slick new condos popping up like dandelions all over Boston and Cambridge. Flynn unclipped a noisy ring of keys from his belt and unlocked the front door, nondescript except for a stick-on aluminum street number. They entered a plain foyer and Flynn strode to the elevator panel to punch the up button.

"What did this place used to be?" Laurel asked, running a hand over the brick and studying the ancient framed picture hung on one wall—a photo of the building from over a century before, carriages passing on the street in the foreground.

"Molasses factory."

Laurel studied Flynn's sour expression, the dark bruise rising along his jaw to match the one ringing his left eye. The ding of the arriving elevator triggered a mental image of him stripped to the waist in the ring.

They stepped into the car and he hit the buttons for the second and fifth floors. The doors closed then eased open at two and he said, "Hold it." Pam leaned an arm in the threshold and Flynn jogged down the hall to the right. Laurel heard him knock three times then he jogged back.

"What was that about?" Laurel asked as the doors slid shut behind him.

"My sister," he said. "She's kind of a basket case on fight nights. Likes to know when I get home in one piece."

"You guys live in the same building? You must be close."

"Yeah," he said. "You could say that."

The bell sounded again as the elevator opened onto the fifth-floor foyer and Flynn led them down the corridor to the very end. He unlocked his door and they stepped inside and he eased the dimmer up on a set of bulbs that hung from the high ceiling. He and Pam dumped their bags on a loveseat that seemed to be there for that purpose, but Laurel held on to her purse, as though it might save her from drowning. The door clicked shut behind her.

She took in the large, open loft space, galley kitchen along the far wall, three towering, arched factory windows offering a view of similar buildings and a sliver of white moon. Exposed pipes and vents crisscrossed the ceiling, making the apartment feel industrial and stark. A couple couches and an easy chair were clustered in one corner around a coffee table. A bicycle, purple with silver Mylar streamers, was propped on its kickstand below one tall window, an open toolbox beside it. Laurel raised her eyebrows.

Flynn clapped her hard on the arm as he passed, heading for the kitchen area. "Don't you go searching for kinks where there aren't any. I got a six-year-old niece."

The apartment was divided by a makeshift wall, a heavy curtain hung from a runner built into the ceiling creating a C shape with the entryway on one side, the kitchen, living area and sleeping area on the other. Flynn's generous bed was against the back wall, a navy comforter tossed across it in a middling attempt at tidiness. Skinny shelves stood to either

35

side and along the wall above the headboard, filled with books and CDs.

"Have a seat." He waved a hand toward the couches. "Bathroom's there," he said, pointing to a door next to the kitchen area. "We're gonna ignore you from here on out. You need to leave, you know where the exit is." He turned to where Pam sat on the couch unlacing her tall, shit-kicking boots. "You want me to shower first?" he asked her.

She grinned. "Not a chance."

He nodded. He went to the front of the apartment and flipped off the lamps so only the dim, sickly glow leaking in from the city illuminated the room. The orange streetlight exacerbated everything industrial and ominous about Flynn's home, made the space feel at once hidden and exposed.

Laurel took a seat on an easy chair, not sinking in but perching on the edge as her eyes adjusted, still clutching her purse for dear life. Pam drank a glass of water at the counter while Flynn sat on the mattress and took his shoes off. Laurel wondered how he had the energy to do *anything* after what she'd witnessed at the gym.

Pam set her glass in the sink. Flynn stood as she approached, looking twice as dangerous now in the shadowy privacy of the space.

Laurel saw his expression shift, eyes narrowing, features hardening. He reached out and clasped Pam's jaw in both hands, thumbs digging into her cheeks. The kiss that followed was less a show of affection than of dominance and ownership. He pressed into her, chest to chest, forcing her backward until she dropped onto the bed. Laurel felt the cushion under her own butt, imagined it was the mattress, that she was the one at the center of Flynn's attention.

"Strip," he said, cold. In her head it was Laurel who peeled her clothes away, skin bared to the humidity and this man's hungry stare. He stepped back a couple paces. "On your knees."

Laurel sucked in her breath, yanked back into her own body for a moment. This was actually happening. A part of her screamed that this was wrong—chauvinistic and cruel. Another part wanted to see him served, wanted to be the one at the mercy of his selfish demands.

Pam knelt before him on the floor and Laurel rubbed her own knees, wishing for the rude bite of hardwood boards beneath them.

"Get me hard, girl."

"Yes, Sir." It was Pam who reached out to unbuckle his belt, but Laurel could practically feel the cool metal releasing in her hands, feel the excitement as she unzipped Flynn's jeans.

"Take it out," he commanded.

She tugged his pants and shorts down a few inches to expose his cock. She stroked him, the gesture worshipful, just how Laurel felt. She got him stiff, made him long and thick and ready. Her lips parted, anticipating, and Laurel's own mouth watered.

Flynn voice came, low. "It's been a whole week. You been missing this?"

"Yes, Sir."

"Tell me."

"I've missed your dick."

Flynn's eyes flashed across the room, right into Laurel's. He held them for just a moment then addressed Pam. "You look hungry, girl."

Laurel swallowed, watching her small hand running up and down his heavy-looking cock. She conjured heat off his skin, the stiffness of him in her hand.

"Suck it," Flynn ordered. As her face lowered he tugged the elastic from her long ponytail and wrapped a hand in her hair, yanking her closer. "Suck it."

"Yes, Sir." Her mouth closed around his head, hand still stroking. Laurel could see from her hollowed cheeks how hard she was sucking, could feel that aggression building in her own body. Flynn sniffed in a harsh breath and a vein rose along his neck.

"Good. Make it nice and wet."

She drew him out and ran her tongue up and down the length of his shaft, bathing him in her spit.

"That's right...now more."

His hand set the pace, drawing her mouth down his dick in slow, deep swallows. Laurel suppressed a moan to match Pam's, pushed a rough hand through her hair, wondering how it would feel to be held that way.

More, she thought. Desire and fear hummed in her pulse and her cunt clenched painfully tight, impatient.

"More," Flynn commanded. His other hand cupped Pam's head, pulling her closer as his hips began to pump. In seconds he had her taking all of him, her lips meeting his base with each thrust. Laurel's neck and face heated, her hands damp as she imagined holding Flynn's sides, feeling the flex of muscle and bone beneath his jeans.

"Good girl. I wanna see you choke on that cock."

More, Laurel thought again. She watched and felt Flynn bury every last inch, shut her eyes and clawed her nails against her own thighs, what she'd be doing to him if she were the one on her knees.

Flynn's arousal began to overshadow his callous self-control—Laurel heard it as his breaths turned raspy. She opened her eyes, frozen as she found his trained right on her face.

He looked back down at Pam, tugged the bottom of his shirt up, giving himself a clear view of her mouth and giving Laurel a spectacular look at his fierce stomach muscles. "That's it. Keep that up. Keep that up and I'll fuck your pussy so hard you'll be begging me to stop."

In her imagination Laurel gave him all this pleasure, sucked him until his composure waned. Even in the dim light she caught his cheeks and neck and ears darken, saw the faint trembling of his arms and shoulders.

"Good," he said. "Good." He slowed her head, made the thrusts shallow then pulled his cock from her mouth. He stroked his head across Pam's lips a few times and Laurel could swear she tasted him on her own tongue.

"You love that cock, don't you?"

Yes.

"Yes, Sir." Pam lapped at his head, kissed the swollen skin.

"You wanna drink my come later, sweetheart?"

She gave voice to the thirsty noise Laurel ached to, lavishing more wet caresses on his dick.

"Good... You give me what I like and I'll reward you with a mouthful."

Laurel nodded, parched for it herself.

"Turn around," he said. "Hands and knees."

Pam shuffled in place and put her palms to the floor. Laurel felt the grit under her palms, Flynn's eyes on her back. He shed his shirt and dropped his jeans and shorts and socks, walked to a shelf. Laurel heard a box being opened, a wrapper crinkling. Flynn turned back, rolling the condom down his erection. There was a stern placidity to his face, that same look Laurel had seen him wear just before the bell rang to start a fight.

He dropped to his knees behind Pam, their bodies in profile to Laurel. He glanced to Laurel and all at once it was her before him, dying to be taken, all that heat coming off his body making her woozy.

"Eyes on the floor," he ordered.

For a second Laurel obeyed, forgetting who she was in all this. As she raised her head she saw Flynn gripping his cock in one hand, the other teasing Pam's pussy.

"Nice," he breathed. "You're always ready for me, aren't you?"

"Yes."

"Yeah." He angled his cock to her, pushing in. He made a sound of bone-deep satisfaction. Pam made a different noise—a sharp intake of breath followed by a sigh and his hips set a rhythm, slow and steady.

"You been thinking about this all week?" he asked.

Fuck yes.

"Yes."

"Yes, what?" he demanded.

"Yes, Sir."

Laurel saw his fingers dig harder into Pam's ass as he fucked deeper, his thrusts echoing through her body, through Laurel's. She watched his driving cock, knowing just how it must feel, all that hot, thick flesh taking what it wanted in greedy strokes.

"Good girl," he murmured, and Laurel blushed from the praise, needing it to be for her. He fucked, steady and calm, for several minutes. Then one palm slid up from Pam's ass to the small of her back, the gesture oozing with possession. He sped up, pumping deep and fast and selfish. "Lower," he said, a new meanness in his voice.

She obeyed, moving onto her elbows, hair pooling on the floor like a curtain and hiding her face.

"Lower."

She dropped to one shoulder, then the other, face and neck turned awkwardly to one side. Laurel imagined it, letting her discomfort be Flynn's pleasure. Pam slid her arms to her sides and he took her wrists, crossing them behind her back and pinning them with one big hand. Laurel held her breath, grasped her own wrist, disturbed and turned on and concerned and *hungry*.

"You want this?" This time Laurel knew the question was meant for her. She held her tongue, letting Pam speak for the both of them.

"No," she said, almost too faint to make out.

Flynn turned to Laurel, expression cold as he nodded, the exact moment the play shifted from rough to far rougher.

He grunted in time with his hard thrusts, his free hand running up and down Pam's thigh. He brought it down on her ass with a harsh slap and she cried out just as Laurel gasped. Chemicals released into her bloodstream, the same confusing mix of adrenaline and shameful intoxication as when she watched a rape scene in a movie. In both cases, no one was really being violated, but she felt that same hot guilt she had her whole life, finding the visual powerful and horrifying but undeniably arousing.

"You like that?" Flynn asked, sneering, body hammering Pam's.

Fuck yes.

"No. Stop."

Flynn laughed, sharp and cold and his eyes darted to Laurel. "I saw the way you watched me tonight." He looked back to Pam. "You were dying for this cock, weren't you?" He pounded her fast, hips slapping her ass for a handful of violent beats.

"Stop. Please, stop."

"You think I can't feel how wet you are for me?" His body slowed, drawing his cock out, easing it back in, controlled and explicit and mocking.

"Don't, please."

"Shut your mouth, bitch. Shut up and get fucked."

"No—" Her protest was cut off by another hard smack of Flynn's palm on her hip.

"Shut your mouth."

Laurel gulped for air, lightheaded and breathless, assaulted by a hundred conflicting emotions. Her awareness flashed in and out of the scene, torn between red-hot curiosity and icy fear. Part of her wanted to run for the door, but she remembered everything she'd been told at the fights, about how women came to Flynn specifically for this treatment. There was consent, a core of respect buried inside the cruelty.

She watched Pam's arms jerk uselessly in Flynn's grip.

"Go on," he said. "Struggle all you want. Just gets me hotter when you fight it." With that, he let her hands go. He pulled out long enough to turn her roughly onto her back before grabbing her wrists again, pinning them to the floor as he shoved his thighs between hers. Even in the dim light, even with her black hair strung across her mouth and her face set in a fearful grimace, Pam looked unmistakably aroused. Her eyes blazed up at Flynn's as she flailed her legs, kneeing his ribs as he tried to get his cock back inside her. Laurel felt her own arousal return threefold, felt the floor under her spine and Flynn's weight against her pinned hips.

"Hold still, bitch." He flinched as Pam spat at him and Laurel saw his eyes narrow as though they were mere inches above hers. "You'll fucking pay for that."

Pam gasped and jerked and Laurel imagined his penetration between her own legs, mean and merciless.

"Yeah, that's what you get." He found a rhythm, graceless now, working against her thrashing body. "Harder you struggle, the harder I fuck you," he warned. "Open your mouth."

She bucked and spat again.

"Don't piss me off," Flynn said. He yanked at her wrist, making her back arch, making Laurel's ache alongside it. "Do what I say or I'm gonna get mean."

She twisted under his hold and he yanked again and this time her body quieted.

"Better," he said. "Now open that mouth."

Both women parted their lips as Flynn lowered to kiss Pam, violent, hips still pounding. For a moment Laurel could feel his firm, wet tongue taking her mouth, then he jerked away with a gruff noise, released her wrist to touch his fingers to his mouth.

"Fucking bitch."

Laurel watched Pam slap uselessly at his slick chest and stomach with her freed hand as he wiped the blood from his bitten lip. Flynn squinted down at his victim, hips going still, his face full of hatred so cold it made Laurel shiver from ten feet away. Without warning, he jammed his blood-streaked fingers into Pam's mouth before moving the hand to her throat, pushing her head against the floor. Her assaulting hand froze between them.

Laurel froze too, body so tight with arousal and adrenaline she felt faint. She tasted copper in her mouth and her throat closed up.

Flynn's next words came slow and dark and dangerous. "Now you're going to do what I say. You understand?"

Pam made a noise, strained but coherent enough to tell Laurel she could breathe just fine, that Flynn wasn't actually choking her.

"Right. Now you be a good girl and reach that hand down and touch yourself." When she didn't respond he seemed to tighten his hold on her neck. "*Now.*"

She obeyed, snaking her hand between their bodies to finger her clit. Laurel ached to do the same, her pussy begging for it. She held back, reminded herself of her role and made her obedience into an unspoken order from Flynn.

"Good." He moved his choking hand to the floor by Pam's shoulder. "Now you make yourself come, bitch. And I'll know if you're faking. You make that cunt clench around my cock or I swear to God I'll make you regret it."

Words gave way to moans and grunts as both bodies turned frantic. Laurel smelled the heady mix of sweat and sex and latex, felt the heat peeling off them against her own dampening skin. Her eyes drank in every shape of Flynn's powerful body as it twitched and tightened, his thrusts looking punishing, the brutality real. Her cunt was screaming to experience him, throbbing deep and hot with curiosity.

Pam came apart. Her breathy grunts matched Flynn's harsh ones and her legs came up, knees at his waist, inviting him deeper. He let her pinned hand go and she moved it to her chest to palm her breasts and tweak her nipples. Laurel's fingers twitched, dying to do the same.

They fucked like nothing she'd ever seen in a porno—technically missionary, technically vanilla, but the intensity between them was incredible, palpable, crackling with electricity. All at once that energy was rerouted, shot straight across the room between Flynn's eyes and Laurel's and she felt him, all the aggression and strength of his body pummeling hers.

Pam groaned beneath him, head turning to the side as the hand stroking her breasts lost coordination.

"Good girl. Come all over that hard cock." Flynn froze, pushed deep inside.

Pam cried out, raked his back as she climaxed. Laurel's mind swam for a second, lost in the details of Flynn—his sweat-damp hair, muscles gleaming in the city's ambient glow. She breathed in his smell, feasted on his body. She wanted him more violently than anything she could recall, as though the need in her were blinding pain and the only thing that could take it away was Flynn.

"That's right," he whispered, hips giving a few gentle pumps as Pam calmed. "That's right. Good girl." He leaned in, kissed her forehead, the gesture sending an odd ripple through Laurel, seeming twice as graphic and raw as any other intimate contact she'd witnessed in the last ten minutes.

Flynn pulled out and got to his feet as Pam made it unsteadily to her knees. She reached out to unroll the condom from his cock, set it aside and stroked his hard flesh. Laurel imagined him in her palm. His balls looked tight and high, telling her how close he must be. His hand took over after a minute, jerking fast and rough, and Laurel felt each bump of his head against Pam's lips. She felt his skin under her nails as Pam dug her fingers into his thighs, saw his need as her eyes stared up at his face.

"Here I come, sweetheart. Open up wide for me."

Laurel ached to see him come but Pam's mouth closed over his head, keeping the moment private, forcing her out of all this borrowed intimacy. She had to be satisfied watching his clenching ass and his tight fist as his hand slowed, listening to his rumbling moan as he released. She saw Pam swallow what he gave her, caught her breath as his gaze jumped to her face for the briefest moment.

"C'mon." He put a hand out and helped her to standing. "Go get cleaned up."

Pam disappeared inside the bathroom, closing the door to block out the light and the whir of the fan. Laurel's stomach dropped and she wondered if she was supposed to go now. She bit her lip and watched Flynn tug on his jeans and buckle his belt. The shower hissed on behind the bathroom door.

Flynn turned to her, still barefoot and stripped to the waist and looking just as dangerous as he did in the ring.

"Still here, huh?"

Laurel tried to keep her eyes on his face, off his gleaming stomach, tried to keep her awareness on the words and off her pleading cunt. "Looks like it."

Flynn nodded and pulled his shirt on as the water shut off on the shower. He gathered Pam's clothes, knocked on the bathroom door. A hand emerged to accept them with a thank-you.

Laurel got up, stepping to the windows to peer at the empty street five stories down.

"You dawdling?" Flynn asked. When she turned to try to come up with a pithy answer she found him smiling at her, thumbs tucked into his pockets.

"It's okay," he said. "You probably got some questions. Run away if you want though."

She opened her mouth to speak just as Pam opened the bathroom door, flipping off the light and fan to emerge fully dressed. She looked different with her hair wet, bangs off her face, eyeliner and dark lipstick gone—vulnerable and heartbreakingly human. She turned to Laurel, her voice softer than it had been all evening.

"Did you like it?"

Laurel pursed her lips a moment and nodded. "Yeah. Thanks for inviting me." She turned to Flynn and held his eyes to tell him the thanks were meant for both of them.

"You need an escort to your car?" he asked Pam.

"No, I'm just across the way."

"I'll watch from the window," he said. "Go on, it's late."

She gave him a last look then turned to Laurel. "You need a ride anywhere?"

"No, I live close," she lied. "Thanks though."

"Take care," Flynn said, and closed the door behind Pam. He braced a hand on the wood and leaned into it a moment as if he were thinking, then walked to the windows. He stared down into the street, raised a hand in a small wave and a car started up outside.

He turned to approach Laurel, crossing his arms over his chest. "So."

"You're bleeding," she said, eyes on the thin stream of fresh blood coming from the gash on his lip.

He wiped his mouth, smearing red. "You traumatized now or anything?"

She ignored his patronizing tone. "Do you have rubbing alcohol?"

He blinked at her a couple times then headed to the bathroom. He crouched at the cupboard below the sink, coming out with a bottle of hydrogen peroxide. Laurel slid past him and rooted through his medicine cabinet, finding antiseptic ointment and bandages. No cotton balls, but she popped the toilet paper roll off its spool and headed back into the main room. She heard Flynn follow as she walked to his bed and sat on the edge. He looked down at her, semi-silhouetted. She patted the mattress and he surprised her by sitting.

Laurel angled his head and inspected the cut. He didn't flinch as she brushed her fingertips over it.

"You a nurse or something?"

"No, I'm a waitress."

"Aren't you too old to be a waitress?" he asked, the tease stinging a little.

"I'm only twenty-nine."

"Yeah, but you can wait tables in Providence. Nobody moves to Boston to become a waitress. Where'd you drop out from?"

"Nowhere. I graduated from Wentworth." She wet a wad of toilet paper with the peroxide and pressed it to his lip. He didn't bat an eye. "I just didn't like my field so much once I got into it."

"Waste of thousands of dollars."

She frowned at him. "I had a scholarship, not that it's your business. Is there a humongous chip on your shoulder I should be disinfecting?"

"Sorry," he said, not sounding it.

"What do you care, anyway?"

"I like to know who I'm playing with, and you seem like you might be sticking around." He watched her smear her fingers with ointment before dabbing it on the cut.

"Well, I'm a failed engineer who waits tables at a tourist trap in Quincy Market," she said, addressing his lips.

"And you don't live around here, do you?"

"No. I live in the North End."

"Roommates?"

She nodded. "I'm pushing thirty and my career's in the crapper and I wait tables and have two roommates. And my longest relationship lasted less than your current fuckbuddy arrangement. Happy?"

Flynn laughed genuinely for the first time and it changed him. It deepened the lines beside his eyes and mouth, revealed his imperfect but white teeth. It also reopened the cut and Laurel glared at him.

"What else have you got?" She touched her fingers to a nasty bruise just above his collar. He peeled his tee shirt up and she grimaced at the collection of black and blues—way more now that she was close up. An ugly scrape traced his collarbone but nothing else appeared to be bleeding. Laurel swabbed the scrape and smeared it with Bactine, eased a bandage on and pressed it in place.

"Why do you do that?" she asked. "The fights?"

"Same reason I do the other shit you saw tonight."

"Which is?" She crumpled the bandage wrapper in her fist and met his eyes.

"Dunno. Just need to."

"Does it make you feel alive or something?" she asked.

"Why'd *you* come here tonight?"

She nodded. "Touché."

"You done fussing over me?"

She screwed the cap back on the ointment and nodded again.

"You drive here?"

She shook her head. "Bus."

"Buses ain't running this late. You want a ride?"

"I can call a cab."

"Or I can give you a ride. Come on." He stood and tugged his shirt back on and she followed, setting the first-aid supplies on his counter. She grabbed her purse from the table as Flynn pulled on his shoes and clipped his keys to his belt.

"Flynn isn't your first name, is it?" Laurel asked.

"No. It's Michael."

"Oh." She'd been expecting a little more evasion or possibly a stranger name than Michael. "Well, my last name's White."

"Right, Laurel White. I'm Michael Flynn." He shook her hand curtly. "You've watched me fuck and we know each other's full names. That enough for your first night?"

She gave him a snide smile. "Sure." They left the apartment and he locked up behind them. They shared a silent elevator ride and walked half a block to a rust-pocked white station wagon. Flynn unlocked the driver's side, slid in and leaned over to pull the lock for Laurel's door. She sat down and glanced at him, then around the car.

He started the engine, grinning. "What'd you expect?"

"Not a station wagon."

"I'm the only non-drinker in a bar full of fighters. Some nights I wish I had a bus for getting people's drunk, limping asses home." He pulled them onto the silent street and Laurel rolled her window down, breathing in that ripened summer city smell. Flynn flipped on a classic rock station and lowered the volume.

"So," she said. "Thank you. For letting me tag along."

He shrugged and they didn't speak for a couple minutes as he drove them over a bridge and through the Seaport District. "Dirty Water" came on, as though they'd crossed into a parody of themselves. Laurel suppressed a laugh.

"Think you're interested in what I do?" Flynn asked, turning to her. "If you are, just tell me what night."

"Are you interested in inviting me?" she asked.

"Pretty sure I just did."

She shifted in her seat and clutched her purse tighter. "I'm interested. I'm not sure how I'll feel tomorrow though."

"Just pick a night. You can always stand me up."

"You must work early," she said, stalling. "So weeknights would be—"

"You're thinking way too hard about it. Just pick a day."

"Okay. Wednesday. I'm off work at four."

He nodded. "Fine. Come over around eight. Or don't. But I'll make sure and be home then."

She nodded and exhaled, feeling all at once relieved. "Is there a...shallow end? You know, to the rough stuff."

He grinned at her. "You need training wheels?"

"Well—"

"Just fucking with you. Of course there's a shallow end. You've seen how I like to screw. But it's a preference, not a fetish. I don't *have* to be a prick to get hard." He turned the car onto Atlantic Avenue, downtown looking as empty as Laurel had ever seen it.

"Regular sex is like jerking off to me," he went on. "It feels good, it gets the job done. But I'd rather be doing something else, you know?"

"Are you part of the BDSM scene or whatever?" Laurel asked.

He made an exasperated noise. "I can't stand that shit. They make everything so fucking complicated. You might as well be one of those Civil-fucking-War..." He twirled his hand, searching for the word.

"Reenactors?"

He snapped his fingers at her. "Three points. Anyhow, I just like stuff a lot of women don't, so I have to make sure I find the ones who do. Like, really do. Do you have a man someplace?"

"No."

"Good," he said.

She sighed, mildly annoyed. "And exactly how many people do *you* see at a given time?"

"Just one for the last few months."

"Oh." Laurel's muscles relaxed a bit. It was ridiculous to already feel a twinge of jealousy over this man, but it was also an undeniable relief to know she wasn't going to be just one in an endless stable. "So what about it gets you off, do you think?"

Flynn shrugged, eyes on the road. "Power, I guess."

"Same with the fighting? You like—"

"I'm not real interested in being psychoanalyzed, kiddo. Dissect my rotten soul all you want but keep it to yourself."

"Sorry. I have an engineer's brain."

He eyeballed her. "What's that mean?"

"I like understanding how things work," she said.

"Well, draw yourself a pretty little blueprint and do me a favor and don't show it to me. I like fighting, and I like fucking. I don't care much for thinking."

"Okay."

He took a right on Hanover into Laurel's neighborhood. "Tell me where to turn," he said.

"Left on North Bennet."

He drove to her building and put the car in neutral, double-parking on the narrow one-way street. She caught the wink of headlights in the rearview mirror and unstrapped her seat belt. "Thanks for the ride."

"No problem. You got your phone? I'll give you my number, case you need it."

Laurel pulled her cell out and he entered his info.

"I never hear it ring, so just leave a message. I'll see you Wednesday at eight," he said, handing her phone back. "If you find the balls."

"I—"

An SUV pulled up behind them and honked. Laurel flung her door open but Flynn grasped her wrist.

"What?"

"Nothing, just making that prick wait. I can't fucking stand impatient people."

The horn blared again.

Flynn leaned out his window. "What's the rush at three a.m. on this gorgeous fucking summer night?" His grip was too tight for Laurel to break.

A series of honks, and Flynn propped his elbow out the window, presumably flipping the driver the bird. Laurel felt her face color. She hated being a part of a scene.

"I can wait all night, douchebag," Flynn sang once the horn quieted.

Laurel's heart beat in her throat. A greedy, primitive part of her relished the thought of the pissed-off driver confronting Flynn, only to get loomed over by a tower of black-eyed, split-lipped muscle. Instead they gave a last honk and reversed, fast, turning down a side street with a petulant squeal of tires. Flynn let her hand go and the blood trickled back into her fingertips. She tried to imagine him holding her wrists in another context and blushed deeper, glad it was dark.

"See you Wednesday," she said.

"Yeah, we'll see."

She got out and slammed the door without looking back. Flynn idled until she unlocked the building's front door and closed it behind her. She heard him drive away as she started up the steps, her body mourning the sudden absence of his smell and voice. Wednesday sounded like a hundred years from now.

And Wednesday sounded far too soon.

Chapter Three

Laurel stood outside Flynn's building, sheltering under the awning from the evening's warm rain, staring at the keypad beside a list of the tenants. M. Flynn, 508. Easy as pie. Just push the numbers and buzz his apartment.

She opened her purse and pressed a button on her phone, illuminating the screen. Seven-fifty-six. Four minutes early. Would that look too eager? It wasn't as though she could control how fast the bus got her here... Still, maybe she should take a walk around the block and be fashionably late. But it was raining and her hair was already fuzzy enough from the humidity—

A knock on the glass in front of her made Laurel yelp and jump. Flynn stood on the other side, staring at her. He made a beckoning motion with his finger as he pushed the locked door open.

"Oh," she said and stepped into the stuffy foyer. "Are you on your way out someplace?"

"No, dipshit, I have an appointment. With you. I saw you walk up the street from my window like five minutes ago. Thought maybe you couldn't figure out the buzzer, Little Miss Engineer."

"Oh," she said, unable to think of a witty comeback or a good lie. "I was just checking my phone messages."

"Uh huh. Anyhow, come on up." He turned and she followed him into the elevator.

"Did you have a good day?" she asked.

"Yeah, not bad. You get dinner yet?"

She nodded. They exited at the fifth floor and walked down the hall to his apartment. It felt different than when she'd been here the last time. More and less intimidating at the same time. Flynn closed the door and took her umbrella, hanging it on a hook to drip-dry.

"You tell somebody where you are?" Flynn asked. She'd left him a message the previous afternoon, wanting to double-check his address, and when he'd called her back he told her do as much.

"I gave my roommate your name and everything," she said.

"Good girl."

Laurel let his patronizing tone slide, pleased he had a clear understanding of how sketchy he was. She followed him to the living area. She cast her eyes all over the space, then at Flynn. "So, do we just, you know…get right to it?"

"I'm not a whore," he said, expression somewhere between amused and insulted.

"I didn't mean—"

"Have a seat, sub shop girl. You want a drink? Soda? Wine?" He walked to the counter and held up a bottle of red as Laurel sat on the edge of his loveseat.

"Yeah, sure. Wine's great."

He uncorked it and poured her a generous measure in a glass with a Christmas holly pattern around the lip. He took a seat kitty-corner from her on the other couch, leaning forward, elbows on his knees.

"So, what are you into?" he asked.

"Sex-wise?"

He nodded.

"I haven't done anything super-crazy before," Laurel said. *Except coming here.*

"Let me know what's off the table. Anal?" he asked, businesslike.

She shrugged her tight shoulders. "Not my favorite, but I'll go there. Just, you know…"

"Be gentle?"

She nodded. "That sounds stupid, since I'm here because, you know. You're into rough stuff."

"I don't wanna hurt you. That's the last thing I want. That's why you need to tell me anything you know of that'll freak you out."

"I gag easily," she offered.

"Does it freak you out?"

"No, I wouldn't go that far."

He nodded. "You want condoms with oral?" He seemed to be going down a mental checklist and Laurel wondered how many times he'd conducted this interview.

"Should I, with you?"

"Your choice." He got up and went to the filing cabinet standing between two windows, returning to hand her a paper with hospital letterhead dated two weeks prior—a long list of tests detailing Michael P. Flynn's negative status for all things contagious and undesirable.

Laurel made an amused face. "Is this what you call foreplay?"

"Pardon me if I kill your buzz, kiddo, but this is important to me. Should be to you too."

"No, it is. Just feels a bit clinical… Anyway I think oral's okay without," she said. "But thanks for offering."

"That doesn't really deserve thanks, but sure."

"What about you?" he asked. "You clean?"

She nodded, folding the letter and handing it back. "I didn't bring a note though."

"Any traumatic experiences I should avoid triggering? Any off-limits words? You know, the C-word or anything?"

"I don't think so. Just don't call me ugly or anything, please."

He raised an eyebrow. "Any fucker ever tells you that, you give me a call and I'll come over and kick the holy hell out of him for you."

Laurel flushed warmer than she had contemplating any of the other aspects of Flynn's brutality.

"Slapping okay?" he went on. "Like just spanking to start?"

Her blush ran so deep she could just about taste blood. "Fine."

He nodded again. "All right. We're not going to get too crazy tonight, but if anything feels off to you, just use my first name and we'll stop. You remember my first name?"

"Michael," she said, praying he couldn't guess how many times she'd repeated it in her mind in the last four days.

"Good. And so you know, there's no hidden cameras or any of that shit. And you're welcome to look for yourself," he said. "For what I am, I'm a decent guy. I don't want you here if you don't think you believe that yet."

"I trust you."

"How do you want it to end tonight?"

"What do you mean?" she asked.

"Unless you tell me not to, I'm gonna come, for one. I'll try make you come too if you want me to. But if you think you'd rather leave hot and frustrated, I can do that too."

"I wouldn't mind coming." She raised the glass to her lips to hide a nervous smirk.

Flynn nodded. "Good. And what about afterward? You want to get tossed out on your ass? You want a lift home? You can stay the night, but I don't cuddle or spoon and I leave at a quarter to six for work."

"Do I have to decide now?"

He shook his head. "Nope. Only if you want this to end with me acting like a jerk and giving you the boot."

"Is that what girls usually want you to do?"

"No, not usually. But it's an option."

"And what...what do you need from me?" she asked.

He made a face then laughed. "Don't think a woman's ever asked me that before... I just need you to be here with good intentions, I guess. Don't make me live the rest of my life feeling shitty about anything I do to you that you didn't warn me not to. That's about it."

"I'll try not to."

"Good. And I'll tell you now, I won't be calling you tomorrow or the next day or the day after that, so don't get in a stink when I don't. None of the normal dating rules apply to this. I know what goes on here is twisted as fuck as far as most people are concerned, and I don't want to be the creepy fucker calling up some girl he accidentally freaked out. If you decide you want to do this again, you call me. You decide I'm a jerk, don't. My feelings won't be hurt."

"Okay." Laurel took a deep drink and grimaced at the sour wine.

A smile melted Flynn's stern, professional expression. "Sorry. I'm useless with booze. I just picked the one with the girliest label."

"Are you..." She trailed off.

"Recovering?"

She nodded.

"Nah. I just don't drink. Not since I was like twenty-five. Just a glass of something at a wedding or whatever. You remember what I said about coffee?"

"Yeah."

"Yeah. I'm twitchy enough without chemicals short-circuiting shit in my head."

"Maybe you should take up smoking," Laurel teased.

He stood. "Don't fuckin' tempt me. Hardest breakup of my life, me and cigarettes."

She offered an empathetic smile. "How long were you going out?"

Flynn looked at the ceiling, doing math in his head. "Twelve years." He went to the sink to fill a pint glass with water.

"Wow, well done." Laurel raised her glass and choked down another gulp in honor of Flynn's abstinence. Gut-rotting or not, the wine was working. She felt heat seep over her skin, loosening her muscles and mouth and inhibitions.

"Can you tell I'm super-nervous?" she asked.

Flynn met her eyes. "I'd be worried if you weren't. But no, you don't seem that nervous."

"Are *you* nervous?"

"Nah." He sat back down with his glass. "I've been on board with this part of myself for a few years now, and I know when a girl's worth getting nervous over."

Laurel frowned, insulted. "What do you mean?"

"You didn't show up with a trench coat, so I know you're not going to whip it off and be wearing some crazy get-up made out of black plastic and dog collars, asking me to parade you down Broadway."

"Oh. But you're not nervous about, I don't know…your performance or whatever?"

"Should I be? You got high standards?"

She considered it a moment and Flynn laughed.

"Neither of us is here to prove anything," he said. "We're here to have fun, and for you to maybe get your motor cranked like you never knew it could be. Or not. Who knows? My ego's not tied up in this going a certain way. The only thing that makes me nervous is hurting you by mistake, and I trust myself enough to think that's unlikely."

"Are you good about knowing? You know, if a woman's about to freak out."

He nodded. "I think fighting's taught me how to read people pretty good."

"You should take up poker." Laurel drained her glass and set it aside. "Do you have some kind of waiver I should sign, Mr. Preparedness?"

"Nah, let's start. If I do something that makes you want to sue me, I'll probably deserve it."

Laurel smiled at him, feeling as if she'd uncovered a new, complex dimension of a man who'd seemed so simple at first glance. He stuck his neck out for this, putting his faith in his partners as much as they did him. Maybe more.

"You're really quite...trusting," Laurel offered.

"And you're really quite attractive when you bust my balls, sub shop girl. Why don't we get down to business and see how this goes?"

The chatting and alcohol had eased the tension in Laurel's body but it flooded back with a vengeance as Flynn sat beside her. His weight shifted the loveseat, reminding her just how big he was.

She cleared her throat. "Can we keep it pretty vanilla, to start? And I could tell you when I might want you to get...meaner?"

He nodded. "Whatever you need."

"Okay, good." She studied his eyes, different than she remembered. Blue with a dark outer ring and a burst of amber around the pupil. She realized she probably looked silly, her eyes crossed from staring at him this close up. Then he kissed her and she couldn't give a good goddamn about anything except his mouth.

Training wheels or not, Flynn only gave her a couple soft kisses before his tongue slid between her lips, hot and wet and aggressive. Laurel sucked a breath through her nose, focusing on her body's thrill and filtering out the fear. His palms felt broad and warm as they grazed her neck, a little taste of the promised roughness in the way his fingers tangled in her hair, freeing half of it from the elastic. She stroked his shoulders and chest, taking in the firm contours as his tongue delved deeper.

He pulled his head back an inch. "Get in my lap."

A shiver trickled through Laurel at that first order. She toyed with saying "Yes, Sir" but wasn't ready to jump into her role quite that efficiently. She tossed a leg over and straddled him. Flynn's eyes and hands roamed her sides, her arms, her small breasts. She touched his face and hair and ears then he grabbed one of her hands and put it to his mouth, sliding two fingers between his lips. He sucked hard, making her fingertips prickle and her eyes widen. She felt his tongue push between the digits, then the drag of his teeth down her skin. He made a throaty noise that raised the hairs along her arms and he pulled her fingers out.

"Take your top off," he said.

Laurel's body warmed from being commanded by this man. She'd done little snatches of role-playing with lovers but it'd always felt cheesy and awkward. Not with Flynn. He wasn't play-acting. She peeled her shirt up and tossed it over the arm of the couch.

"Nice," he whispered, eyes darting over her skin. His rough palms swept up her stomach and ribs, cupped her breasts. He smirked. "Didn't anybody tell you it's July?" He meant her pale skin.

"I'm not really a beach person." She glanced down at her freckled arms and the white skin of her trunk that never saw the sun.

"I like it," he said, still staring. "You must be Irish."

"I'm a mutt. And don't forget the red hair's not really mine."

He ignored her attempt at self-deprecation. Reaching around, he got her bra clasp open. Another husky, appreciative noise escaped him as the garment dropped. His

Cara McKenna

touch started light, the graze of his fingers stiffening her nipples. He cupped her breasts, squeezing and kneading softly, then a bit meaner. Laurel got her first taste of physical dominance when his palm slid to her lower back, jerking her closer. His mouth took one breast as his hand teased the other. She felt hard suction, then a glancing of teeth.

"God," she muttered.

His mouth broke away a moment. "Say my name," he said.

"Flynn."

A smug laugh warmed her wet skin. "Keep saying it. It gets me so fucking hard."

Heat burned in her neck and cheeks as she thought of arousing him. She shifted her hips, wanting to feel the evidence. Pressing their pelvises close, she ground against the stiff ridge behind his fly.

"Flynn."

"Yeah." His mouth moved to her other breast, even rougher than with the first. His thick thighs fidgeted between hers, his swelling cock craving more space or more friction as the tension escalated.

"You feel big," Laurel whispered.

He pulled his head away. "You wanna see me?"

She nodded.

"Push that table back and get on your knees."

Laurel got off his lap, slid the coffee table away and knelt between his feet. Her heart raced, a hundred percent excitement, zero fear.

Flynn scooted forward so his thighs flanked her ribs. He tugged off his tee shirt, offering the sight of all that powerful muscle, the smell of his skin.

Laurel didn't wait for an order. She reached for his belt, getting the buckle open and letting the worn, heavy leather fall aside. She freed one button then the next and the next until she spread his jeans open, revealing a strip of black cotton and getting her first hint of his scent, one that kicked her salivary glands into action. He eased his jeans down a couple more inches and adjusted his cock, centering the impressive bulge in his open fly.

She glanced up and met his eyes a second, wanting an order this time.

"Touch it." Cold.

Laurel swallowed and put her fingertips to the ridge, feeling his flesh react. She flattened her palm, surveying his broad, heated erection and listening to his sharp inhalation. His hand covered hers, wrapping it tight around him, making her feel how thick and hard and ready he'd grown.

He moaned above her. "Yeah… Fuck, I've been thinking about this all week, making you touch my dick. Get it out, girl."

She tugged his waistband down, exposing every throbbing inch, wrapping her hand around him again and loving the smooth texture.

"Good girl." His hips flexed into her slow, gentle exploration. "Harder." He guided her hand again, tightening her grip and quickening her stroke. "That's good. That's good. I want this so bad." He made their shared rhythm fast and rough and groaned in time with the pulls. "I've been jerking off thinking about this. About making you taste me." Pre-come beaded at his slit then slid down his head to slicken the motions.

"Flynn."

"I'm so fucking ready, you're gonna get me off before we start playing. Taste me," he ordered.

Laurel lowered her head, brought her mouth to him as their hands continued to work. She kissed his head, gave him a light lick.

"Yeah. More. Tongue me."

She lapped at his slit, lavishing it with wet caresses.

"Good girl. Tease it. Tease it and I'll reward you with a nice mouthful."

Her face burned as she took his orders, the sounds of his panting breaths and the salty taste of him making her lightheaded. She flicked her tongue over him, savoring a thrill of power as his bossy hand faltered and his grunts turned to shallow gasps.

"God, fuck." His hand released her and he tangled his fingers in her hair, holding her head but not forcing her mouth. Not yet. "Keep it tight," he said, and she squeezed him harder. "Keep teasing me."

She fluttered her tongue across his slit, the taste of his pre-come greeting her in steady bursts. She freed her mouth for a second.

"You taste so good."

"Yeah. Take more of me. Suck my cock."

Bitch, she added to herself, the word seeming implicit from his harsh tone. She took him into her mouth, sucking hard. Any discomfort was worth it just for the sounds he made.

"More. Nice and deep."

She worked her mouth lower, letting his head bump the back of her throat and trigger her gag reflex. It didn't ease as she bobbed her head, but the sensation only heightened the experience, the taboo.

"All of it," Flynn ordered, starting to force her. Though he was rough, he knew what he was doing. His demanding hands made her swallow every inch but he withdrew with each protest from her throat, gave her a chance to find her breath. He pulled out after a minute and got to his feet, making Laurel shuffle back a pace on the hard floor. He brought his cock back to her lips, adding his own thrusts and showing her the deep rhythm he craved.

"I love it," he whispered. "I love fucking that sweet mouth of yours." His hips sped up for a few beats, emphasizing, overwhelming Laurel a moment before he returned to a tempo she could handle.

"You're so good at sucking that cock, girl." He traced her lips with his thumb. "I'm gonna reward you. You want that?"

She moaned an affirmation around his shaft. He pulled her hair, yanking her head back and holding it at arm's length. "Jerk me. Hard as you fucking can."

She wrapped her hand around his slick cock and stroked so aggressively she feared she'd hurt him.

"Good. Keep going. Keep that up."

A desperate, needy feeling clouded her mind as he held her hair, keeping her mouth just out of reach of his cock head. She jerked him until she could see his hips and stomach trembling, his breath racing from her mean strokes.

"You're gonna get it," he rasped. "You're gonna get a big fuckin' mouthful of me." He groaned, the sound reverberating in Laurel's bones. His free hand pushed hers away, taking over the pulls as the other hand brought her head close, forcing his cock past her lips as he released. His stroking fist bumped her chin as the come lashed her tongue, a long, hot stream of him bathing her taste buds and sliding down her throat. The roughness of his commands blended with the helpless sound of his moan, making Laurel feel in control for the briefest of moments. His hands released her as his body stilled.

"Clean me up," he said, panting.

Laurel reached out and took his softening cock, laving it until he stepped away. She watched him walk to the sink and fill a glass from the tap. She looked to her top and her bra slung over the loveseat and wondered with a stab of panic if the evening's activities were already over—if she was supposed to be getting dressed and making a decision about whether or not she was staying. Flynn set his glass on the counter and turned to face her.

"Okay. We've got about twenty minutes before I get mean again."

She laughed, relieved the night was still young. "What are you, some kind of sex-werewolf?"

He let out a heavy sigh, blinked a couple times and walked over.

"Here," he said, putting out a hand. "Get up. Looks weird having a topless girl on my floor when I'm not in barbarian mode."

He helped her to standing and she dusted her knees off before meeting his eyes. "So. What do we do for twenty minutes?"

Flynn's eyes dropped as his hand went to Laurel's jeans, undoing her button and zipper. She giggled.

He looked up. "What?"

"Sorry. I can't get over how big your fingers are."

He stared at his hands a moment.

"Not just your fingers, I mean. All of you." She looked to his eyes, probably eight or nine inches above hers, and she wasn't particularly short. "How tall are you?"

"Six-three-and-a-half."

"Damn."

He shrugged and went back to her pants, pushing the snug garment down her hips. He sucked in a soft breath.

It was her turn to ask, "What?"

"I dunno. Just your skin. You're so…white."

"One of my roommates calls me Ghostie."

He shook his head. "You're like that famous chick, what's her name?"

Laurel knew exactly what name he was looking for but refused to supply it. Pale skin and red hair, but she lacked Nicole Kidman's height and bone structure and glamour and didn't feel like hearing their differences listed if Flynn made a project of comparing them.

"So what do we do now?" she asked again.

"You get in my bed and I figure a few things out about you before the beast returns. If you're still in the mood."

She kicked off her jeans with gusto and jogged to toss herself across his rumpled comforter. She heard him laugh at her enthusiasm as she stared into the maze of pipes and vents traversing the ceiling, anticipating. His footsteps faded and the lights went out. More steps, and a dim reading lamp clamped to one of the bedside shelves flipped on. Flynn sat on the mattress, the heaviness of him thrilling Laurel deep down to her marrow.

"Lie on your side," he said. "Away from me."

She complied and he slid up behind her, pressing his bare chest into her back, pushing a hard, jean-clad thigh between her knees. He ran his warm palm up and down her hip and made a soft noise, a whisper crossed with a grunt. His hand slid up her ribs to cup her breast, the sensation tightening her legs around his.

"I wanna know what you like," he said.

She realized that with his mouth this close and his tone hushed, the voice she'd found brash and a bit grating was actually rather sexy. She cleared her throat. "Well, I'm here because I want to see what it's like to be with someone, you know...like you."

"Have you thought about it? Since the last time you were here?" His fingers pinched her nipple gently, then rougher.

"Yeah, I've thought about it. A lot." She'd gotten off about ten times in the last four days, imagining fucking Flynn. No, not fucking Flynn—being fucked *by* Flynn.

His hand moved down her belly to rest on her mound. "Tell me."

Laurel hesitated. She'd always been lousy at dirty talk.

"Listen, kiddo," he said. "I'm a selfish prick, and I want to be the greatest fuck of your life and ruin you for every man who comes after me. But I'm not a mind reader, so I need some help. Otherwise I could end up as the douchebag who's got shitty taste in wine and totally traumatized you when you were thirty."

"Twenty-nine."

"So tell me," he breathed, right behind her ear. "What do you want me to do to you?"

She took a deep breath, held it as his hand slid low, two fingers just barely pressing into her lips through her underwear. "I thought about everything you did with her," she said. "And what it'd be like to do that with you."

"What else?" His fingers turned and ran up and down her crease, flooding her pussy with heat and pressure. Confession became far easier.

"I thought about you making me get on my elbows and knees, on your floor, like you did with her."

"Uh huh." His touch intensified, his thigh pushing her knees wider as his fingers strained against the cotton.

"Except you tie my wrists," she said. "And instead of telling me to keep my eyes on the floor, there's like a mirror against the wall in front of me, so I have to watch you while you fuck me." Her throat was tight, as tight as her pussy under his touch.

"And how do I fuck you?" he asked, voice turning harsh, hand slipping beneath her panties, tickling her pubic hair before his fingers found her folds and banished all other thoughts and sensations from reality. She moaned.

"Tell me how I fuck you."

"Hard," she managed to say. "And mean."

"Am I forcing you?" Two fingers penetrated.

"Oh God."

"Tell me. Do you want me to force you?" He pushed deeper.

"Yeah," she said, barely able to form the syllable as his fingers thrusted into her.

"You're so wet," he whispered, sounding smug. "I can't wait to ram my dick inside you. See your hot body below me as I take you."

He fucked her fast, his slick fingers curled into a hook, the pad of his hand stroking her clit each time he withdrew. Against her ass she felt him growing hard. The buckle of his belt made her think of her hands bound again, escalating her excitement. She groaned with each exhale, drunk from his touch and his smell, his voice. He was turning back into the other Flynn, just as he'd promised.

"You like that, don't you?" She could hear his sneer. "Bet you wish that was my cock, don't you?" His fingers fucked her hard for half a minute and she writhed against him, desperate. "You sucked me so good before. I loved watching you take every inch."

"God, Flynn."

His dick was stiff, as hard as it had been when she'd sucked him.

"You'll say my name just like that when I make you come, bitch."

Her breath hitched at the word but the intimidation wasn't unpleasant.

"You want to live out that fantasy tonight?" His hips pumped, rubbing his erection against her bottom.

"I'm not sure."

"We can do the training wheels version," he said.

She gasped when he pulled away, turned her onto her back and knelt between her thighs, spreading them wide and bringing his groin to hers.

"I love your fantasy," he said, looking down at her, fire in his eyes. He thrust his cock against her, the layers of fabric taunting. "I wanna watch you in that mirror, watching me. Close your eyes and think about it."

She obeyed. His cock rubbed her pussy with hot, frustrating friction. Flynn's face was fresh in her mind, that mean smile, dark expression. Plus his bare body with all those strong muscles, flexing with each thrust.

"I want that," she said, and opened her eyes.

"Good." He changed, suddenly businesslike. He stopped thrusting, wedged a knee under hers to kneel wide before her, put a hand on each of her shins. "We're gonna keep things pretty tame tonight. I won't actually tie your hands, but you're gonna pretend I am. And you're going to set the tone. You think you want to pretend I'm forcing you, you make it clear and I'll play along. Okay?"

She nodded.

He slapped her calf. "Okay. Go make a trip to the ladies' room if you need one, and I'll get things set up. When you come back it's game-on."

"Okay."

"What's your safe word?"

"Michael."

He slapped her calf again. "Good girl. And if for some reason you can't say it and you need to, you grunt three times, fast, or hit your foot or your hand against something, three times. Okay?"

She nodded again.

He got his legs out from under hers and stood beside the bed. "Bring me back a towel. A big one."

Laurel grabbed her purse and went to the bathroom, tidying her makeup for a couple minutes, the whirring fan drowning out whatever Flynn might be doing in the other room. When she emerged with the bath towel he was crouched by the open closet near the sleeping area, a toolbox by his foot. He unscrewed the bottom of a full-length mirror from the door then stood and detached the top. He walked it over to a bare stretch of wall and leaned it there. Turning to Laurel, he took the towel and lay it on the floor, apparently thinking her having her knees and elbows savaged by the not-so-recently swept hardwood was too varsity for her first night.

Flynn straightened up and the cold look on his face said the fantasy had begun. A chill trickled down Laurel's spine as she stared into his narrowed eyes.

"Sit on the bed," he said.

She hesitated a second and it was enough to earn herself some correction. Flynn took her by the shoulders and forced her back a couple steps, pushing her onto the edge of the mattress beside a pair of wrapped condoms, a bottle of lube and a roll of duct tape. The sensation of being physically controlled by someone she knew she couldn't ever hope to fight off was both arousing and terrifying. This man could *actually* rape her, if he was so inclined—he was physically capable of it. She felt her throat constrict as if a fist had closed around it.

"Michael."

His posture transformed in an instant. He sat down next to her on the bed, hands clasped between his knees, wary eyes on her face. "Too rough?"

"I'm not sure. I think mostly I just wanted to test the safe word. I think I needed to know you'd stop, if I asked you to."

"Always."

Then Laurel did something that surprised even herself. She turned and reached out a hand, setting her palm on his jaw. She brought her face up and drew his down and kissed his mouth. A first-date good-night kiss, no tongue, just lips finding their way for a few moments. Flynn set a hand softly on her arm, taking all her cues. Laurel pulled away feeling safe, knowing she was calling the shots. Her relief morphed to curiosity as she stared at his naked chest and arms. Fuck, those arms.

"I'm ready," she said. "You can do whatever you were planning on." She squared her shoulders and looked expectant, as if he'd just pushed her down onto the bed. He licked his lips and nodded, seeming satisfied that she was back on board. He stood and put his knees between hers, a hand coming down to hold the back of her head.

"Take me out and get me hard." Laurel's new favorite order.

She undid his belt and fly, let his jeans drop to the ground. Cupping his bulge, she rubbed her thumbs across his ridge, feeling him go stiff. She stroked her hand up and down his length as he grew, measuring and anticipating. A pang of sadness struck her as she realized that the first time he penetrated her they wouldn't be face-to-face. She'd miss out on that cautious, awe-filled, one-time-only moment between new lovers with this man.

Flynn eased his waistband over his straining cock and pushed his shorts down his thighs. His hand wrapped around hers as before, gripping to dictate her strokes.

"Yeah, good." The weight returned to his voice. "Make it nice and big." He wound her long hair around his other hand, rough and possessive.

"What are you going to do?" she asked, eyes on his swollen head above their two fists.

"Depends on if you cooperate or not. You gonna get on your hands and knees for me, girl?"

She glanced at the duct tape then nodded.

He let her hand go after a couple more strokes and she got to the ground, all fours on the towel, facing the mirror. Flynn kicked his pants and shorts away and grabbed the tape, kneeling behind her.

"Sit up," he said.

She leaned back on her haunches. She heard the rip of tape being yanked and detached, glanced over her shoulder to watch him fold the three-foot length in half the long way, closing the sticky side in on itself. He reached around her waist to press her wrists together, wrapping them with the tape, tucking the ends beneath her thumbs so the only things keeping her bound were her own fists. Staring down at her hands, Laurel thought it looked pretty damn convincing.

"Back on all fours," he said.

She settled on her knees and elbows, keeping the bindings tight. Strong hands yanked her underwear down her thighs and out from under her knees. A hungry noise rattled out of Flynn's chest, the closest thing to a growl Laurel had ever heard a man make.

She watched his face in the mirror, his eyes cast down at her ass or her pussy, his ready cock just inches away. He reached for the condom, unwrapped it. As he rolled it down his erection his other hand fucked her, fingers thrusting into her wet folds. She pushed her hips eagerly into the touch, watching his roped arms in the mirror, his contracting stomach and tight chest. She'd never really prioritized a guy's body when choosing a lover before, but right now Laurel wished the whole world could see this man. Powerful. That was the only word for him. Then his eyes caught hers in the reflection and she forgot all about his body.

"Beg me," he said, holding her gaze.

"Please, Flynn."

"Please what?" His let his dick rest along the cleft of her ass as he grabbed her hip. He tugged her hard onto his fingers as his cock slid along her crack, balls bumping her. His fucking hand reached around to spear her from the front.

"Fuck me, Flynn. Please. I want you so bad."

"I know you do. I can feel it." The hand on her hip rose to come down with a moderate slap. "You're so tight and hot for me."

"Please."

"Or maybe you mean somethin' else," he said. His hips drew back and his fingers left her pussy. She felt them fan across her butt, his thumb slipping into her crack. The wet pad teased her asshole. Trepidation tightened her body but with

Flynn in control the hesitance felt right. She gave herself over to whatever he wanted, trusting he'd sense her boundaries.

His patient voice returned for a moment. "Breathe, sweetheart."

She exhaled, pushing the anxiety out of her lungs. His thumb rubbed in a tight circle.

"Again," he said.

She pushed out another deep breath and he pressed his thumb inside. Laurel swallowed and winced, accepting the violation, trying to welcome the sensation. Still not her favorite thing, but with Flynn she didn't feel pressured, as though he were trying to talk her into it. He was just *dirty*, ready to take, seemingly without permission. For some odd reason it made Laurel trust him more than any boyfriend who'd ever tried to win her over by enumerating the many spurious feminist virtues of taking it up the ass.

He must have felt her relax. "Good." His pushed his thumb in a little deeper, gave her a few slow, short thrusts. "Good. We'll get you there sometime, but probably not too soon. Not 'til you're begging me for it."

A wave of relief engulfed Laurel as he eased his thumb out and took hold of her hip. She felt the tip of his cock tease her lips.

"Please, Flynn."

She watched his reflection. His mouth was open, eyes on the juncture of their bodies. His broad chest rose and fell, deep and steady. He pushed in, the penetration explicit in its slowness.

Laurel moaned. "Oh God."

He was big, seeming even bigger now that his matching frame wasn't distorting the scale of things. In the mirror his entire body looked tight and strained, his face mean. He eased in another inch, the thick, powerful feel of him making Laurel drunk.

"Fuck, you're tight."

"More," she whispered.

He grunted, pushed in, gave her another couple inches.

"Don't stop, Flynn."

"Yeah." He eased out, pushed back in, over and over until he had her filled. As good as his arms and stomach looked in the mirror, she wished she could see his cock, his ass, his back muscles. He gave a few long thrusts, all the way in, nearly all the way out, making her feel every slick, hard inch as it slid deep then withdrew.

"Tight and deep," he said through a labored breath. He sped up, setting an even pace, hands stroking her ass and thighs as his hips found their rhythm.

She craned her neck to meet his eyes, unreflected. "Flynn."

"God, I love your cunt. You're so fuckin' hot." One hand left her flank to reach around and tease her pussy and he brought his thumb back to her asshole, slick. It slid inside, rougher than before, the feeling intensified tenfold by the thrust of his cock.

"Oh God."

"That's right." He pushed the digit in deep and kept it there as his cock pounded. "I'd fuck your mouth too, if I could."

Laurel turned back to the mirror, adrenaline whirling through her body, making her feel crazed and unafraid. She clenched her thumbs tight around the tape and thrashed her hips.

Flynn missed a beat but started right back up, harder than before. "You keep still."

Laurel moved again, walking a knee forward only to get yanked back on the towel by Flynn's hand.

"I said don't fucking move," he warned, cold eyes trained on her face in the mirror.

She let the feelings crash over her, fear and excitement heating her from the inside out, the chemical rush in her brain compounding it all, getting her high. She struggled again, this time trying to break away for real, needing to feel how easy it was for him to stop her. Both his hands shot forward as he leaned over her, grabbed her behind the elbows and folded her arms up beneath her, her shoulders and head coming down, chin landing just above her bound fists with a soft thump against the towel. He pushed down on her back, pinning her as the fucking turned harsh, each impact punctuated by the slap of his damp skin against hers. Laurel turned her head, willing to put up with the uncomfortable position if it meant she could see his face. She saw control in his eyes, cool beside the hot flush of his skin.

"Don't," she whispered.

"Shut up."

She moved the only bit of herself she had power over—her legs.

"Don't make this hard," he warned, keeping her in place with his weight.

Laurel gave a desperate thrash and Flynn's hands left her back. He shoved her knees together and widened his stance, clamping his thighs beside hers and locking them. She had a second to put up a fight with her bound arms before he pinned them down again.

"Now you're gonna get it," he said.

Laurel made a fearful, breathy noise and was rewarded with a few violent thrusts. "Stop," she panted. "Please."

"I said shut up."

"Please, stop."

"Fine. Gets me hot when you beg, anyway."

She alternated pleading with helpless noises, the role-playing arousing her more than she'd imagined possible. Flynn felt godlike behind her, insanely strong and powerful. His dick drove deep, over and over, the heat built with every excruciating minute, sweat making their skin slippery, exertion changing his breathing and voice and rhythm.

"God, yeah. I can't wait to shoot in you, bitch."

Laurel sensed him getting close. Her own body was as tight as she'd ever been without touching herself. The sensation was maddening but ecstatic and the second he let her go she was going to get a hand free and tease herself over the edge.

She made a couple useless attempts at struggling, too excited by his arousal now to put on a good show. One of Flynn's hands left her back, his damp palm sliding across her stomach, fingers finding her clit. She bucked and yelped at the contact.

"Yeah, that's right. I knew you loved it." He fucked her fast, rubbed her clit in a mean circle and drew all the heat of her body into a pounding, swirling mass against the pads of his fingers.

"God, Flynn."

"Good. Come for me. Come all over that big dick I'm fucking you with."

She groaned as the climax rose, the sweet burn tingling up her thighs and bursting open against his fingers, around his cock.

"Yeah, yeah, yeah." He pounded her deep and fast as the orgasm tossed her, teased her clit lighter and lighter as her cries died away. "Good girl."

To her surprise, he let her go. His thrusts stopped and his hands left her. He stood. "Can you get up?"

Laurel oozed out a delirious breath and rocked back onto her knees, registering the crick in her neck and the blood pooling in her fingers. She opened her hands and the tape fell away. Flynn helped her to her feet and she looked to him for instruction.

"Wanna lie down? On the bed?"

"Sure." She sat on the mattress and shimmied herself into the center on her back. Flynn climbed on after her and got his knees between hers.

"Feel okay? Not too roughed up for me to finish?"

"Oh," she said, "you better fucking finish."

His brows rose. "Guess that's a yes."

"I want to see you come," she said, all the urgent desire from before her climax bubbling right back up.

Flynn angled his cock between her thighs and she watched as he drove inside, slow, filling her.

"God, you're big."

"That what you like?" he asked, starting to fuck.

"I guess." She reached down to circle her thumb and finger around him, squeezing to feel how stiff and thick he was. "And you're so hard."

"You can have this big hard cock anytime you want," he promised, hips hammering fast. "Say my name."

She did. She said it again and again as he drove himself to the edge. She took in the strong arms locked at her side, his slick chest, his face as he lost control.

"Fuck, yeah." He yanked himself out, leaning back to strip off the condom and jerk himself home with a rough fist. He came hard with a strangled noise, come lashing her belly in warm spurts until the aggression died away.

"Oh God." He composed himself a moment, panting, then made it off the bed to grab the towel and wipe Laurel's skin clean. He tossed it aside and collapsed onto his back next to her.

She listened to his racing breath. "Wow."

Flynn laughed, the sound turning into a brief coughing fit. He cleared his throat. "Yeah," he said. "Wow." He folded his arms under his head and Laurel did the same and they both stared up at the vents.

She turned to study his face. "So I did okay for my inaugural night?"

He returned the scrutiny. "Yeah, that was fantastic. You liked it then?"

She nodded.

"Good. I hope you'll give me a call sometime."

Laurel decided she rather liked Flynn's unambiguous style of flirting. "I bet I will... And what you said before—is it okay if I crash here? My legs feel like their bones fell out."

"Sure thing. Just be prepared to get up real early. I can run you back home before I start work."

"You can just dump me at the nearest T stop."

"You live ten minutes' drive from my site, dummy. I'm not making you take the subway. Damn thing's always derailing and catching fire anyhow."

"Fine then." She yawned deeply. It was probably only nine but she felt as if she'd been up all night. "I don't suppose I could borrow a tee shirt to sleep in?"

"Course."

She swallowed and watched his face a moment. "You know, you're really a very nice man."

He laughed. "That orgasm must have fucked you up in the head."

Laurel smiled. She was mindful to obey his non-cuddling rule but inched her top half over a little so their shoulders touched. "Thanks." She felt sleep drawing its cloudy veil over her brain.

"You're welcome."

She closed her eyes and breathed him in, the musky smell of their sex and the subtler ones of his apartment and sheets. "I'm definitely going to call you," she murmured.

"Good. I hope you do."

"Definitely," she said again, dreamy. She felt Flynn leave the bed, heard a drawer scrape open then cool cotton flopped over her arm and breast.

"I'm gonna take a shower," he said. "Looks like you'll be out cold when I get back."

"Good night then."

He wandered off and she heard the fan kick on in the bathroom. Laurel managed to fumble into the shirt and under his covers. She had just enough lucidity left to think of something that intimidated her more than anything else Flynn had offered tonight.

I like him.

She liked him enough that knowing he could be with another woman tomorrow would sting if she let it. But right now, he was hers. Until he dropped her at her door the next morning, she was the only one who got him. She smiled into one of his threadbare pillowcases and let the smug comfort of the thought carry her into sleep.

Tonight he was hers. Tomorrow could go fuck itself.

Chapter Four
ॐ

"Hey. Sub shop girl."

Laurel opened her eyes to find Flynn standing beside the bed, dressed.

"Rise and shine, kiddo."

"What time is it?"

"Five-ten," he said. "You got time for a quick shower if you need one."

"Can I use that time to sleep?"

"Sure."

Flynn wandered away and Laurel buried her head deeper in the pillow, but she didn't sleep. Her heart rate spiked as she registered what they'd done last night. Then it eased as she realized there didn't seem to be any reason to panic. After a minute she tossed the covers aside and sat on the edge of the bed, looking around Flynn's apartment. It was dark, just the light above the stove switched on. The city beyond the windows looked purple and sleepy, sunrise hidden by a hundred tall buildings behind them to the east.

Flynn was on the couch, lacing his boots. Laurel padded to the coffee table to grab her purse. She caught Flynn's eyes dart to her breasts beneath the tee shirt she'd borrowed then a glance at where the hem brushed her upper thigh. She smirked at him.

He smiled and went back to his laces and Laurel closed herself in the bathroom. She scrubbed her face and freshened her makeup, finger-combed her tangled hair and thought its messiness looked rather fashionable. She dug out her travel toothbrush and got her mouth in order, lifted up the shirt to check for any marks on her body and didn't find any. She pouted, a bit sad about that.

Her clothes were still slung over the loveseat, including the panties she'd lost on the floor by the bed. She gave Flynn a smug look, stripped off the shirt, pleased by his rapt expression as he watched, his hands clasped politely between his knees.

"Subtle," she teased, adjusting her bra.

"You sleep okay?"

"Yup." She pulled her tank top on then her jeans. "Very roomy in that bed." She sat down across from him and slipped on her flats. "Okay. I'm ready."

Flynn went to his dresser, found a checked button-up and slipped it on over his tee shirt, grabbed his loaded key ring off the counter and clipped it to his belt. Laurel followed him out. She stole glances at his face as they rode the elevator down, looking for signs of awkwardness or regret, but he was tough to read. He unlocked her side of the station wagon first then slid into the driver's seat.

"Thanks for the lift," Laurel said, feeling shy.

"Thanks for the hot sex," Flynn replied, paused a moment, then grinned at her. He flipped his headlights on and started the engine.

She laughed and shook her head. "You too."

"Still not traumatized?"

"No."

"Good."

Laurel stared out her window as he steered them down the near-empty streets of South Boston, thinking it was a strange time of day, lit like dusk but with none of its energy.

She turned to him as they drove over the first bridge. "Can I ask you a question?"

"You just did."

"Have you always known that's how you are? Like, in bed?"

"No."

"When did you figure it out?" she asked.

"Well," he said, "maybe I sort of knew, when I was younger. But I wasn't one of those guys who was into that kind of stuff."

"What kind of stuff?"

"You know, like if those fucked-up *Saw* movies had been out when I was a teenager, or websites with creepy-ass rape fantasy shit on them, I don't think I would've been into it. I sort of knew what turned my crank, but I didn't like that it did. Plus like I said, it's not a fetish. Less rough stuff can get me off, so I sort of shoved it away in the back of my skull."

"Until?"

"Until I was about twenty-two, and I was dating this girl, and one night she asked me to boss her around and hold her down." Flynn stopped to let a woman cross the road with her dog. "And I dunno, it was like a light switch got flipped. Like a light switch attached to my dick flipped on and I fucking caught fire."

"Wow."

"Yeah. I didn't know anything about safe words or any of the rules people have around masochism, and eventually I think I just freaked her out, asking way too often if we could do that again. It totally took over the relationship and she dumped me and said I was a sick-o and a sex fiend and to go fuck myself. Which was fair. I can see how being too eager about wanting to pretend-rape your girlfriend could be creepy as fuck."

Laurel nodded.

"That wasn't like an epic breakup. I mean, we'd been going out for a couple months. But she demonized me enough that I got insecure about how things ended and I tramped it all down again, worried I was some kind of a latent rapist."

"When did you get all well-adjusted with it?"

Flynn pushed a breath through his nose. "When I was twenty-six, I think it was. I started seeing this woman—not dating, just sort of friendly sex. It was sort of like with you. She came with another guy to the fights one night and she saw whatever it is about me, and I got to her, I guess. So she approached me after a couple weeks and we started hanging out and messing around. She was a couple years older than me and about ten years smarter about sex, and she was the first woman who ever asked me, 'So what are you into?' And I was honest, for the first time, and she was into it, and she sort of set me straight about how rough stuff is supposed to work."

"Ah." Laurel tried to ignore the knot of jealousy squirming in her stomach. "How long did that go on for?"

"It was kind of random, like we'd hang out every week or two, for quite a while. Six months, maybe."

"Why did it end, do you think?" she asked.

"She moved to San Francisco."

"Oh. That'd do it." Laurel stared out the window, wondering what this mystery sex goddess looked like. "Were you in love with her?"

Flynn paused before answering. "I thought I was...not while we were hooking up, but when I found out she was leaving I was pretty upset. I thought she was the only woman on Earth I'd ever find who'd let me be how I wanted in bed, and it felt like something monumental was being taken away. But I mean, I didn't try to follow her or anything. And eventually I learned that those magic words—what are you into?—are all you really need. You just keep asking people that and eventually you find someone who fits with you." He looked at her pointedly.

"Yeah," Laurel said. "Or maybe you don't know you're into something but then you stalk some stranger all through the Financial District until he gives you the address to his shady underground boxing syndicate."

"I hear that works too. Anyhow, I'm at a point now where I know what I like, and I can admit it's a deal breaker if a woman I'm getting to know isn't into it." He stopped at a red light and met Laurel's eyes. "I'd rather go without and be lonely than not be how I really want with someone."

She felt a laugh bubble up but turned it into a huff. "You get lonely?"

He glowered at her a moment before it melted into a smile. "Course I do. I don't drink, so I don't get shitfaced and start like cryin' and singin' with my drunk-ass guy friends. Sex is…I don't know, it's like the realest sort of human experience I got, aside from fighting. It's hard, going without. I got nothin' against sitting up 'til one a.m. playing canasta with my sister, but it's not exactly a satisfying substitute."

Laurel nodded again and studied the waking city as they drove down Atlantic. "I'd like to come watch you fight again," she said. "Is there a Saturday night when Pam's not going to be there?" Something sour gurgled in her gut. She'd put off thinking about sharing this man pretty well until now.

"I can talk to her on Friday, tell her to take Saturday off."

She nodded, the politics of the thing feeling uncomfortable and awkward. "What time does it usually start? Right at eight?"

"Pretty close. But I never fight before nine, nine thirty. I'm like one of the main event type guys, I guess. They do all the younger guys first, the more amateur kids. Not that I'm a pro or anything."

"Are any of the guys who fight there pros?"

"Sure. Not like, *major*, but we've got a few regulars who make some money off it. There's a guy from Dorchester who won the Golden Gloves a couple years ago, middleweight. He gets some paid fights. Gets his ass kissed a little when he comes back to town."

"Do you ever fight him? Oh, or are you in different weight classes? You must be a heavyweight."

He raised an eyebrow at her. "You been doing your homework?"

She grinned, busted. "You've got to weigh at least two hundred pounds."

"Two-eighteen. And weight classes don't count for shit in that gym. Everybody just steps in with whoever else is up for it. Within reason. And yeah, I've fought him."

"Wow." She looked him over again, wishing she could see his arms. "What class would I be, if I boxed?"

"What are you, like a hundred and twenty?"

One-thirty-two, but Laurel nodded.

"Featherweight, depending on who's running the fight. Why? You wanna learn?"

"Ha—no thank you. I can't even stand to get into arguments with my roommates over the dishes. Confrontation gives me hives." She realized with disappointment that they were nearly at her building.

"Coulda fooled me," Flynn said. "You sure came on strong in that sub shop."

She shrugged. "You don't scare me."

He pulled up to the curb and leaned over, close. "Never?"

"Well, sometimes. But only in a good way."

He grinned indulgently then pecked a hard kiss into her temple. "God, you smell like something. What is that?"

"Something bad?" she asked.

"Hell no. Something awesome."

"Beats me. Probably some sex pheromone."

"Maybe," he said. "Well, I got to get to work. Come by this Saturday. You can ice my bruises."

She rolled her eyes at him and unstrapped her seat belt. "I'll see you later."

When she crept through the front door of her third-floor apartment, Laurel was surprised to be greeted by Anne's round, expectant face.

"What are you doing up?" Laurel asked, looking to the microwave clock.

"What are *you* doing, just getting home?" Anne grinned, blue eyes full of happy suspicion. She was by *far* Laurel's favorite of her two roommates. Christie had morphed into some kind of mutant *Ally McBeal* wannabe since discovering her brand-new life-long dream of going to law school.

"I was...out," Laurel offered, dumping her bag on the counter.

"Who with?"

"Just some guy."

"You've got sex hair," Anne said, doing her mischievous little thumb-biting thing, practically glowing with triumph.

"I've got *messy* hair," Laurel corrected, mussing it further with her hands. "That's all. And me and my messy hair need a shower."

"You smell like..." Anne came in close for a whiff. "Like the nastiest cocktail ever invented."

"It's Bactine." She hoped that wasn't what Flynn had smelled in the car.

"Have you taken up with a nurse?"

Laurel pushed her shoes off, resigned to the grilling she frankly owed her friend after months of romantic flatlining. "It's nothing to get excited about. It's nothing serious or anything." She ignored Anne's skeptical eyebrow. "And what *are* you doing up so early?"

Anne made a murderous face. "The fire alarm went off again. Four fifty-two in the frigging morning. You might've got away with your little midnight rendezvous if I hadn't barged in there to see if you were on fire. You want coffee?"

"God yes."

Anne pulled the canister out of the fridge. "So let me guess. It was so bad you caught the T as soon as it started running? I hate those mornings."

Laurel was tempted to run with the proffered excuse and be done with the conversation, but she wasn't much on lying. "No, he gave me a lift. He just works really early."

"How was the sex?"

"Who said I had sex?"

Another accusing eyebrow.

"Fine. The sex was great, actually. He's just not, you know, boyfriend material."

"What's wrong with him?"

"Depending on whose criteria you're going by, a lot. But I think he's all right. He's just not in the market for that, I don't think. It's not an exclusive thing."

Anne filled the pot and flipped the coffeemaker on. "Sounds sordid."

"It is, actually, and that's exactly how I want things to be right now."

"How liberated of you. You working today?"

Laurel nodded then yawned. "Not 'til one."

"Job searching this morning?"

"Sadly," Laurel fibbed. She wasn't above a fib. She'd been blaming her quasi-permanent delay in going back to engineering on the crappy state of the economy, but really the mere idea of it made her sick. "Not getting my hopes up though." She wandered to the fridge, read Christie's latest angry Post-It then rolled her eyes at Anne. "We're labeling our butter now?"

"She must be boning up on dairy liabilities." Anne's ability to shrug off other people's psychoses was her best trait. She set two mugs on the counter and Laurel stood the half and half carton beside them. They both crossed their arms and stared at the burbling coffeemaker.

"So can you tell me *anything* about your mysterious new conquest?" Anne asked.

"He's tall."

"Okay."

"And he's from here," Laurel said. "And he's kind of a meathead."

"Wow, sounds savory."

Laurel nodded. "He's gawt a wicked heavy accent."

Anne pulled the pot out before it was done brewing, drops of coffee hitting the burner with a sizzle, another offense Christie would surely want to make note of. "Pissah."

"Yes indeed." Laurel grinned as she poured cream into her cup and earned herself a nudge in the side.

"Look at you, little miss smiley. I'd like to meet the guy who made you do that for the first time in like a whole year."

"Well, you won't, so get over it."

They took their coffees into the living room and Anne switched on the TV, scanning through her roster of recorded shows. "Is six a.m. too early to watch *The Bachelor* and mock all the giggly, desperate women?"

"Go for it. Though I bet it'd work better as a drinking game," Laurel said. "One shot for the flirty arm touch. Chug if they strip and bum-rush the pool."

Anne hit play. "Like they'd get their hair wet."

Laurel stared at the screen, laughed at Anne's comments but felt another weird pang upset her insides. "Would you say this show makes something incredibly complex—you know, relationships—into something mind-numbingly vapid? Or does it make something actually rather simple into a big fucking circus?"

"Both. That's why I love it."

"I couldn't stand competing for a man like that," Laurel murmured. "I don't have the right...programming for it. Like to fight like that. Some people get an adrenaline rush and they're like *foosh*, give me somebody to beat down. I just, like, curl up into a ball and want to hide."

"I'm somewhere in the middle," Anne said. "I'm like a ninja. I'll, like, come out of my shadowy hiding space and beat you down, bitches. You won't even see me."

"The guy…"

Anne's head turned a fraction. "What about the guy?"

"He's a fighter," Laurel said. "Like, a boxer."

Anne swiveled her whole body to face Laurel, almost comically impressed. "Oh shit, that is *sexy*. Is he all, you know?" She mimed some Hulk Hoganish flexing, a funny look for a heavy girl.

Laurel nodded.

"Well done you."

Laurel watched a blonde woman have a breakdown on the TV, confessing her never-ending but tragic love for the show's sole male to the camera, to millions of viewers. "Like I said, it's not anything. I mean, look at that chick. Even if it was an option with this guy, I'm just not up for all that. All that messiness." She waved her hand at the on-screen meltdown.

"You're way less of a spaz than her," Anne said. "I so hope she goes next. Or actually, no. What am I saying—where's the fun in that?"

Laurel took a sip of her coffee. "Anyhow, it doesn't matter. This one's not exactly the guy you'd bring home for Christmas."

"Ah. Jewish?" Anne teased, then jerked her head around. "Is that you?"

"What?"

"Is that your phone?"

Laurel strained and picked out the sound of her ring over the television. She set her cup down and jogged to the kitchen counter. The last name she'd have expected blinked on the phone's screen.

"Hello?"

"Hey, sub shop girl."

She walked to the far side of the room to lean on the sink, keeping her voice low. "Hey. I thought you didn't do calling."

"I assumed you were beyond the potential freak-out stage. Was I wrong?"

"I guess not. What's up?"

"I'm at the Dunkies by my site and I figured out what you smell like."

Laurel made a noise only she heard, a little laugh caught in her nose. "Oh. What's that?"

"That gooey stuff inside a Boston crème donut. That's what you smell like. Now I'll get a hard-on every time I eat one."

She snorted. "Did you just call to sexually harass me?"

"I'm allowed now, ain't I?"

"Go to work, Flynn. Go…go drink some decaf."

"Yes, ma'am." Laurel heard a smile in his voice before he hung up.

She flipped her phone closed and aimed a goofy smile at the sink, composing her face before heading back to the living room.

Anne batted her eyelashes demurely as Laurel flopped onto the couch. "That was him, wasn't it? Your mister he's-not-anything."

"So what?"

"So you are so doomed, Laurel. You look like you just put on a whole tub of rouge."

"Stupid traitorous complexion."

"I think it's cute. I think you like him," Anne teased.

Laurel pointed her eyes at the screen, as stony as she could manage. "Shut your face, please."

"Oh man, you have it bad. I bet his arms are like..." Anne cupped her hands as if she were trying to grab hold of something big.

"Silence, please? I'm trying to watch this documentary." Laurel nodded at *The Bachelor*. "I believe one of the females is about to present to the alpha."

"Fine," Anne sighed. "Be that way. But don't think for a second you're any good at hiding that shit-eating grin."

"I am cool as a cucumber," Laurel said loftily.

"Bitch, you are fucking doomed."

* * * * *

When Laurel descended the metal steps to the gym on Saturday night, the smell made her dizzy. Enjoyably so. She found Flynn still dressed in street clothes, talking to the same young ref from the week before, demonstrating some combinations in the air between them. She walked over, waved as she caught Flynn's eye. He gave the kid a clap on the shoulder and he and Laurel were left alone.

"Hey there, sub shop girl. You're early. It's barely seven-thirty."

"Both my buses came really quick." Technically true, though more accurately she'd left early, wanting the pre-fight time to hang out with Flynn, to see how he changed from the start of the evening to the end. And to be seen with him.

"Well make yourself useful," he said. "Come on."

He led her to a metal rack loaded with free weights, grabbing one in each hand and nodding to say she should do the same. She selected a smaller pair, fifteen pounds apiece, and followed Flynn, shuffling behind him into a side room filled with workout equipment. They slowly emptied the rack of dumbbells then carried it to the room, shutting and locking the door.

"They should really just put wheels on that thing," she said.

"Where's the fun in that? Now why don't you get the beer station set up?" He pointed to the folding table leaning against the far wall, plastic bags of Solo cups and a keg sitting beside it.

Laurel did as she was told, pleased to be a part of the evening, a part of the gym. Part of some secret, shady club, so much more interesting than her own life lately. She wandered to where Flynn was chatting with another fighter, a stocky guy already dressed in shorts.

"I can't lift the keg by myself," she said and offered a small wave to the other man.

"Laurel, Jared, Jared, Laurel," Flynn said, and they shook hands before Flynn walked to the beer table with her, hefting the keg by himself while Laurel basked in the glow of having been introduced, of being someone worth introducing.

"That closet's full of folding chairs," Flynn said, nodded to a corner. "You want to stack about twenty of them against that bare wall?"

"I don't see you doing much work for this boxing co-op," she teased.

His brows rose, smug. "The minute you start getting punched in the face for everybody's entertainment, I'll quit bossing you around."

She stepped close. "I like when you boss me around."

He smirked. "Well you just keep up the bitching and you'll get what you like."

She headed to the closet so he wouldn't see how broad her grin grew. By the time she finished arranging chairs Flynn had disappeared and come back changed, same tee shirt but wearing track pants again, running shoes. People were trickling in, boxers warming up. Flynn grabbed two chairs and carried them to his little corner. He and Laurel sat side by side in comfortable silence, watching as everyone's excitement primed.

"Which is better," she asked, "Friday or Saturday?"

"Saturday. More folks come, and that's the night when the virgins — the first-timers — get to step in. Friday night's just for regulars, and newcomers only get to watch. The energy's way better on Saturdays. Fresh blood."

She laughed. "How old were you when you first fought?"

"Here?" He squinted into the middle distance, thinking. "Maybe twenty-four."

"What about the first time you ever fought somebody else, anywhere?"

He frowned. "Shit, I dunno. When I was six?"

"Wow, aggro much?"

"You ever been in a fight?" he asked.

"Not a proper fight… I got detention for kicking Shelly Walker in the butt with my muddy boot when I was in fourth grade."

Flynn laughed. "What'd she do to deserve it?"

She smiled down at her hands. "I think she badmouthed Joey McIntyre or something. I was a *hardcore* New Kids fan."

Flynn made an amused, judging face. "I hope it was worth it."

"Oh yes. Nobody puts Joey Mac down and gets away with it."

"You're a passionate woman, sub shop girl. Your parents give you hell for it?"

Laurel worked hard to keep her smile from drooping too noticeably. "Nah, they didn't care." She was relieved when the fights kicked off. Two guys in their twenties climbed into the ring, one tall, one short, both pretty slender and ropey.

"Are either of these guys newcomers?" she asked Flynn.

"Guy in the red shorts is a virgin. He'll win though."

"How can you tell?" she asked.

"Because the other guy's scared."

"He doesn't look scared."

"Watch how much he swallows and blinks," Flynn said, "and how tight he's got his shoulders."

She studied the man a moment and nodded.

"Plus he didn't even warm up. When a young guy shows up and doesn't warm up, it's because he's already decided he's going to lose, so he doesn't try. Like if he tries and loses, it's worse than just saying 'fuck it' and pretending he doesn't care what happens. Fucking pathetic."

"Do you hate quitters as much as you hate impatient people?"

Flynn smiled. "I try and hate everybody equally."

He was right about the match. The spectators made a noisy show of heckling the young fighters but the newcomer earned an easy victory and scattered, half-assed applause. The crowd multiplied as the clock neared nine and Flynn stood, stripping off his shirt and tossing it on top of his gym bag. Laurel gave his prep routine her full attention, ignoring the action in the ring.

She watched him wind tape around his palms and wrists. "You have no clue how manly you are, do you?"

He cocked an eyebrow at her but didn't reply.

"Are you up next?" she asked.

"Yup." He tossed a few punches in the air in front of his face, stretched his arms and back and jogged in place.

"Who are you fighting?"

He peered around the relative darkness, still jogging. "Not sure. Never sure until you step in there. You turn up and they give you a few slots, don't tell you who you're up against."

"Is there anyone you're afraid to fight?"

Flynn stopped jogging and gave her a supremely patronizing look. "You want me to find you a dull blade so you can just hack my nuts off?"

"No, just curious. You're not afraid of anybody?"

"Like I'd tell you if I was." He waved an arm around the basement. "You might as well open up a vein in a tank full of sharks, talking about fear around these guys."

"Oh sorry."

He shrugged and Laurel sensed she'd made a faux pas, touched a nerve if not insulted him outright. She bit her lip, feeling stupid.

"Don't look like that," Flynn said. "You're still getting your brains fucked out when we leave here, kiddo."

She blushed and grinned down at her hands. She jumped as Flynn surprised her, grabbing her arm and pulling her to standing. He took her face in his cotton-wrapped hands and claimed her mouth in a deep, territorial kiss. He broke away looking mean. In the ring, the ref called a winner.

"You're up," she said.

He nodded and grabbed his gloves from the ground, ripping apart the Velcro straps that linked them together.

"Aren't you supposed to wear a mouth guard?" Laurel asked.

"This place isn't much on rules." Flynn tugged his gloves on. "That's why I like it."

She frowned. "That's just stupid. You could get your teeth knocked out."

He gave his neck a stretch that popped something audibly. "I hate those things. They make me feel like I'm choking on something."

"Guess I'll never get you into a ball gag, huh?" she asked.

Flynn met the remark with a withering sneer. "Keep that snark up and you'll get yourself punished, missy."

She offered a sarcastic quaking-in-my-boots pantomime and he punched her gently on the shoulder then wandered to ringside. Laurel studied his back muscles and triceps and tried to guess if he got nervous before he boxed. She suspected not.

The ref shouted over the din. "Next fight!"

The crowd murmured, air crackling with anticipation. Bloodlust. From the other side of the ring, Flynn's opponent approached. They climbed up and over the ropes at the same time and Laurel felt her stomach fold in on itself with sudden nerves.

The other man wasn't as tall as Flynn but probably weighed a few pounds more, some of it muscle, some straight bulk. He looked about twenty-five, with bleached blond hair and dark roots and sharp, closely spaced eyes that lent him a weasely quality. They tapped gloves and backed into opposite corners. Flynn's posture changed, shoulders hunching, feet shifting restlessly.

The ref whacked the bell with a wrench and the match was on. Flynn straightened up, dropping his guard and acting casual as the two fighters circled. The other man looked punchy and eager and took the offensive for the round, coming fast at Flynn a few times and threatening some jabs. Flynn kept himself relaxed, pulling his head back from the strikes but leaving his guard largely open. After a minute of this the crowd got impatient, as did the blond guy. The second he made a real rush, Flynn got serious. He snapped his guard up and hunched his shoulders, upped his footwork. Unlike when he'd fought the big black guy the week before, he didn't take any punches on purpose. He dodged and blocked until the bell rang to end the round, not having thrown a single punch of his own. Laurel met him in his corner with water.

"Thanks, kiddo." He downed half of it and handed the cup back.

"You gonna do something soon?"

"When I'm good and ready." He offered a smug grin that heated Laurel's insides like liquor.

The next round was much the same as the first. Flynn continued to hold back, his inactivity pissing the blond guy off as the seconds wore on—Laurel could see in the set of the man's jaw that he was getting tweaked. Toward the end of the three minutes he lost his cool. He came at Flynn with his whole body, a torrent of powerful but graceless punches. Flynn blocked a couple and took a hard hook to the neck and jab to the nose, then came back with a combination that landed on the blond guy's chest and temple with two wet thwacks. The guy dropped to his knees for a short count, finding his feet seconds before the bell rang. Flynn knocked his gloved hands together, aiming a look at his opponent that Laurel couldn't make out. The ref rang the bell again and both men retired grudgingly to their corners.

"'Bout time," Laurel said as she gave him his water.

"You can't rush a symphony like this."

She shook her head at his aggrandizing tone, pretending to disapprove. Flynn crossed his arms on the rope and looked down at her, as casual as he might if they were waiting on a subway platform.

You are some fucked-up kind of magical, she thought.

Flynn handed the cup back and turned away as the bell sounded to signal the third round. He didn't waste the final three minutes. Laurel wondered if he had some philosophy to prove...that a good fighter only needed one round to lay another man out. Or maybe this was a big fuck-you to his opponent, letting him know he didn't think the guy deserved a full fight's effort. At any rate, he didn't even need the three minutes. He needed just over two, then a terrifying right hook snapped the blond guy's head to the side, left him staggering a few paces until he toppled over as though his legs simply stopped working.

The normally surly crowd offered the most enthusiastic applause Laurel had heard yet. She clapped awkwardly with the cup in one hand, eyes on the fallen man. He blinked groggily after a half a minute but didn't make it to standing before the ref called the fight and thrust Flynn's arm into the air. Flynn helped his opponent to his feet, rewarded with a sour look as the man yanked his arm away. They exchanged a couple words Laurel didn't catch. Flynn ducked between the ropes and hopped heavily to the concrete floor.

"Well done," she said, handing him the last of the water.

He held the cup up in a weary toast and drained it. They wandered to the corner together and he let her blot his sweat-beaded forehead with the towel.

"Do you ever lose?"

"Not a lot, but sometimes. Few times a year, sure. I've been doing this since I was twelve, so I'm pretty good." He touched his fingers to a clot of blood at one nostril, opening the flow and frowning at his red fingertips.

"Oh gross," Laurel said. "And twelve? Really? Is that even legal? Well, I guess if karate's legal..."

"That kid over there?" He pointed at the teenaged ref. "That used to be me. So fucking eager and hardly anybody around small enough to fight. My sister's ex, Robbie, he managed a gym in Southie way back then. He let me hang around because he was so nuts about her, and she thought it'd keep me out of trouble."

Laurel stared at the kid, feet at the edge of the ring, hands wrapped around the top rope, antsy as hell. "Did you ever want to fight professionally?"

"Nah. I'm too territorial to ever leave this neighborhood to go on the circuit."

"Really?"

"I think so. Why, you plannin' on marrying me and dragging my ass down to Providence to make babies?"

Laurel's mouth fell open and she felt her cheeks burn. Flynn laughed at her shock and gave her a clap on the shoulder. "You're too easy to freak out, kiddo."

"No I'm not."

"Yeah, you are. It's cute." He stared into the basement's dim chaos. "Think you'd never been flirted with before."

"Not about marriage. Not by a man who's actively bleeding." She frowned at him and dabbed at his nose with the towel.

"Yeah, well, it's cute that that scares you when all the other shit I've done to you doesn't. Makes my heart all fluttery." He smirked at her. "Mrs. Laurel Flynn. Nice ring to it, don't you think?"

She wasn't sure what to say to that. Part of her was flattered he wasn't afraid to tease her about something that serious, but mostly she felt insulted. There wasn't a doubt in her mind that she and Flynn wouldn't ever go beyond regular fuckbuddies, but the fact that he could snark about marriage stung…not that she'd been bookmarking dresses online or anything. But a bottle of conditioner to keep in his shower, maybe, some tiny symbol of her significance. *Idiot.*

Laurel shrugged off her angst, made a decision to enjoy herself. So what if Flynn didn't belong only to her? She could always ask him not to mention that he had another lover if it kept hurting. She didn't want it to hurt though. She wanted to not give a shit, to be as well-adjusted and relaxed about their arrangement as he was.

Laurel went through all the same motions for the rest of the evening's matches, joking with Flynn, fetching his water when he was in the ring, clapping when he inevitably won his second and third matches, inventorying his fresh injuries. The bitterness faded and she found herself excited and happy again, happy just to be here, so far out of her element but seeming to belong somehow, among all these sweaty, battered ruffians, permanence and significance be damned.

Flynn changed into street clothes around twelve thirty and they left, the back door closing behind them and cutting off the sounds of other men's violence.

They walked to Flynn's building without speaking and he punched the floor buttons for two and five. He made his usual stop to knock on his sister's door then returned, a hardness to his expression.

"You okay?" Laurel asked.

"Second we get in that apartment," Flynn muttered, "it's on."

"What's on?"

The growl in his voice was all the answer she needed. "You fucking know."

Laurel held her breath the whole way down the hall, heart hammering as the door shut and deadbolt clicked. She turned to face Flynn. He tossed his bag by the door and approached her with slow, even steps. Laurel swallowed. His eyes were wild in the faint light leaking in from the city.

"Michael," she said. "Sorry. I just really need to use the bathroom. Hold that glare."

She peed and tried to gargle away her beer breath with a mouthful of tap water, checked her makeup and stepped back out into the dangerous dark. The absence of the bathroom light left her momentarily blind and she gasped as a hand grabbed her wrist and twisted it behind her back, rough, almost painful. Flynn had taken his shirt off—she felt his damp skin plastered against her bare arm as he leaned down to speak just behind her ear.

"Scream and I swear I'll kill you."

The blood drained from Laurel's face and fingers, her extremities going numb as her pussy clenched and flooded with heat. He smelled dangerous, like sweat and blood and dirt, and Laurel forgot how to breathe for a moment. She found the barest squeak of her voice as his hand tightened around her wrist.

"Don't," she whispered.

"Don't what?" he jeered. He pushed her, walked her roughly to the bed, forcing her down onto her chest, legs hanging over the edge. He let her wrist go to reach beneath her, both hands tugging at the button of her jeans. Adrenaline surged through her veins, mixed with her excitement, made her tingle with aggression and fear. She thrashed, flailing onto her back and wedging her feet against Flynn's stomach, trying to push him away, determined to make him work for it so she could feel the power and danger of his strength. He yanked her jeans down her thighs and off her calves, hooked her around the waist as she made it to her feet and tried to run. His arm half-knocked her wind out and she blinked herself to coherence to find her back against the bed again. Flynn's knees pushed between hers, one hand unbuckling his belt as the other pinned her by the shoulder. His black silhouette blocked out the jaundiced glow from the windows and made him seem anonymous, deepening the pulse throbbing between Laurel's legs.

She slapped his arm with both hands, buckling it a moment with a hard hit to the inside of his elbow.

"Bitch." He ignored more strikes, finishing with his pants and wrestling to get her wrists in his grip. He'd gotten his hard cock out—Laurel felt it pressing against the crotch of her panties as he brought his body down to hers. He made a deep, hungry animal noise that raised the hairs all down her arms. She yanked and pushed as violently as she could, barely budging his arms.

"Don't make this harder than it needs to be." He held both her wrists in one fist, pinning them above her head as he reached for the shelf. He ripped the condom open with his teeth and got it on so fast Laurel was impressed. She forced herself back into character, bucking her body under his.

"Fucking lay still," he whispered. He reached down and pushed the crotch of her panties to one side, big fingers

Willing Victim

finding her pussy wet and ready. "Oh yeah, you're gonna feel beautiful."

Two fingers slid in deep, thrusting, and Laurel did what she hoped was a convincing job of feigning disgust and terror. He had her pinned so effectively she couldn't move anything but her head more than an inch. She did the only thing she could and spat in his face.

Flynn froze and Laurel was suddenly glad she couldn't see his expression. He held both their bodies so still his flaring breaths rang out like shouts in the dark. Anticipation held court for a moment then he lowered, fearfully slow, covered her mouth with his as his hand left her panties to clasp her jaw. He forced his thumb between her lips, got her teeth apart even as Laurel bit down as hard as she thought she could without breaking his skin. His tongue slid into her mouth, finding hers and giving her as explicit and dirty a kiss as he could manage. He pulled away, keeping his face close, pressing his forehead to hers and sliding his thumb out of her mouth.

"You don't wanna know how rough I can play, girl." His lips brushed hers. "Now I'm gonna let your hands go and you're gonna be good, or else I'm gonna be real bad. You got that?"

"Don't do this."

Flynn ground his rock-hard cock against her pubic bone. "You didn't give me a choice, bitch."

He released her numb hands, leaned back and pulled her underwear aside again. She felt the head of his cock pressing hard between her legs, seeking her entrance. Laurel hauled off and slapped him dead across the face, harder than she'd ever hit anyone in her entire life. The noise must have been scarier than the force, as Flynn's head barely moved. A sound that belonged to a pissed-off bull hissed from his nose.

His whispered words came out smug and dangerous. "You're so fucked."

Laurel grabbed hold of both his arms as he angled his dick and pushed inside. Fuck, he felt amazing. She stifled a moan as he forced his way into her clenched pussy.

"You're so tight when you fight me, girl." He took the whacks and slaps she laid on his arms, all his energy focused on the penetration. He eased in slow, halfway, then pulled back and rammed himself home.

Laurel cried out, the surprise all real.

He made a filthy, satisfied noise and thrust again. He yanked his arms out of her grip and grasped her wrists, pinning them together again above her head, one hand free to wrap around her throat.

"Tell me you love it," he ordered.

Laurel gave a good thrash then froze as the hand on her neck tightened. Not hard enough to choke but plenty hard enough to intimidate.

"Tell me."

She swallowed, the motion thick and labored under his palm. "I love it."

"I thought so. Tell me how I feel, bitch."

She whimpered, the noise utterly authentic. "Hard," she managed to say.

"What else?"

She swallowed again. "Big. And thick."

"Yeah." He pumped her deep, seeming to luxuriate. His hips felt powerful, thighs strong and hard, spreading her wide. He released her throat, took a wrist in each hand and held them on the mattress on either side of her butt. Laurel wanted to drown in the grunts that punctuated each rough thrust. She kept her arms tugging and her pussy clenched and kept her ecstasy to herself.

After a couple minutes' hard fucking Flynn released her tingling hands, pulled out, lifted her legs and flipped her onto her stomach. He yanked her panties down her legs and pinned her thighs together with his clothed knees. His hands found hers again, bringing them together at the small of her back, forcing her head to one side. She was too turned on to muster much of a fight, just moaned as his dick brushed her butt, slid between her thighs and plunged back inside her pussy. His zipper scraped against her ass.

"God yeah." Flynn sounded close to release, the words strangled, his body losing coordination. Laurel felt drops of sweat land on her back and wished she could see that hard body working, all those glistening muscles and his angry cuts and bruises.

"Oh fuck, I'm gonna come in you. Fight me, bitch. Fight me."

Laurel did her pathetic best to struggle and the little resistance she managed was enough. Flynn pounded her for a half minute and came apart, hips hammering as he groaned through his release. Laurel expected him to collapse but the opposite happened. He let her go and rolled her onto her back, ditched the condom and curled his body beside hers. She relaxed her head into the pillow as his hand found her pussy. He dipped two fingers inside to wet them then teased her clit, fast and frantic.

"Oh God—" His mouth cut off her moan, kissing her hard and deep. Laurel touched his face, his damp hair and skin, let her legs twitch as his hand set her on fire. When his face drew away she watched his slick arm flexing to pleasure her, the contour of his side and hip and jeans-clad ass in the ambient light.

"God, don't stop."

His fingers rubbed harder, bringing the pleasure to a rolling boil.

"Use your thumb," she stammered. "Fuck me with your fingers."

He tucked his body closer, got two fingers inside, then three, then all four, thrusting rough for a minute before pressing his thumb to her clit.

"Flynn. God, fuck me."

"Come on, girl. Come on." He circled her clit, the sensation so intense she felt a wall form between her mind and reality. Pleasure jerked her deep into the climax, bubbled up from her core and spilled into her arms and legs and out her mouth in a long, animal moan. His hand slowed as her clenches became twitches, until the last drops of her orgasm were wrung from her quaking body.

"Holy fuck."

He slid his fingers out, wiped them on the bedspread. His warm, slippery chest pressed against her as his arms wrapped around her waist. He rested his mouth against her collarbone and oozed out a long, satisfied sound that heated her skin.

"Shit, you're so hot."

Laurel giggled, smiling up at the ceiling. "You're real pretty yourself."

"Let's quit our jobs and fuck all day."

"Works for me. Think somebody will subsidize that? Maybe we could apply for some kind of research grant," she said.

Flynn made a happy noise and his arms tightened. They lay quietly for ten minutes, until their collective breathing was even, sweaty bodies cooled. Flynn pulled away, got to his feet, wandered across the apartment to switch on the lights. Laurel sat up and watched him putter, tossing clothes from his gym bag into a hamper. He disappeared into the bathroom briefly and the sound of the shower left Laurel sad, made her wish his smell wasn't being washed away. He came out with a towel wrapped around his waist, hair dripping. She studied his body, those familiar injuries like angry, transient tattoos.

She rolled herself off the bed, went to bathroom to tidy herself and retrieve some first-aid accessories. Flynn glanced at the items as she emerged and he took a seat obediently on the coffee table.

"God, you're such a mess." She sat at the edge of the chair and soaked a wad of toilet paper with peroxide, tilting his head up to swab his latest cuts. She smeared Bactine over the deep ones, studied his eyes under the guise of scrutinizing his injuries. He moaned as she daubed at a scrape on his throat, not a sound of pain.

He pressed his neck into her touch, spoke through a heavy sigh. "I like when you do that."

"Do what?"

"You know…" His words faded to a mumble. "Fuss over me."

"Take care of you?"

He nodded, just the briefest dip of his chin. Laurel wasn't sure what to do with this information. It was tough to write things off with Flynn as he so rarely made sentimental proclamations, and the ones he did couldn't be blamed on alcohol. She finished swabbing the scrape, blotted his skin until none of the tiny lines offered any fresh blood.

"You're a strange man, Michael Flynn."

"Can I call you Nurse White? That's such a good porno name."

She rolled her eyes at him. "I bet there isn't much porn out there that does it for you, huh?"

"Why d'you say that?" He raised his eyebrows, skeptical.

"Because the normal stuff's probably too boring, and the things that you *are* into…well, I just imagine it would be icky, watching other people pretending to do rape stuff and all that. I mean, I feel grossed out just trying to imagine Googling the keywords for that."

"You're a smart girl," he said, nodding.

"Plus I don't think you own a computer. Or a TV."

"There's a laptop around here someplace," he said, sounding suddenly sleepy and distracted. "I haul it to the coffee shop if I need to do something online."

"You know," Laurel began, then trailed off.

"What do I know?"

"I was just thinking, when I first met you, you seemed really…obvious. And you're not. Not just how you are in bed," she said, rambling. "On the outside you're like über-macho, Mr. Toolbelt-and-Boxing Gloves with your bossy accent and your attitude and your…tallness."

"My tallness?"

"And your body and everything. But you're really something else on the inside. Sorry," she said. "That sounded way more squishy than I meant it to. Should I insult you, to take the edge off all that squishiness?"

"Nah. I'll just take it out on you next time."

She smiled to herself. "I'm sure you will." She eased a bandage over his worst cut, pressed it carefully into place. "Done fussing."

He nodded. Laurel carried the things back to the bathroom, took a quick shower and reemerged naked. Flynn was stretched out on the bed in his shorts. He sat up as she flipped the bathroom light and fan off. As always, his gaze lacked subtlety and as always, she liked it.

"Can I steal another shirt to sleep in?"

He managed to stare even more pointedly. "Fuck no." But he rose after a moment and tossed her a tee from his dresser, looking disappointed as it swallowed her torso.

"Thanks."

"Hit the lights and get over here."

Laurel turned the overhead lights off, came back to the bed, wiped the dust from her feet and lay back on the rumpled covers. Flynn rolled to his side, coming close. He wrapped his arms around her waist and buried his face in her damp hair, his breath flaring in hot, slow intervals.

"You said you don't do spooning," she said.

He made a shushing noise.

"Are you the only one allowed to break the rules you make?" she asked.

"I dunno. Try sometime and find out."

They lay in silence for a long time. As Laurel grew drowsy she felt Flynn's body calm then turn restless. His sticky arms shifted around her.

"You okay?" she asked.

"Christ, your skin smells so fucking good."

Before Laurel could offer a sleepy reply she was turned onto her back and Flynn was braced above her. Her body roused a few seconds ahead of her brain. "Hello."

"Like vanilla custard."

"So you say."

He leaned in and kissed her, light and slow, a drag of his warm lips against hers. "You too sore?" he asked.

"Nope. Have at it."

He smirked. "You need lube?"

"Find out for yourself."

The smile deepened and he slid a hand between their bodies, two fingers dipping inside her pussy. "Oh fuck."

His warm body left her as he found a condom and kicked his underwear away. Laurel peeled her shirt off and watched him stroke himself stiff, knowing the mere fact he hadn't ordered her to do it marked this occasion as different. By the time he rolled the condom on, his breathing was labored, heavy and impatient. She propped her legs open as he knelt between them, palms flat on the mattress beside her ribs. His hips angled his cock at her pussy, sinking him in, slow.

"Goddamn," Laurel muttered. "I love your cock."

He lowered to his elbows and pushed his face against her neck, muffling his words. "I love your cunt. You're so fucking warm. I can't get enough of this."

She whispered above his ear. "Do you want me to struggle?"

"No. I just want to fuck you."

She ran her hands up and down his body, admiring his back muscles, his ass, the week-old rope-burn scar still raised along his shoulders, his soft, short hair. Eventually her palms settled on his hips. She memorized how he felt. She brought her legs up, wanting to wrap herself around him, possess him as he was possessing her. He took his time, pumping her deep, savoring, giving his stiff cock whatever it demanded. Each breath huffed out as a shallow grunt against her collarbone. In time his thrusts shifted, turned frantic, the change in this domineering man fascinating her. She clawed her fingers against his skin and released a shudder from the power she felt, feeling and hearing him turn so helpless.

"Michael."

Flynn shot up, propped himself on his arms and froze.

"Oh God, sorry," she said. "That was supposed to be a sweet-nothing, not a safe word."

She felt his tight thigh and arm muscles release. "You scared me."

"Sorry. Is it okay if I call you that? Can I change my word?"

"To what?"

She thought a second. "Parakeet?"

"Fine." He leaned in close again, bringing his slick chest back to hers, breathing into her shoulder. "I'm not used to being called that though."

"What, parakeet?"

He snorted. "No, genius—Michael. Doesn't really feel like my name."

"You'd rather I called you Flynn?"

He pushed back up on to his arms. "Yeah."

"Okay. I will. But let's keep the new safe word. In case I slip up again."

His body pumped once more. The desperate quality from before hardened, transformed at least partly into Flynn's usual, aggressive sexual style. He felt good, but she missed that little taste of what she suspected was a rare glimpse into some softer side of Flynn. Of Michael, maybe. But she made a mental note to not get her hopes up about seeing too much of this man's gentler alter ego.

Above her, Flynn moaned. He hammered her deep, thighs slapping hers with each thrust. "Take my fucking cock."

She grasped his hips, tugging in time with his body to urge him on.

"God, I wish I could fuck you bare. Come right inside you." He slammed into her then suddenly stopped, pulling out and moving back on the mattress.

"Is everything okay?"

He was already lowering himself, moving his face between her legs. "I need to taste you."

She gasped as his tongue lapped her clit, hot and wet and hungry. He hooked his arms under her thighs and clamped his hands to the creases below her hipbones. Laurel had gotten plenty of head in her time, but never like this. Flynn *fucked* her with his mouth—tongue driving deep, lips suckling, the stubble of his jaw scraping her tender skin to fan the flames. He set a rhythm of firm licks from her lips to her clit, punctuating each with a grunted, "Yeah."

"God, Flynn."

"You taste so fucking amazing." He brought his head up and Laurel could see the violent rise and fall of his chest. "Sit on my face," he said.

She sat up and they swapped places, Flynn lying back with his head just below the pillows. She swung a leg over and wedged her calves under his arms, settling her pussy against his mouth and grasping the edge of a shelf for balance. She fussed with the position until he yanked down on her hips, pulling her closer. "Oh God."

His voice was thick and desperate. "Fuck my mouth." He made his tongue stiff, spearing her, nose grazing her clit, and Laurel rocked her hips and let the sensations and textures of him drive her insane. One hand left her and she felt the motions behind her back, knowing he'd started jerking. She let go of the shelf and leaned back, craned her neck, wishing she could see more. A flash of pumping fist and swollen cock, the condom stripped away—then her balance faltered and she aimed her face forward again and grabbed the shelf.

Flynn broke away to suggest something that unnerved her a little. "Turn around."

She obeyed, still unsure which of them was in charge but happy to hand over the keys. She got in position and tried to ignore how vulnerable she felt, spread open with her ass in his face. But as she braced herself on her palms, facing his feet, the view made it entirely worth it. Flynn's mouth went back to work, followed by his hand.

"Yes," she murmured. "Gimme a good show, Flynn." It wouldn't be hard to stroke or suck him herself, but Laurel wanted to make him do the work, to be served and indulged by this bossy man. She watched his tight fist pulling on his thick cock, luxuriated in his flicking tongue and sucking lips on her cunt. Her brain projected a screen over the visual and she imagined him coming. Each time she conjured the image of him shooting, bathing his stomach in all that hot cream, she edged closer to climax. When the pre-come glistened at his tip she reached out to rub it into his head, teasing his slit with her thumb, loving the moan he rewarded her with.

"I can't wait to watch you come, Flynn."

His grip seemed to tighten, the pulls slowing for Laurel's enjoyment, turning more explicit. She cupped his tight balls in her palm, squeezing, fondling, rubbing the smooth skin just behind them. His body jerked beneath her, suddenly sending her tumbling into her release. Her thighs fluttered around his face as the pleasure pulsed through her clit and pussy, clenching her hand around the bedspread and his sac. He bucked again at the touch of her climax. His fist cranked into overdrive, fucking his cock fast and rough, getting him there just behind her. His chest and stomach clenched as if he were trying to do a sit-up beneath her, then the first spurt shot come against his damp skin, followed by two more spasms, a deep groan, then peace. He swore softly.

Laurel crawled off him and flopped onto the mattress. Flynn grabbed the towel and cleaned himself up, then his body wrapped around hers again, warm and sticky.

"Man," she mumbled. "That visual should keep me going 'til the next time I come over."

"Pervert."

"Oh right. Me, the pervert." She reached back to pat his damp hair. "You keep telling yourself that."

They fell silent, sleep coming down hard on Laurel like a narcotic curtain. Clothes, covers and no-cuddling rules abandoned, she fell asleep to the rhythmic sound of Flynn's breaths against her hair.

* * * * *

Laurel woke first the next morning, lazy light from the tall windows coaxing her eyes open. She peeled her body from Flynn's, still in the same positions as when they'd fallen asleep. He groaned as she stood from the bed.

"What time is it?"

She squinted at the microwave. "Nine-thirty-two."

"Oh fuck." He sat up, confirmed the time and swung his legs to the floor. "This is real obnoxious, but we have to get going."

Laurel hid a pang of hurt. She'd been looking forward to a lazy couple of hours before she had to get home and dress for work and face reality. "Seriously? It's Sunday."

"I know. I gotta drive my sister to frigging church." He yanked his underwear and jeans up his legs. "I can drop you at home, if that works for you."

"Oh. Sure." She dressed and threw on some mascara and concealer, frowned in the bathroom mirror at her hair, parted weirdly from being slept on damp.

Flynn looked ready to go when she emerged.

"Sorry about the rush," he said. "I don't usually sleep so late, but you must have fucked the sense out of me."

The compliment pushed away some of her disappointment. "No problem. I have to work in a while, so I should probably get going anyhow."

She assembled her purse and Flynn locked up behind them. They took the elevator down three flights and she followed him to apartment 202. Flynn knocked and female voices flared behind the door.

"They're never fucking ready on time." He thumped a couple extra times. "Jesus can't wait all day, ladies."

Laurel raised an eyebrow at him. "What was your stance on impatient people again?"

"Punctuality trumps patience."

"And where exactly does hypocrisy fit in?"

Flynn's smirking retort was cut off as the door opened and a harried-looking woman appeared before them. She was tall and pale like Flynn but with unconvincing auburn hair and at least an extra decade's wear and tear.

"You have to pound my door so fucking hard, Mike?"

"It's nearly ten of. Heather, this is Laurel, Laurel, this is my sister, Heather."

Heather put out a hand and gave Laurel's a firm shake with a faint bite of acrylic nail. "Nice to meet you. Kim's just putting her face on." Heather left the door open and disappeared inside, replaced by a faint whiff of stale cigarettes.

Laurel raised an eyebrow at Flynn. "Putting her face on? I thought your niece was like six years old."

"That's my grandniece, I guess. Great-niece? That's Kayla. She's usually at her dad's on the weekends, or with his mom, at any rate. My niece Kim is twenty-two."

"How old is Heather?" Laurel asked, keeping her voice low.

Flynn did a calculation in his head. "Forty-six."

"Wow, big gap."

"There's a few more of us in between, but I'm only close with Heather."

His sister reappeared in the doorway. "Yeah, I raised his ass."

Flynn nodded. "Yeah, she raised my ass. Fine upstanding citizen you created too."

Heather gave him an unimpressed look. "Sober, employed, no record. I did just fine, thank you."

A plump young woman materialized behind her, looking more prepared for loitering outside a convenience store than for church. Snug jeans with overdone fade marks, brassy-blonde hair pulled back in a sort of tight-bunned Latina style, two long corkscrew curls hanging down in front of her ears. Her makeup suggested she was looking to make an unlikely impression on her Lord and Savior.

"Hey," she said. "I'm Kim."

"Laurel." They shook hands as Heather locked up.

Flynn led them to the elevator and a minute later they piled into the car, shotgun entrusted to Laurel. Flynn started the engine and made a U-turn onto the street.

"So where's Ricky these days?" he asked, eyes on the rearview at one of the women. No one spoke. "What's a shrug mean?" he asked. "Prison? Rehab? Cult?"

Kim spoke, sounding theatrically bored. "No. He's around."

"Around where?"

"I dunno," she sighed. "Someplace."

"He still in school?"

Another sigh, angstier than the last. "If I see him I'll ask him."

"Where's Kayla? With his mom?"

Another silent reply via the rearview.

Laurel stared straight ahead at the road, wondering how often Flynn's fly-by-night lovers drove around with his family on a given Sunday morning.

"Your eye looks better," Heather said.

"This one's been playing nurse, taking good care of me," Flynn said, tossing a thumb at Laurel.

She blushed, glad the women wouldn't see.

Flynn pulled up beside a stone church five minutes later.

"Thanks, Mike," Heather said. "Nice to meet you, Lauren."

"Laurel," Flynn corrected. "See you at twelve. Pray for my soul."

The women climbed out and Kim mumbled a goodbye before the doors slammed.

"Right," Flynn said. "Straight home, or you need a lift someplace special?"

"Home's fine. I have to work at one."

Flynn flipped on the radio and they drove into Boston without speaking. His silence seemed comfortable but Laurel's felt melancholy. She blamed the damp air and the flat gray sky. She turned to him as they passed the hotel, steps from where they'd met.

"I sort of get why you were so hard on that idiot couple, that afternoon I bought you lunch." As soon as the words came out she worried he'd hear it as an insult, that she was calling his niece obnoxious.

But Flynn just said, "I want to shake her sometimes. And her douchebag boyfriend."

"Is your sister married?"

He shook his head. "But they were together for a long time, her and Kim's dad—Robbie, the guy who taught me to box. On and off, but mostly on. Really good dude. They broke up maybe five years ago. I try to bust Kim's balls as much as I guess he would, if he was here."

"Was he like a father figure to you or something?"

Flynn gave a dismissive sort of snort. "No. He was just my sister's cool-ass boyfriend, who treated me like a grown-up when I was twelve. Every guy I knew whose dad was around, they made me pretty sure a father's just there to yell a fuck of a lot and to have a bottle surgically attached to their hand the second they got home from work. *If* they worked. Robbie found Jesus or something when he was like eighteen and I never saw him drink anything harder than Red Bull in the twenty years I knew him."

"Are you religious?"

He shook his head. "Not since I was like ten."

"Your tattoo looks religious," Laurel said. She'd Googled the Latin already but decided not to share this fact in case it sounded like something a stalker might do.

"It is," he said. "It's Saint Michael."

Laurel grinned. Archangel Michael. Holy ass-kicker.

"That's actually Robbie's fault too," Flynn said. "When I was in high school he photocopied that picture for me out of some old art history book, since it's my namesake or whatever. I think he was trying to make religion seem bad-ass or something."

"Maybe it worked. You did get the tattoo."

Flynn shrugged.

"He sounds cool. Robbie, I mean. I'd like to meet him sometime," Laurel said.

"Wish you could, sweetheart, but he's dead."

She recovered from the psychic punch to her gut. "Oh. I'm sorry."

Flynn kept his blue eyes firmly on the road. "He shot himself a couple years ago." He crossed himself in such a reflexive-looking fashion Laurel wondered if he even knew he'd done it. "Cool motherfucker though. He went with me for a school thing when I was in like eighth grade. I forget why but he chaperoned, and I felt like the hottest shit happening, showing up with my sister's twenty-five-year-old tattooed welterweight boyfriend to go to the aquarium or whatever."

Laurel studied his smile from the passenger seat. "Was he much like you?"

He shrugged. "I hope I'm something like him."

"Sounds like you are. Fighter, tattoos, non-drinker."

"It's a start. Anyhow, he was in the Army Reserve and then everything went and fucked its own ass in 2001. He got shipped out, came back after a couple years, all different. Real angry. He mellowed after a while, but he was always sort of...tired after that. He always cared more about stuff than everybody else around him—you know, tried harder. Just gave more of a shit than everybody else. I think it fucked him up to be over there, then to come back and see everything the same here, everybody still fucking around, being idiots, pissing their lives away, after he saw whatever he did in Iraq."

"Ah."

"You know when you spill like cleaning fluid or butane on something plastic, and it takes all the shine off it?" Flynn asked. "It's like Robbie was shiny when he left, and he came back dull."

Laurel frowned at this sad scrap of poetry and watched the pedestrians flash by as Flynn turned them down this street and that into the North End. He pulled up at her building and put the car in neutral.

He wrapped his arm around his headrest and turned to her. "When do I see you again?"

"Oh um…I'm off Wednesday night again, if that works."

He nodded. "I've got training from four to six then I'll grab some dinner and a shower, see you around eight again?"

"Sounds good. Well, thanks for the ride."

He dropped his arm and leaned in, took her face in his hands and gave her a long, hard, tongue-less kiss, fingers shoved deep in her hair. "Don't you take any shit from any tourists."

She smirked at him. "Only from townies."

He ran his thumb over her chin and smiled. "Fucking right. See you in a few days, kiddo."

Chapter Five

Laurel shifted the paper grocery bag in her arms and fumbled for her phone, checking its screen. Five twenty-eight. Flynn should be nearing the end of his training, but hopefully not so late that she'd miss watching some of it. She let the butterflies swirl in her stomach, enjoying them. Then she reached the bar and they turned to rocks. Closed.

"Fuck." What sort of a shady bar wasn't open by this time? A man emerged from the alley, a huge white guy with a shaved head and tattooed neck and a gym bag slung over his shoulder.

"Hey!" Laurel said. "Excuse me."

His eyes met hers then took a brief trip down the rest of her body, wary but intrigued. "Yeah?"

"Is Flynn down there?" She nodded at the building.

"Yeah."

"Is there some way I can get in? I'm...supposed to meet him." *In three hours.*

"Sure, there's a keypad." He stepped in close, looking around, his proximity and rather potent body odor making Laurel's flight instincts hum a warning. "Punch in four-nine-nine-two-two-five, then the pound key," the guy said, voice private.

"Thanks." She offered a smile and sidestepped him, heading into the alley. The keypad was beside the heavy metal door and she entered the code. The box beeped and a lock released. Laurel heaved the door open and stepped into the dim stairwell and that familiar cologne of sweat and Tiger Balm.

The place felt different by day, still seedy and dingy but brightly lit, definitely a gym now instead of a venue for shadowy violence. She leaned in the threshold for a minute. Two men sparred in the ring, wearing head gear unlike on fight nights. She clutched the bag tight as her eyes found Flynn. Track pants and no shirt, just as when he fought, and just as when he fought his body made her weak. He was working out at one of the tall leather punching bags, throwing combinations, hooks and jabs and uppercuts interspersed with blocking motions from his fists and elbows. He'd wrapped his hands but didn't wear gloves. Laurel frowned, conjuring x-rays of fractured knuckles in her head. When he stopped to grab a bottle of water from the floor she walked over. Flynn set the bottle down and went back to punching. He didn't look at her until the third time she cleared her throat.

"Oh," he said, eyebrows rising. He dropped his guard and hiked his pants up an inch, cinching the drawstring and retying it. "Hey. How'd you get in here?"

She offered a warm smile. "Some gigantic guy with a shaved head gave me the code."

Flynn spotted the grocery bag and took a step closer, giving her a deep whiff of his insanely attractive smell. "What's all this?"

"I thought I'd save you some time and money and cook dinner at your place. If that's okay." Her heart stopped at a sudden possibility. "Unless you were like meeting someone for dinner…"

He shook his head. "Nope. Cook away."

Her pulse started up again. "Oh good."

"I hope I have all the pans and things you need," he said.

"I'm sure you will. It's just chicken pot pie, and I brought aluminum pie plates."

"Shit, from scratch?" He made an impressed face then leaned in close. "I hope you're prepared to get your daylights fucked out, showing up promising home-cooked meals."

"I did factor that in to the planning."

He straightened up. "Fantastic. Do you mind if I finish here? I'm sort of a Nazi about my routine."

"Oh yes, pummel away. I'll just watch the sparring." Yeah, right. Like she'd take her eyes off Flynn when he was stripped to the waist and kicking the tar out of something.

"There's chairs in the corner," he said.

Laurel set up a seat with a good open view of the ring and a fine surreptitious view of Flynn. He finished his bag workout and headed to the far side of the gym, to the huge rack laden with free weights. It was easy to watch him through the ring's ropes, staring past the men fighting to study his arms as he ran through reps with dumbbells. Laurel was confident she wouldn't be able to lift the ones he used even with both hands, at least not without risking a slipped disc.

After the weights Flynn lay on his back on a bench off to one side, hooking his feet under a T-bar and doing a long series of complicated sit-ups that made Laurel's abs ache just to watch. He finished ten minutes later and walked back to her side of the gym, grabbing a towel from the ground beside his water. She hurried over.

"Can I do that?" she asked, her eagerness drowning out any fear of seeming smothering.

"What?"

"You know. Like dab you dry?"

He laughed once, hard enough to double over.

"Unless that's totally embarrassing," she said as he straightened.

"Only for you, fan-girl." He tossed her towel. "And I like when you blush, so go ahead. Mop my sweat, you kinky beast."

She did, happily, liking that he let her. Liking that it seemed like a girlfriendly intimacy and he wasn't afraid for the other guys to see.

He left her to drag his gym bag over and pull out an undershirt.

"How often do you train?" she asked.

"Every day I don't work overtime, which is most days, lately."

Laurel made an impressed face. "That must be exhausting, after working a physical job all day."

"Clears my head. The dudes I'm working with right now are total assholes. Feels good to pound the shit out of something after putting up with those jerk-offs all day. Wanna head out? I'm all set here."

She nodded. She folded her chair and stowed it by the wall, hoisted her groceries as Flynn shouldered his bag. She followed him through the back hallways and up into the sunshine.

"I hope that wasn't…uncool. My showing up here."

He cocked an eyebrow at her as they came out on the sidewalk. "What, some hot woman showing up to be my towel girl? Yeah, you're really cramping my style."

"I didn't know if there's some sort of man-code down there."

"Nah. The girls who work out there wouldn't put up with it."

"There's girls who go to your shady underground gym?" she asked, and a warm, unwelcome murmur pulsed up her neck.

"Not many, but three or four."

"They must be bad-ass."

"They are," he said.

"Have you ever, like, dated a female boxer?"

Flynn smirked at her, squinting in the late afternoon sun. "Why, you jealous?"

She answered far too quickly. "No."

"Chicks who box, you're right, they're bad-ass. They're way scarier than the dudes, and they're total pit bulls. Now think for a second what I like in a woman when the bedroom door's closed."

She nodded. "Too aggressive?"

"Too many motherfuckers fighting over who gets to wear the pants," Flynn said. "Or tie the ropes."

"Gotcha."

They paused, waiting for a walk sign. "So never fear, sub shop girl. There's no competition to be found down there. Your alpha sub status is safe."

"I wasn't jealous," Laurel said.

He smirked again, playfully skeptical. "Could you pretend you are? Makes me feel fuckin' ten feet tall."

"Fine… So you said before, on fight nights, there's not really any rules."

"Not really," he said. "Gloves and shoes, hit above the belt."

"What about steroids? Some of those guys are huge. Do they do any testing or anything? Do they care if people are clean?"

"Don't ask, don't tell, fight whoever's slot you draw," Flynn said.

"That seems unfair."

"It's a bar basement, sweetheart, not the Olympics."

"You haven't ever used anything, have you?" She looked at his arm, big but not in that lumpy, veiny way she associated with 'roided-out body builders.

"Nope, never. Too much of a Boy Scout."

She smiled up at the sun. "Obviously."

They walked the last couple blocks in silence and Laurel liked the stares they got. Questioning stares, probably asking where Flynn had gotten the bruises on his jaw and arms. Nosy stares, dying to know if Laurel had bruises of her own hidden beneath her clothes, evidence of abuse. She couldn't care less what people wondered, though—she just wanted to be seen walking beside this man, knowing what his body was capable of, wishing everyone else knew too. He pushed the elevator button and Laurel enjoyed being in the tiny foyer with him, so close to his smell and energy. He peered into the bag again.

"Can't remember the last time somebody cooked for me."

"Heather doesn't?"

"My sister spent her teens and twenties raising me and my older brother, then her daughter. I think she's all set cooking for ingrates. Now I bet every takeout joint in Southie recognizes her voice." The elevator arrived and Flynn punched the buttons for the second and fifth floors.

"It's not a fight night," Laurel said.

Flynn shrugged and dropped his bag as the door for two slid open. "Hold it."

Laurel pushed in the door-open button and listened to Flynn knocking down the hall. A lock clicked and he said, "The sexy one's cooking me homemade chicken pot pie." Then he said, "Ow," and Laurel heard the door shut.

He returned rubbing his arm.

"The sexy one?" she asked.

"That's what Heather calls you."

"Did she bite you or something?"

"She pinched me," Flynn said. "She's always been a pincher." The doors reopened at his floor.

"You get socked in the face twice a week," Laurel said.

"You don't understand. That bitch can fucking *pinch*." He unlocked the apartment and Laurel carried her groceries to his counter.

"Tell me what you need," he said as he eased the lights on above the living area.

For a second she thought he meant sexually. "Oh, for dinner? Nothing. Well, a measuring cup, if you have it. And a saucepan. That's it. I'm sure I can find everything else."

She unpacked ingredients—a little bag of flour, a box of butter, chicken, gravy, vegetables, a pack of aluminum pie plates.

"I'm going to make three. You can keep one in the freezer and heat it up whenever." *And think about how awesome I am when you eat it.* "Three-seventy-five for forty-five minutes," she added, turning to him.

Flynn was unlacing his sneakers on the couch. "Think I can handle that. I'll take a shower while you're playing housewife, if you're all set over there."

"Yup, knock yourself out."

He disappeared into the bathroom as she got the crusts made, using a pint glass in lieu of the forgotten rolling pin. Flynn emerged in a towel and flicked on the radio on top of his fridge, scrolling until the Sox pre-game broadcast emerged from the static.

"You know," Laurel said, "this wasn't the smartest idea for dinner in July. This is really more of a winter meal."

"It's so hot when you fret about girl crap."

Her breath turned short as he drew close, wrapping his bare arms around her waist from behind. "Smells fucking phenomenal."

"Good."

"So do you," he added, pressing his nose into the space behind her ear. Everything that had happened after Saturday's fight replayed itself in an instant across Laurel's cavewoman brain.

"I've been thinking about tying you up when I jerked off all this week," he said, "but maybe I'll have to replace the ropes with an apron, after all this."

She whacked the back of his hand with a spoon and he obediently pulled away. She sneaked little glances as he dressed in jeans and a fresh undershirt. He passed her to go to the fridge and pull out a can of something that fizzed when he opened it. Laurel recognized the smell of ginger ale. She smiled unseen to herself as she listened to Flynn flop onto the couch and sigh—a tired, satisfied noise.

When she'd stopped at the grocery store to pick up the ingredients she'd succumbed to a kind of easy excitement she hadn't experienced for the past couple years. Flynn had become the most enjoyable feature of her life in recent weeks. Before he appeared she'd been feeling restless and disillusioned. Pathetic, maybe, but seeing him gave her something to look forward to...something that offered a challenge and a change a pace, a spark of dark excitement and a taste of self-discovery after months and months of half-assed floundering. She wondered what she'd have thought a few weeks ago if someone had shown her a video of the gym and the bloodied, muscly man she'd soon after be sleeping with.

"You know," Laurel said when an ad break interrupted the radio commentary. "Every time we've hung out, you spent all day either working and training, or you spent three or four hours beating people senseless in that torture-chamber basement."

"Yeah."

She doled filling into each crust. "What are you like when you just have a day off? No training or fighting."

"Insufferable."

She laughed. "You must have crazy baseline energy."

"I think I'm a bit manic," he said, sounding thoughtful.

She turned to study him, his eyes lit up blue and gold in the early evening light flooding in from the west-facing windows.

"Like, really?"

"Yeah," he said. "I think so. I'm just glad I grew up after everybody started going ape-shit with the ADD diagnoses."

"You're sort of straight-edge," Laurel said.

"I suppose."

"So is beating people senseless a good substitute for Ritalin, do you think?"

He met her eyes. "You tell me. You seem to think I'm worth cooking for."

He caught her blush and smiled indulgently.

"Yeah, you are," she said then made her face devious. "But only because I know I'm going to get massively laid later."

Flynn laughed. "You're a fucking brat. And yeah, you are. Getting massively laid, I mean."

"You know," she started and paused, needing a deep breath.

"What do I know?"

"You were talking about your friend Robbie. Who died."

Flynn nodded.

"Who killed himself." She clicked the oven on to preheat. "My mom killed herself too. A couple years ago."

Flynn's eyes widened and he stood. She prepared herself for an awkward hug but he went to turn the radio way down then took his seat again. "Sorry, kiddo. That sucks."

She nodded.

"Your dad still around?"

"Yeah, somewhere, but we're not close. I never saw him much when I was growing up." She turned her attention to crimping the top crusts onto the pies.

"Brothers or sisters?"

She shook her head.

"What was she like? Your mom?"

"Sorry," Laurel said. "I wasn't trying to like start a conversation about it. I don't know why I brought it up."

"Because we're friends?"

"Maybe... Anyway, she was..." She shrugged, feeling a hundred years old.

"Wonderful?"

Laurel laughed, hating the bitterness anybody could hear in her voice. "No, she was really hard to live with, actually." She finished one crust and moved on to the next. "She had a really nasty kind of depression. She hardly ever could keep a job for more than a month, and she was needy and demanding and she sucked the life out of everybody around her."

"Oh," Flynn said simply.

"When I was like ten years old I already knew how to forge her handwriting so I could write the rent checks. She'd go on these weeks-long jags where she'd just lock herself in her room."

"Sounds awful."

She nodded, hating the stinging pressure in her sinuses. But she decided to tell Flynn something she hadn't told anyone, not her roommates or friends, not even under the influence of drunken sentimentality on any number of wine-soaked girls' nights. "It was sort of a relief. When she died."

"Oh," he said again. "Did you love her?"

She hissed out a long breath. "I don't know. I don't really think so." Laurel sealed the last pie and stabbed vent holes in all the tops with a fork. "Sorry."

"Don't be. You need a hug or something?"

She kept her back to him so he wouldn't see how pink her face must be. Her lips felt thick and tight from the emotion she was holding in. "No, thanks. I *would* like some beer though. If I give you some cash would you mind going out and grabbing me a six-pack?" She turned her face halfway to meet his eyes, away from the light.

"Course. You brought dinner. You're *making* me dinner. I'll buy you whatever you want."

"Just Newcastle or Bass or something like that. Bottles."

"Sure thing."

She heard Flynn move around the apartment then leave. Laurel slid two pies into the oven, set the timer, wrapped the third in foil and scrawled the cooking instructions on its top with a Sharpie from Flynn's junk drawer. She made a home for it in his freezer and leaned against the counter, staring at the strip of linoleum under her feet. The pattern reminded her of her kitchen growing up. She'd play in there for hours, pulling pots and pans out of the cupboards and building cities with them on the floor. Then hunger always set in and she'd abandon her project to go in search of food. *Self-raising toddler, just add water.*

Laurel walked to the loveseat, gave the padded armrest a couple lame punches and burst into tears.

* * * * *

When Flynn got back they made small talk about the neighborhood and listened to the game while the pies cooked. Laurel savored the cool slide of bottled beer down her loosening throat. Though the topic had closed, she thought about her mom. She thought about herself, craving a drink when she probably needed a slap up-side the head. She wondered if she was depressed...but the thought was too heavy. At any rate, she knew why she was attracted to Flynn now—attracted to being with a guy who could completely dominate her in bed. It was what she'd been doing in every aspect of her life lately, wanting to hole up in the backseat and not be asked to drive. Just hand over the keys to someone else. She glanced at Flynn, wondering if that made him her pusher or her therapist.

"This was fucking amazing," he said, scraping the last of his pie out of its tin.

"You want the rest of mine?" He accepted her dish and finished the few bites she couldn't cram in. It felt oddly comforting to be taking care of somebody again. Somebody grateful, who could give something of himself back.

"I love cooking," she said, turning her bottle around in her hands. "Or I used to. I used to cook something good every night. Then I got out of the habit when I started waitressing and my schedule got all wonky. Now I look at food and all I see is people's orders."

"Well if you change your mind, you can cook for my ass any night you like." Flynn cleared the coffee table and did the dishes. He looked to Laurel as he dried his hands on a towel, something cautious tightening his features.

She felt hesitant too. They had a routine of sorts and she estimated it was eighty percent fucking, most everything else—the fights, this meal—mere foreplay. The transition into sex was complicated now, Laurel's fault for introducing a downer topic. She wished she hadn't brought it up, even if it was a relief to have told someone. But Flynn shouldn't have been that someone. As stupid and impossible as the impulse was, she wanted to be perfect for him. She wanted to be what he was looking for and that surely didn't include crying unless it was part of some fucked-up role playing scenario.

She stepped to him, knowing it was her job to give him the green light but also trying to gauge exactly what she could handle without risking a meltdown and really wrecking the evening. She put her hands on his chest, tilted her head up. He kissed her slow, soft. Laurel made a decision to stop over-thinking everything and respect her body's wishes. She pulled her mouth away.

"Flynn."

"Yeah?"

"I'm not sure I'm up for anything too rough tonight. I'm sort of jangled."

He nodded, leaned in, cupped her cheek and pressed his lips against the crown of her head. "No problem."

"Sorry."

"Don't be sorry. I don't look at you and just see chicken pot pies and rape fantasies, you know."

She swallowed, determined not to cry. "What do you see?"

"I dunno. Just Laurel, I guess. The smart, good-smelling redhead who's been nice enough to put up with me for the last couple weeks... Don't get me wrong, I'm thrilled to find somebody who seems to be in to what I like, but just knowing I get to have that once in a while is enough. Not every meal has to be Thanksgiving."

"You can still be bossy though," she said. "I like that. I like...you know, giving up control. It feels good, not having to be in charge."

He tucked her hair behind her ears. "Sure. Whenever you're ready. Whatever you want."

"Can we make out for a while?"

Flynn put out his hand, inviting her to head for the bed and get comfortable. He kicked his shoes off and lay down beside her, and Laurel felt the tightness in her body intensify, then ease nearly to nothingness. He propped himself on an elbow and smoothed her hair back from her face with his other hand, and smiled.

"What?"

"I sort of like when you're all vulnerable," he said.

"I'll bet."

"No, not like that. Just when you're all..."

"Weepy?"

Flynn rolled his eyes. "When you're off your guard, I mean."

She blinked a moment. "Do I come off as guarded, usually?"

He nodded.

"Oh."

"That surprise you?" he asked.

"Kind of." She thought of people she knew, worked with...of hyper-defensive Christie and her guerrilla Post-Its. "Do I seem prickly?"

"Nah. You just seem like you've got an extra layer on, sometimes. Not like armor, but like you're wearing an invisible sweater. Like you've got your arms crossed over your chest, even when you don't."

"Oh," she said again. Even as she ached to deny it, she could feel herself tugging that psychic sweater down over her head and burying her arms in its sleeves. "I guess you're right."

"I'm always right."

Laurel didn't reply, not in the mood for Flynn's sanctimonious tone, no matter if he was kidding.

"It hit eighty-six today," he said a few moments later.

"Oh?"

"Yeah." He leaned in close, eyes watching his fingers as he played with her hair. "Too hot for that extra layer you just put on."

Laurel sighed.

"Good thing I know how to get you to take it off." Flynn put his lips to her neck.

She sputtered out a derisive laugh at the playboy tone he'd adopted. "Smooth, Romeo."

Flynn shut his eyes and half whispered, half sang the chorus to *Sexual Healing.* Laurel smacked him on the chest and crushed her head into the pillow, rubbed her palms over her face.

"Fine, keep your shield on. But get your clothes off, huh?" He plucked at the strap of her tank top. "You could use a distraction right now."

Yeah, right. More like *he* could use an escape from her unsanctioned show of emotion.

"Fine. But don't think for a second that you're tricking me into believing this is some huge sacrifice you're making for me." She cracked a smile at him but looked away quick, anxious from the eye contact.

They shed their clothes and came together. Flynn's mouth tasted just like her own when they kissed, and his hand against her face pushed all the hesitation from her head. Laurel pulled away to stare down at his body, to put her fingertips to his ribs, to the damp skin stretched over his oblique muscles, the yellowing bruise just below his armpit. So many details, intimacies…only they weren't hers alone.

His cock hardened as her palm drifted to his belly, rousing her in turn as she felt that new power—power to excite such a strong body. She wanted him helpless for a change—a tiny taste of revenge for how he'd made her feel the other night, teasing her about marriage at the gym, being tacky enough to point out her defensiveness just minutes before in bed.

"Make me come, Flynn."

He spoke against her throat. "You want me to fuck you?"

"No. You have to wait your turn tonight."

She felt and heard him laugh, a quiet, happy noise.

"Yes, ma'am." He slid his body farther down the bed beside her, face at her chest, free hand creeping up her thigh.

Laurel folded her arms behind her head, intending to be as lazy and selfish as possible.

Pleasure overshadowed intention as Flynn's tongue traced a curve along the side of her breast. She brought a hand down to touch the back of his head, hummed out a sigh as his lips closed over her nipple. Her fingers raked his short hair, fisted it as he suckled, as his hand edged close, teasing the sensitive crease where her thigh met her hip.

"Don't keep me waiting, Flynn."

But he did. His mouth dominated the action, lips sucking, tongue flickering, teeth grazing until Laurel writhed against him, so ready for his fingers she felt crazed.

"Touch me," she said.

His mouth retreated by millimeters, breath cool on her wet skin. "Ask nicely."

"Touch me, Flynn, please."

His hand inched closer, the tips of two fingers glancing her lips. Her hips bucked and Flynn moaned his satisfaction against her breast. Even when he was the one taking orders, he still had all the control. Or nearly all. Laurel grinned, surveyed his body, the stiff, beading cock at attention between his legs, surely hurting with insistence. Two big, warm fingers flirted with her entrance, the touch still slow, still light, tightening her with need and impatience. She memorized his face, the arch of his eyebrows, the bridge of his nose marred surprisingly little given how many times it must surely have been broken in the last two decades. A little white bandage next to his sideburn seemed to glow against his skin. Laurel forgot her arousal for a moment, hypnotized by him.

Fall in love with me.

His fingers pushed inside, pushed the ridiculous thought from her head. She gasped and jerked as he penetrated, two fingers thrusting then curling, caressing and teasing and coaxing the little knot of nerves inside her pussy. Shit, he was good. Heat flashed across her skin, then chills, then pure, maddening need. Tension pulsed through her veins and made her fingers and toes tingle, collected in her belly, pounded in her clit. She felt the weight and the smooth, hot skin of Flynn's cock on her thigh, just above her knee, and imagined him ramming it in deep, all hers.

"Fuck, you're good, Flynn."

He intensified the touch, setting a steady pace he echoed with his own body, small thrusts of his hips that rubbed his erection against her leg. His mouth stayed hungry, moving to her other breast to make the pleasure burst in to bloom all over again.

"Make me come, Flynn. Touch my clit."

He made her wait again. When his thumb finally grazed her hard clit she gasped, gripped his hair, raked his neck with her nails. He gave her a couple more light teases and stopped.

"Jesus, Flynn, please."

She could feel his smile from the way his lips tightened over her nipple. He pulled away, kept his fingers teasing as he got his body lower, lower, until she felt his cheek scrape her inner thigh. Two licks against her clit and the pleasure tore her in two. Heat and electricity boiled through her cunt and shot down through her legs, clenching them around Flynn's back. His hand and mouth kept working, coaxed a second, borderline-painful orgasm from her, hot on the heels of the first. When he released her Laurel watched white spots dance in front of her eyes and realized she'd stopped bothering to breathe.

"Oh," she said dumbly.

She melted back into the bed as Flynn lay down beside her, one arm shoved beneath her head and the pillow, the other draped across her stomach, fingers fanning over her ribs.

"Hot."

Laurel mustered a wrung-out laugh and tapped her knuckles against his temple. He rested the side of his face on her sticky shoulder and she could sense his smile in her periphery.

"You're pretty pleased with yourself, aren't you?" she asked.

He shrugged, way too innocent.

"Well," she sighed, "you should be... So what would *you* like? You broke my brain, so I'll do just about anything right now."

"Nothing fancy," he said. "Just play with me, I guess."

Laurel turned her head to meet his eyes. "I can do that."

She pushed up on to her side. Flynn covered her mouth with his as her hand wrapped around his half-hard cock. That familiar heat grew against her palm, inside her own chest as he stiffened. He abandoned the kissing to stare down at her hand.

"Good," he mumbled. He rolled on to his back and Laurel sat up straighter so she could stroke his hard stomach as her other hand masturbated him. She gave him sensual, slow pulls, taking her time, loving how he changed as he got closer, how his breathing went shallow and his face flushed, arms twitched.

"Good, Flynn."

"Harder, sweetheart. I need it rough."

"Do you need me to pretend—"

"No," he said. "Just hard and fast. I need it rough to get off."

She tightened her fist and upped the pace.

"God, yeah. Just like that. Fuck… I want to watch. In the mirror."

Laurel looked to the floor in front of the bed. The full-length was still leaning against the wall from the last time they'd used it. "Okay."

She let his cock go and Flynn got up, grabbed the comforter and tossed it on the floor. They sat down side by side, Flynn's thighs spread, inviting her hand. Two pairs of eyes watched the reflection as she resumed his torture with hard strokes. She rested her chin on his shoulder.

"You're so big, Flynn."

"Yeah."

"Look at that thick cock." She gave him slow, luxurious pulls, worshipping his length with a greedy hand. "I love it."

"I love watching your hands on me. Wanna watch when you make me come."

Even hotter than Flynn's ready cock was his face. Laurel studied his tensed features, all the evidence of his excitement and desperation. His eyes looked unfocused, hungry lips parted, nostrils flared. He dragged a hand across his flushed chest, stroking his own skin, his ribs, his nipples, his neck.

She brought her lips right to his ear, made her voice sweetly evil. "You gonna come for me? Gonna let me see all that hot come shoot across that gorgeous stomach?"

"Fuck yeah."

"Oh good," she whispered. "That's what I fantasize about when I'm getting off, thinking about you." She tightened her fist to hear his moan.

"Please."

"Yeah, it's your turn to beg now," she said.

"Please. Make me come. Please." His hand moved lower, covering her small one for a few thrusts before he cupped his balls, kneading as he came undone. "Fuck yes."

"Good. Let me see." She eased her pulls as he came, keeping her fist tight to milk every last drop, watching in the mirror as it lashed his skin and feeling the wet heat pour over her knuckles. Fever flooded her face and breasts and pussy and she bit her lip just to feel the tiny sting of pain.

Bossy Flynn returned after a few labored breaths. "Fuck yeah... Clean me up."

Laurel relocated, getting to her knees between his legs, leaning in to lick the come from his skin and hers. His hand cupped the back of her head, warm and possessive.

He sighed, sounding tired in the best way. "You're staying the night, right?"

Laurel straightened up, swallowed and nodded.

"Oh good. No way I can operate a car now," he said.

They made it to their feet and he collapsed back across the bed. Laurel knelt next to him, dragging her fingers through her sex-tangled hair and staring down at the length of Flynn's naked body. She'd miss this when their arrangement came to an end. She'd miss feeling like the temporary owner of this strong man, if only for an evening at a time. And she'd miss selfish things, like how easy it was for him to get her off. He was the best lover she'd had by miles and the pain that came with knowing she'd eventually lose that shifted Laurel's mood again. Her armor didn't snap on this time. Instead she felt as if her skin was falling away, leaving her a tangle of exposed nerves and brittle bones. She gazed out the tall front windows, wishing she wasn't flooded with ridiculous, manipulative impulses, like the desire to suddenly decide to leave so Flynn would rush after her, try to talk her into staying. If he would. He might not.

"What're you thinking about, sub shop girl?"

"Nothing."

"There's a vein ticcing in your neck."

She turned to frown at him, hoping she looked bored and that the hurt didn't show.

"Everything okay?"

"Yeah, just not looking forward to work tomorrow."

"Shit, I must be losing my touch if you're already thinking about work two minutes after we stop fucking," Flynn said.

She flopped back down against the mattress. "No, you're still the best lay of my life."

He clenched a triumphant fist in the air and they fell silent for a little while.

"Is it about what you said earlier?" he asked. "What you told me about your mom?"

"No."

"You want me to not ask you if anything's wrong?"

"Nothing's wrong," she said. "I'm just a bit off today."

"Would you like me to compliment your taste in shoes or listen while you bitch about your female coworkers?" he teased.

"Fuck off." Laurel pretended she was teasing back but rolled onto her side to stare at the wall, knowing her face was no good at keeping secrets. Flynn shifted a minute later, his hand closing around her arm, voice by her shoulder.

"Can I tell you something that really annoys me about you?" he asked.

Unseen, Laurel grimaced, utterly confused. "I guess so."

He exhaled against her skin. "I really hate that you spent the time and money — well, the government's money — to get a degree you don't even want."

Her body tensed. "I want my degree. I'm proud of my degree."

"How come you're wasting it then? Taking a shitty waitressing job away from some other college kid?"

Laurel felt a fever growing, hot and defensive. She opened her mouth to reply but Flynn went on.

"You know what I wanted to do when I was little, more than anything?"

"Grow up to be an engineer?" she asked, making her tone intentionally bitchy.

"Kind of. I wanted to build buildings. Not like I do now. Not hanging drywall or pouring foundations so I can end up with a bad back and no insurance when I'm fifty. Like be an architect or whatever. It pisses me off that you basically have that, and you're shitting it away."

"Engineering wasn't what I'd expected."

"And waitressing's a beautiful fucking fantasy land?"

"I stopped after my mom died, okay?" She rolled onto her back and glared at him. "For the first time in my life I decided to stop working my ass off for other people and be fucking irresponsible for a change. Happy?"

140

"Maybe you got depressed, like her."

She yanked her arm out from his grip. "Fuck you. I thought you hated analyzing people."

"I hate being analyzed."

"Then you must know how fucking annoying it is." She propped herself up on an elbow and stared at him in the near-dark. "It's none of your business what I do with my life."

"It's none of your business if I wear a mouth guard. But you're right to be a naggy little bitch about it."

"I'm sick of this conversation, Flynn."

He made an innocent face. "You shouldn't have said yes when I asked if you wanted to hear my opinion."

"Like you really gave me a choice. Why did you even ask me that? What was that about?"

"I wanted to know what was up with you," he said. "You went all quiet and it freaked me out. Usually when I make women go all quiet it's a really horrible sign."

"So you...you crammed your dirty fingers all inside my open wound, like I'm going to open up and cry about stuff if you antagonize me hard enough? Can't you just respect that I don't want to talk about it?"

"Sorry." His jaw clenched and released a few times. "I just wanted you to say something and stop being all shut-down. I wanted to know if I upset you."

"Well, that was a stupid fucking way to go about it."

"Sorry... Would you like to tell me something about me that annoys the living fuck out of you then?"

She squinted at him, chewing her lip. "I think it's really obnoxious that you never became what you wanted and you're being a douche about it now, taking it out on me. In *bed.*"

He nodded. "Good. We even now?"

"I also think it's irritating that you treat me like your girlfriend sometimes, when I know I'm not."

That shut him up. He didn't reply and she could see the dark circles of his irises drift toward the wall—not eye-rolling, more like escape-route-plotting.

Laurel sighed, half sarcastic, half petulant.

"What do you *think* we are?" Flynn asked. His tone was odd, diplomatic and calm and unreadable. Laurel's pulse ground to a halt.

"I didn't think you did girlfriends," she said.

"Why not?"

"I dunno. Because I'm not the only woman you're banging, for starters. Or what if another willing woman came along? You said it's hard to find people who'll go there with you. Wouldn't it...be a waste to let yourself get tied down, in case a new woman showed up?"

"Wouldn't it be a waste to not try and stay with one I liked?" he asked.

She entertained a dozen images in five seconds—a smiling Flynn walking down the street toward her, sliding onto a barstool next to her, shaking hands with Anne. She shifted onto her side again, staring blankly at her hand against his sheets.

"What about Pam though?" she asked.

"I'm not seeing her anymore."

Laurel shook her head. "Yeah, right."

"I'm not. Not since Friday, before the last time you and me hung out."

"Oh." She swallowed, hard, choking on hope and disbelief. "How come?"

"We had a rough talk, at the fights. When I asked her to not come on Saturday. She wanted to know about you, and if we'd hooked up, and I gave her the gist and she flipped out on me."

Laurel blinked, staring at her hands. "Shit."

She felt him shrug. "I'd seen this coming awhile."

"What did she say?"

"That's her business."

"Well, I'm stuck in the middle now, so make it mine too. I mean why on Earth did she ever invite me along then?" Laurel asked. "She made it seem like she was all in favor of you and me...you know."

"She plays the part of the liberal free spirit real well. So well even *she* thinks she's above sexual politics. Or that's my take, for what it's worth."

"Oh." Laurel breathed deeply for a couple minutes, turning it all over in her head. "That's all well and good for your little boyfriend-girlfriend speech," she said, "but I mean, would you have kept seeing her if she hadn't freaked out?"

"Not if it seemed like you and me were turning into something. Not if you'd asked me not to."

Laurel laughed, not convinced.

"You think I'm some sort of sex maniac, don't you?" he asked, defensiveness sharpening his voice.

"No."

"You think I don't know how to date? You think the kind of sex I like is like some condition? Like a fucking dialysis machine I have to drag around behind me, making everything into a big fucking hassle?"

"Do you...what do you think of me as?" she asked.

"You're the nice, smart, hot, funny woman I'm sleeping with. If that's still true in a couple weeks, and maybe you throw in a night when we sleep together but don't get around to fucking...yeah, I'd probably tell people you're my girlfriend."

"Oh."

"You going to finally freak and run out the door? Let me know and I'll get my shoes on and drive you."

Laurel didn't reply. As much as she liked Flynn, as much as she liked what he was saying, there'd been a safety to imagining he'd never entertain the idea of coupledom. Now she'd inevitably look at him differently and the whole ugly dynamic of who-likes-who-more would come into play. She didn't want to wake up in a month and realize she cared more about him than he did her, that she might lose him. And she didn't know if she was ready to have someone in her life who'd hold her to a higher standard than she'd been doing herself the last couple years.

His hot sigh warmed her neck. "What're you thinking about, sub shop girl?"

"Nothing." Tons.

"You know I said two weeks ago or whenever that if you came and watched me fight, and you still wanted to ask me out after that, you could. We've hooked up like three times since then and you still haven't asked me out."

"I thought the sex counted as dates."

He made a little noise, a miniscule laugh. "Jesus. Just ask me to go out to dinner or something, somewhere besides here or the gym. Or if you don't want to, tell me now so I know where I stand. I'm happy to be your fuckbuddy, Laurel, but I'm not afraid of getting attached to you either. I'm a pretty simple creature."

She stared at the wall, unsure what to say or do or think.

"I'm not afraid of angry pricks kicking the shit out of me," Flynn said. "And I'm not afraid of you." His body shifted, breaking their damp, sticky bond and turning her on to her back. His hand held her jaw and a thumb stroked her cheek. Flynn brought his face down and kissed her mouth, slow and shallow.

Against the rush of her quickening breath and her pounding heart, Laurel formed words, sticky and fearful. "Would you like to get something to eat next week?"

He laughed and she could make out the shape of his smile. "Sure."

"Wednesday? At six? Lucky's, across from the Dunkin' Donuts on Congress?"

"Sure," he said again.

"And maybe afterward we could come back here and not have sex."

"Sounds fucking sensational," Flynn murmured, pulling her tight against him so she felt his hardening cock. "Can't wait to not have sex with you."

"Clearly." She swallowed, wanting to embrace the fresh wave of excitement but still distracted by the gears ticking in her analytical brain.

"You got your force field switched on again," he said.

"Yeah."

"You said before you like how when we fuck, you don't have to be in control of anything."

She nodded.

"Let me give that to you again. Now. Let me be in charge."

"Maybe."

She sucked in a breath as his mouth closed over hers, a taste of that tempting offer. She shut off her mind, melted into what he was giving. Then a stray thought cut through the haze of arousal—a truce. She pulled her head back a couple inches to hold his gaze.

"If you start wearing a mouth guard, I'll start looking for engineering jobs."

His eyes jumped back and forth between hers. "Oh yeah? That a promise?"

"Yeah." She ran her hands down his body, cupped her hand over his warm dick. She watched his face in the low light, loving that familiar glaze to his eyes, the heaviness in his lids. "Not, like, next week. But soon."

"You keep busting my balls and I might just trick you into sticking around."

She laughed, embarrassed and flattered. Relieved.

"But don't worry, not 'til we get better at not having sex."

"That might be awhile," Laurel said, tightening her hold.

He moaned. "Probably. So don't worry, you're safe for a couple years at least. Now how about it? Let me give you what you need. Let me take you out of your head for a few minutes."

Laurel smiled and bit her lip, nodded.

Flynn got to his feet and eased the dimmer switch down until the lights were barely on. He went to his closet, came back with a short length of rope in each hand. He knelt at her feet, staring until her eyes left the ropes to meet his.

"You trust me?"

She gave it a second's serious thought, already knowing the answer. "Yes. I do."

"You want this?"

She nodded.

"Sit up."

She did. She let Flynn bind her ankles, tie her wrists behind her back—real this time, no way out. He connected her arms with enough slack that when she lay back down her fists rested at her sides, the rope between them pulled taut beneath her ass. She tested the bindings and felt a scary thrill from the sensation, true physical helplessness. The bite of the rope as she tugged was taunting, as cruel as the heat in Flynn's expression. His knees were spread wide between her own, hands kneading her thighs. One left to move to his cock, stroking until he was stiff and ready. His eyes traveled along her body from her pussy to her belly to her breasts, up her throat, stopping at her lips. His body followed, strong legs straddling her chest and pinned arms. He angled his cock to her mouth and brushed it across her lips.

"Taste me."

She slid her tongue out, savoring his excitement. He held himself there and she teased his slit, sucked his swollen head until she roused his moan.

"Fuck, that's so hot. You want more?"

She answered with suction, wrapping her lips tight around him.

"I'm gonna fuck your mouth," he whispered. "If I do something you can't handle, use your teeth. You know, gentle—but let me know."

She freed her mouth enough to say, "I will."

He leaned over, braced one arm at the top of the mattress, guided his cock with the other hand. He adjusted his knees until he got the distance right. She took what he gave her, four thick inches, sucking as his hips slid him out, then back in, setting the pace. She wanted her hands free to touch his body but accepted the frustration, made it part of the thrill. Flynn wrapped a fist around his base, either to keep from thrusting too deep or give himself pleasure, perhaps both.

"Oh that's so good. Keep taking me. Moan for me."

She obeyed, offering a deep, vibrating noise as he fucked her mouth. He worked himself deeper a half an inch at a time and Laurel kept the suction hard, finding it reduced the gagging. Flynn's hand moved to his balls. He squeezed and rubbed, making Laurel ache to touch him. She reveled in the warm weight of his thighs against her arms, the presence and energy of him.

"Yeah. Yeah. Take my cock. Suck me." He moved his hand to her face, her temple, her hair. His thrusts came slow, deeper, deeper still until his head bumped the back of her throat, triggering a protest. He pulled out and rested back on his haunches.

"I like seeing you tied up, sweetheart."

Heat bloomed in her chest at the words. "Good," she murmured. "Do you want me to pretend I don't want it?"

"Not tonight. Right now I just want that look. Helpless and hungry."

He leaned over to grab a condom off the shelf. She watched him roll it down his cock, her body tightening with anticipation, studying all that hard muscle, hers by some filthy miracle.

"God, you look amazing," she whispered.

"You like my body?"

"Yeah."

"Good. I like when you take care of me," he said. "And I love fucking you more than you can possibly know. You make my cock feel so *fucking* big when you look at me like that." He turned her by the hip, coaxed her legs to the side, bent, shoulders still mostly on the mattress. He planted his knees wide behind her ass, a hot palm on her hip as the other hand stroked his erection.

"Fuck me, Flynn."

"When I'm ready."

"Please. Now." She licked her lips, so ready to feel him slide into her pussy and ease the hunger.

He teased his tip up and down the crack of her ass. The hand on her hip slid between her thighs, big fingers finding her wet, getting slick before they rubbed her clit, pinching the hard nub, giving her that mix of pleasure and pain he was so damn good at.

"Give me your cock, Flynn."

"Be patient." Wet fingers toyed with her folds, taunted with shallow exploration.

"Fuck patient, Flynn. Gimme that hard cock."

"Fine." Threat, not surrender.

She watched his face, stern and calm as he smeared her wetness between her thighs then all up and down his shaft. "Fine," he said again, barely audible.

Laurel gasped at the sheer heat of him. Each inch of hard, thick cock pushed between her thighs, drove hard into her pussy until he had no more to give. He held there a full minute, letting her feel him throb and twitch, making her wait.

"C'mon, Flynn, please."

"Turn on to your side."

She shifted her shoulders, facing the wall. His dick slid out, all the way out, then rammed back in to the hilt.

"God yes—"

He cut off her triumph with a mean tug on the rope stretched between her bound wrists. It pulled her arms back, tweaked her top shoulder and sent a little burst of pain like static shock straight down to her fingertips.

"Don't rush me," he warned.

"I need more."

Another tug, slow this time, stopping when Laurel gasped at the strain.

"You know how I feel about impatience."

She held her breath, relieved when he let the rope go. His hands grasped her hip and waist, kept her still as he started to fuck.

He held his composure a few moments before a harsh, hissing breath told Laurel the pleasure was trumping his intent to act cold and controlled.

"God, I fucking love your cunt."

She squeezed herself tighter around him, earning a fierce grunt, then a hard slap on the ass.

"Keep it tight like that," he ordered.

Laurel obeyed, making her pussy a fist, intensifying the pleasure for both of them. He spanked her again.

"God, Flynn."

"That's right. Say my name. Tell me who's fucking that tight cunt."

"Flynn." Each time she said it, his palm came down with another slap. By the tenth strike the sting turned savage, leaving Laurel teetering on the threshold between pleasure and true pain. She held her tongue and winced, unsure if she could expect another slap for disobeying.

Instead she felt a tug at the bindings. She steeled herself for the punishment, but after a few seconds' gentle fumbling her wrists were free, the rope strung between them gone. Flynn's cock left her and she flexed her fingers, reclaiming circulation as he moved to untie her ankles. She turned on to her back and he came down on her, his huge body spreading her thighs, dick driving home.

"Touch me," he said.

"Where?"

"Anywhere." He was frantic, all that cool self-possession gone, his face buried against her shoulder. "I want your hands on me."

She slid one hand to his ass, fisted his hair in the other. She tugged until he brought his head back and she kissed him, rough, ending with a little bite on his lower lip.

"I wanna get fucked," he moaned.

"Fine."

He flipped them over, lay back while Laurel found her balance, straddling his hips. She fanned her fingers over his ribs, knowing he could handle her weight as she took charge of the sex.

"God yeah. Use me, sweetheart."

They fell silent, lost in each other's bodies. A slideshow of emotions passed over Flynn's damp face—need, pleasure, desperation, then a warm look of unmistakable fondness. He smiled up at Laurel, seeming exhausted.

"What?"

"You mean what you said? About looking for jobs?"

"Yeah."

He made a greedy noise and grinned, hands guiding her hips for a handful of thrusts.

"And maybe after a few more months and a fresh pair of blood tests," she said, "you might get that other wish of yours." She clenched her pussy tight and gave his cock slow, long pulls, imagining how he'd feel, releasing inside her, bare.

His hands grabbed her waist and he moaned, pushing deep.

She watched his eyes close, his face turn helpless. And she wanted him. Wanted to be here to patch him up, to call him on his bullshit and get called out in return, to explore the darker depths of her mind and body with this patient, real, occasionally obnoxious man.

"I love when you look this defenseless," she murmured, grinning evilly at him.

"Not many women ever manage to get me on my back," he said, voice shallow and scratchy.

"You better keep me around then."

"Why d'you think I was so keen to tie you down?" The words hitched with his uneven breaths. "Fuck, Laurel."

The sound of her name, two choked syllables rising from his throat as he gave her all the power felt like a filthy, sacred proclamation. She stared at his strained face. *Fall in love with me.*

"Laurel."

Fall in love with me.

"You keep—looking at me like that—and I swear—I'll let you wear the pants—any night you want."

She froze in mid-pull, holding him still, deep inside her body. She grinned down at his sweaty face. "Beg me."

"Laurel."

"Beg me and I'll make you come so hard you'll lose your fucking mind."

He sounded as though he already had. "Please. Fuck me, please."

She eased her pussy off his cock then claimed his hard length again, rough.

"God, fuck. Please, Laurel."

"Fall in love with me." Horror slapped her hard in the face as the words tumbled out of her subconscious into the air between them.

"I will," he said, still panting, still lost in the fucking.

"I didn't mean that."

He laughed, sounding exasperated. "Fine. But you keep treating me the way you have been, and I will. Whether you like it or not." He groaned. "But I won't say it in the middle of getting my brains fucked out, so relax."

She didn't reply, kept her body moving as her head overheated. As always, he could read her. Her fears stacked up like bricks between them but he took the wheel. He flipped them over, gave her the reassurance of the bed against her back and his weight on her body, the relief of not being in charge.

"Thank you," she mumbled.

"Don't be ridiculous... Actually," he said, "be as ridiculous as you want. I'll still want you. Be as irrational as your little heart desires. I'll keep buying you beer and driving your ass home."

She smiled at him and shook her head. "Now might be a good time to try out that mouth guard."

He half masked his grin with an insulted glower and let their bodies take over communicating. Laurel gave herself up to the sex, dissolved like sugar into the blissful knowledge that tonight, she was enough. When his chest brushed hers she wrapped her arms around his back, grateful for his strength. Grateful he might be in her corner when she decided she was ready to learn how to be strong again herself.

CURIO

Dedication

∾

For the surprising number of people who chimed in to express their enthusiasm when I first mentioned I was working on a "Parisian man-whore book". Here you go, you glorious perverts.

Acknowledgements

∾

Great thanks to my editor and one-woman bomb squad, Kelli, for snipping my green wire, mere seconds before my head asploded.

Equally heartfelt thanks to Amy and Ruthie, for their willingness, time, encouragement and invaluable (yet somehow free) feedback.

Enfin, most grande thanks à la belle Liz, pour aider avec my hideous mots franglais.

Thursday
The First Visit

Didier Pedra is the name of a male prostitute who lives at sixteen Rue des Toits Rouges, in Paris.

It's a relatively quiet street amid the greater bustle of the Latin Quarter, his flat on the top floor of a long tenement, two blocks from the river. I'd never expected to find myself standing on the stoop of a prostitute's building in the rain, on what should have been another unremarkable Thursday evening in March.

Then again, I'd never expected to be five weeks from my thirtieth birthday with my hymen still intact.

As I stood on Didier Pedra's front step—precisely six minutes early for my appointment and unwilling to go in, lest I appear too eager—I knew only a few things about him. I knew he's in his early to mid-thirties, that he's always lived in Paris and that he has a reputation for being supremely good in bed.

As if I have any basis for comparison.

I knew also, beyond the shadow of a doubt, that he's gorgeous. I use that word without gushing, without girlishness. I say *gorgeous* as though I'm speaking of the most luscious and decadent cake you ever laid eyes on, one you can taste from ten feet away. So beautiful that not only do your salivary glands tingle, your eyes water. So beautiful that cutting a slice and consuming it would feel wrong, because you are beneath such a specimen.

As an aside, you might wonder what sort of woman would visit a male prostitute. I can only speak to the one I know, which is of course myself.

I'm not what I pictured.

I'm younger than I'd have guessed, not quite thirty as I said, and I suspect I'm better-looking but less well-off. I'm not beautiful, but I'm an inch or two taller than average, perhaps a bit underweight, though in this city of chain smokers my measurements seem standard. I have curly hair, neither short nor long, neither blonde nor brown, neither sloppy nor tidy. I pin the sides back with a barrette behind each ear. For some reason I dressed this evening more for a job interview than a first date, likely because Didier intimidates me tremendously. My flats collected rain on the walk from the Metro and the cuffs of my slacks were wet and shapeless by the time I reached number sixteen, Rue des Toits Rouges. The Street of Red Roofs.

I was scared and thrilled, shaky from excitement and nerves and anticipation.

There was no doubting Didier's aforementioned gorgeousness. I work at a museum in Paris—no, not the Louvre but still very nice—and two of my best friends work in the gallery next door. Paulette is from near Provence and Ania is Polish, and they are both insatiable perverts. I say that affectionately. When customers wander out of earshot, Paulette and Ania are never more than a breath from discussing some man or other or the exploits of a mutual friend.

Ania first told me about Didier Pedra when the gallery displayed a half-dozen daguerreotypes. You may have seen some—photographic images burned onto shiny silver plates, like dark mirrors. It's a delicate, temperamental, antiquated medium. The artist behind the exhibit was a local woman and her model was Didier.

He is without a doubt the most stunning man I've ever seen, both burned onto metal plates and in person, burned forever onto my retinas. He's so beautiful I actually felt an ache in my chest when I viewed those images.

Noting my fixation, Ania had declared herself the model's greatest fan and disappeared into the storeroom, emerging with a large binder filled with prints. Didier has sat for many photographers and other artists since he was in his late teens. Ania plopped the portfolio down on a table and proceeded to flip through the images. I'd immediately wondered how I might possibly steal the binder and sleep with it beneath my pillow, though of course I never would. But if given the chance, I might borrow it on a long-term basis without permission.

Definitely without permission, because there's some defect in my personality that prevents me from admitting my attraction to handsome men. I've always been that way. I was an extremely homely kid, growing up in northern New Hampshire. I wasn't quite the ugly duckling who blossomed into a beautiful swan... I merely developed into an okay-looking duck. But back then I was inarguably gawky, and because I knew it would be laughable for me to profess my love for the cutest, most popular boys at my school, I chose to act as though I couldn't care less about them. That I was above such nonsense.

In truth they intimidated me, because they had the power to disappoint and humiliate me, and confirm everything I feared about my own awkwardness. I carried this facsimile of haughty superiority with me through college and beyond, and though I shrug off accusations that I might have a crush on this man or that and pass my attitude off as contempt, secretly of course I'm simply terrified to hear it made official that they're out of my league.

Beautiful men terrify me because, deep down, they're the only kind I want.

I could probably do well, dating guys as passable-looking as myself. I even suspect they're nicer people, yet I have what feels like an affliction—an affinity for beauty. A fetish, perhaps, to further belabor that overused term. It's what led me to museum work, to art appreciation, to entire weeks of my life lost window-shopping for mouthwatering furniture and trinkets that could bankrupt me with a single swipe of my bank card. I have expensive taste, my father always said. Though surely he'd meant my refusal to settle for less than the fancy brand of macaroni and cheese, with its seductive silver packet of gooey Velveeta cheese. Not home furnishings or Parisian prostitutes.

But that's enough about me for now.

When it finally struck six fifty-nine, I gave myself permission to enter Didier's building. I shook my umbrella off on the stoop and studied the tenant list. I pressed the brass button beside *5C Pedra, D.* and waited, my breath held. I should mention that Didier and I had only corresponded in postcards, because a) I hadn't had his number at first; and b) once he gave it to me, I was too chickenshit to use it. The voice I'd speculated and fantasized about didn't greet me, though the door buzzed as it unlocked and I let myself in.

It was probably once a dazzling building, now thoroughly worn around the edges. In addition to attractive men, I fear elevators, especially the ancient kind here in number sixteen, with the accordion-style door, so I found the slightly less claustrophobic stairwell and dripped my way up four flights.

Flat 5C is at the very end of a long, dim, narrow corridor with a ceiling at least a foot shorter than the lower levels'. As I took my final breath, knuckles poised to knock, the door swung in.

Didier was taller than I'd anticipated. He was more of everything than I'd anticipated. Which is saying a lot, because I'd purposefully built him up in my mind, so grand he could only fail to measure up and hence give me permission to do as I always do and declare myself above the bothersome magnetism of lust.

But Didier did not disappoint. My mouth went dry and I must have looked stoned, standing there with the blank expression I rely on when desperately trying to appear unaffected.

"Good evening," he said. "You're Carolyn?"

I managed to say, "I am." My name is, in fact, Caroly, a misspelling on my grandmother's prospective baby name list that my mother found exceedingly fetching. No sympathy for her daughter, doomed to be addressed as Carol or Carolyn for the rest of her days. And because of how "Caroline" is pronounced in France—*Caroleen*—nobody here ever gets my name right when I introduce myself. But that's fair, considering how badly I mangle their entire language every time I open my mouth.

"I'm Didier." He shook my hand and I marveled at the gesture, how he could manage to make it feel so casual yet confident. "Come in." His English is strong, though his accent heavy. Ania told me he speaks several languages, and that his father was from Spain.

He closed the door behind me as I stepped into his garret.

It's the single most sensual space I've ever been in. There's nothing fancy about it, yet sex seems to drip from every square inch. His furniture is all dark wood, a mix of mahogany and walnut. More estate sale than antique broker, but it works. It matches the stained beams of the sloped ceiling and sets off the walls, painted the deep red of a dying rose, two weeks past Valentine's Day. The lighting is perfectly inadequate, allowing the eye to take in only a handful of immediate details at one time. Very soothing, like blinders. The living room is long and narrow, and through the few windows not shrouded by gauzy curtains, you can see an enviable skyline view to the east. It smells nice, as well, something I couldn't place, the oddest mix of clean and musty.

I'm babbling about Didier's décor because I was afraid to look at him at first, and those were the minutiae I lost myself in. But eventually I turned to face him.

"You have a lovely flat."

"Thank you. Would you like a drink?"

"Sure." I'd never needed a drink so badly in my life.

"Have a seat." He waved toward the settee and armchair in the corner before heading for another room. "And you prefer English?"

"If you don't mind. Thank you." I set my umbrella and purse by the door and crossed the room to sit on the chair. Pigeons paced on the ledge outside the window, their little bird motors idling, purring and cooing their contentment. I envied their ease.

Didier's voice carried from the far room. "I see you did not escape the storm."

"No, sadly."

He reappeared with two glasses of red wine, handing me one as he took a seat on the couch.

I have avoided describing Didier, I know. That's because I worry I'll never be able to paint him properly, to do him justice. But here goes.

I'll start with his voice. It's deep and gentle, warm and relaxed. I'm terrible at guessing heights, but he's tall, over six feet. His image in those photos and sketches from the gallery binder are elegant, which he is in real life as well.

I can't find the right word for his build. Though he's quite trim, he has a large frame—wide shoulders, broad hands— making him seem heavy and strong. In person, his muscular body was of course hidden, and it was maddening to know what he looked like nearly naked and to then have to suffer his sweater and slacks. He had on socks but no shoes, which for some reason I found reassuring.

We sipped our wine and I have no idea what we talked about. The rain, how this spring was stacking up to previous years, perhaps. I took in only what I was looking at.

I know you must want to know about his face, one worthy of so many artists' awe and my clumsy prose. It's a stern face, as you'd expect of a male model. A strong jaw, though not square. Cheekbones that bend light, of course. Expressive eyebrows, black in the dim room. His hair is a shade lighter than his brows, and not as unruly as mine—a wavy sort of curly, long enough to clutch but not to wrap around one's fingers. His eyes are deep brown with heavy lids that give him a slightly sinister, slightly sleepy expression. His nose is strong, not quite *big*, with the slightest hook to it. Like so many Parisian men, he has an air of caustic wisdom about him. Unlike many Parisian men, he does not have an aroma of cigarettes to accent the attitude.

Didier is the type of man who, even if you can't stand seafood, makes you crave oysters. There is something raw and primal yet utterly refined about him that leaves you hungry for such a thing. He pairs with liver and black caviar and hundred-dollar champagne, this extraordinary delicacy of a man. A rare animal, worthy of hunting to extinction lest anyone else lay claim to the beauty of him.

"So tell me what exactly brings you here," he said.

Ah, a question I had no answer for. "I saw pictures of you at a gallery, and heard that you... You know."

He nodded.

"You've modeled a lot," I said.

"I did. Not so often anymore." The only imperfect thing about him is his teeth—white but a bit crooked, which I don't mind at all. Mine are just the same.

"Have you lived here long?" I asked, aiming my gaze all around his flat.

"Ages. Nearly ten years." Didier has a way of leaning forward, bracing his elbows on his knees and locking his eyes on yours even as he sips his wine. Though it sounds unnerving, it makes you feel you're the most fascinating woman on earth. Normally I shy from a stare as intense as his, strong as a floodlight, but all I felt then was blank.

"And you?" he asked. "How long have you been in Paris?"

"Two years, next month."

"School?"

I shook my head. "Work. At a museum. Assistant curator."

He made an impressed face. "And so what brings you to me?"

My delusions of charisma faded. "Um… Do you have a confidentiality thing with your clients?"

A smile that melted my muscles. "We never met," he said simply.

"Right. Well. This is embarrassing…"

He let me trail off, no prompting, merely sipping his drink while I gathered my thoughts.

"I'm not very experienced with men."

Didier nodded, as though he were fluent in evasive English. "You're looking to change that?"

"Maybe. To be honest, I don't know what I'm looking for."

He leaned back against the couch cushions and crossed his legs. "Not to put too fine a point on it, but it is a flat rate." I pictured the check in my purse, ready to be dropped discreetly in his mailbox upon my departure. "You get me for the evening, and what we do is entirely your choice. Nothing is off-limits with me." He gestured with his free hand, presenting his body as a package.

"Right."

"But that goes the other way as well. It's your time, and if all you want to do is talk and drink, then that's what we do."

I considered that. I wondered how often that *was* what women wanted from him—a date with no pressure, no fear of rejection. That's what I wanted, after all. I've even heard that plenty of men who patronize female prostitutes want simply that, companionship.

"That would be good, to start."

He nodded, stern face striking and sage. "Do you mind my asking, how inexperienced are you? Or what would you like to learn from me?"

"I've kissed men, but that's really all."

Let me pause here and explain how it felt to admit that. I'm sure plenty of girls lie about how many guys they've messed around with when they're younger, not wanting to seem too easy. Well, there's another stigma that comes later, as you edge closer to true adulthood, especially if you run with a liberal, artsy crowd. I always pray my friends assume I'm a real freak behind closed doors, just stingy with the details. I think you can get away with being a virgin until you're, say, twenty-three or so, and still pass it off as choosiness or cautiousness or plain old willfulness. But twenty-nine? That's when people start to wonder what's *wrong* with you. Including yourself.

Didier is the first person I've actually admitted the extent of my inexperience to, ever. I even lead my gynecologist on. When she asks, "Are you sexually active?" I always reply, "Not at the moment." If the truth is embarrassingly apparent, she's kind enough not to tell me so.

And it was in *that* moment in Didier's living room that I realized, maybe not tonight, but some day not too far off, I could leave this place with that weight lifted from me. I could walk down his street and be like everyone else. I could have a *lover*. This is Paris, after all. Having a lover is like having a pancreas. I was suddenly very ready to quit being a medical anomaly.

All Didier said to my pronouncement was, "That is very interesting." He paused and squinted in such a way that it seemed he were taking a drag off a psychic cigarette. I worried he was about to tell me he had a policy against deflowering his clients, but instead he went on. "It's very flattering that you've come to me."

"Oh. Good."

"Yes. I would be very honored to corrupt you in whatever ways you like."

I laughed at that, relaxing further. The wine instantly tasted extraordinary, and it dawned that I was actually turned-on. I'd worried that wouldn't happen and I'd officially get stamped DEFECTIVE and sent back to the factory.

I cleared my throat. "I have no idea what ways I'm looking to be corrupted. I'm usually pretty nervous around men."

"That's very normal, for the first date."

Ooh, *date*. I liked that. I'd happily pretend I'd scored a date with this perfect man.

"There's no rush, by the way," he said. "I rarely get to bed before five a.m., so if you want to just sit here and drink and talk all night, you're not wasting my time or keeping me up in the least."

"Okay, great." And necessary. I'm a slow thaw.

"Here." Didier stood and crossed the room to switch on a radio. I love listening to French talk radio. Even after two years, I struggle to follow the pace of the language but I adore the sound of it. He kept the volume low, and I felt he'd read my mind, meeting some need I hadn't even realized I had. He filled the silence without making it feel like a pointed seduction or an awkward distraction, and my brain quieted.

The etiquette is odd, when you visit a prostitute. On the one hand, Didier was mine to do with what I wanted. That was my right. But even if I wanted to treat him like a piece of meat, I suspected I wasn't capable of it. He might be a slice of cake, reserved specially for me, but it felt very strange to actually consider enjoying him. Which of us was I worried about demeaning?

He fetched the wine bottle from the kitchen and set it on the table before us, taking his seat. "So tell me. You're an attractive woman. You seem successful and clever."

"Thanks."

"May I ask what it is about men that's made you cautious? Do you not like being touched, or you simply haven't met the right one? Is it a religious decision?"

"No, definitely not religious. And I don't think I mind being touched, really… It's hard to explain." I folded my legs beneath my butt and addressed his hands. "I guess I don't want to settle for a man who isn't really, truly attractive to me. But I'm afraid to try to date those guys, because I'm afraid I'll find out I'm not enough for them. I'm probably just afraid of rejection. It's always been easier and less scary to just not take the chance."

"You won't be rejected here."

I nodded. "That's the appeal. Well, and you." I looked up to meet his eyes. "I'm sure you've heard a million times that you're handsome. You, um… I think you may be the most attractive man I've ever seen."

His smile was warm and humble, and it gathered the skin beneath his eyes into adorable little rolls. "That's very kind. I hope it pleases you that I'm yours to enjoy."

"It does. It scares me, too."

"Of course."

I drained my glass and Didier refilled it. His mix of matter-of-factness and perfect calm was exceedingly disarming. I'd feared he'd be cocky or sleazy or aggressively flirtatious…I mean, countless women pay to sleep with him. How could that not give a man a gigantic ego? I'd also feared he'd be a sweet-talking, God's-gift Don Juan and I'd feel as though I were being coerced. But I didn't. If this was a seduction, it was very covert and exactly my speed.

We chatted some more about the city and when the sky grew dark, Didier lit at least a dozen candles, a mound of them all melted together on an old metal card table behind the couch. Beeswax — that was the pleasant, musty smell I'd noted.

Didier by candlelight is obscenely stunning. At long last, my mind was wandering. I studied the tendons in his neck in the warm glow and recalled the images of his bare chest that I'd seen. He must be used to such scrutiny, as he merely sipped his drink and watched me watching him.

I feel so predictable saying it, but add wine and candles and a Parisian skyline at dusk and this prude is suddenly a hussy.

"I don't suppose you could, um..." My voice dropped to a mumble. "Take your sweater off?"

Didier nodded and stood, stripping away his top and undershirt in one motion.

As he sat, I gave myself permission to be curious, not bashful. I decided to treat him as what he was to me—living art. His bare skin looked warm in the flickering light, and I understood with true clarity what artists mean by "muse". He's magic. A man who poses merely by sitting, a hundred thousand angles waiting to be discovered. I wished I were more artistic so I could capture him, every last shadow and contour.

"You're beautiful," I finally said.

"Thank you."

"It's okay if I only want to look at you tonight?"

"Of course. I'm yours for whatever you wish to do. Or not do."

When you're as inexperienced as I am, there's a ton to learn from a man before you even touch or kiss him. I considered what I wanted. To see him naked, but not too soon. To watch him bathe. To watch him masturbate, above just about everything else. That's always turned me on, and I'm sure it's because I nearly never fantasize about actually being with a man. Even in my own imagination, I fear rejection. My mental porn is almost exclusively comprised of one-man shows, with an occasional faceless woman stepping in as choreography demands.

"Could you take your pants off?" I asked him.

"Of course."

Before I knew it, he'd stripped to his underwear. And it's the sexiest underwear I've ever seen on a man. Nothing fancy, just briefs, but they must be made of silk or some other fine, explicit fabric, the way they cling. His thighs looked strong, his shorts full. He was an Armani campaign, lounging on his old couch in this moody, elegant apartment, candles flickering. Note to self—find out if clients are allowed to take photographs.

"Is it weird," I asked, "having people stare at you?"

"No, not really. I modeled for so long, I'm used to it now."

"And you don't model anymore?"

He shook his head. "Very rarely. My priorities have shifted."

"Oh. Well, I guess it's just weird for me, then, doing the staring."

"You're here with permission to do far more than stare," he reminded me with a smile. "Believe me, I'm not bothered."

"Would you feel weird if I asked to watch you, later? You know, like watch you..." I couldn't find the right verb, all of them sounding too clinical or too juvenile.

"Touch myself?"

Oh, that'll do.

I nodded.

"No, that would not bother me at all."

I sipped my wine and considered something. Male prostitutes can't fake it the way female ones can. For a second I was filled with fear that the time would come for Didier to take me and he wouldn't be up for it, as it were.

"Something is worrying you," he said.

I smiled dopily, owning my nerves. "Sort of. I was just thinking about how... About what happens when you're not attracted to your clients."

"Whether or not I can perform?"

I nodded again.

"Well, I have a few unwritten policies. The first is that no one in this flat does anything they aren't comfortable with. If I don't think a woman is absolutely, perfectly ready for me to do what she's asked of me, I won't do it."

"And what about if *you* aren't into it?"

Another smile, but this time he lowered his gaze to the glass in his hands. "If I've managed to make a woman really, truly ready to have me, I'm into it. It's very seductive to me, a woman who can make demands of my body."

"Oh. That's a good answer."

He met my eyes again. "The truth always is."

"Have you always known... When did you first realize you're, you know. Good-looking?"

He made a thoughtful face, just another intriguing flavor of handsome seasoning his features. "I suppose when I was about fourteen, I started to realize, or people started to tell me."

"Did you always want to model?"

"No, it was very accidental. Photographers kept asking, and I kept being broke. It seemed a natural solution."

"What about..." I gave a little nod to mean this room, the two of us and what brought me here.

"That was accidental as well. It never struck me as such a great divide, the step between modeling and selling my physical body. And I never had a drug problem or anything so desperate, if you were curious."

"That hadn't actually crossed my mind."

"But I've never been modest, and I've never felt that sex is something so precious it needs to be reserved for some mysterious 'one'. That's a very American way of thinking, isn't it? This modern obsession with monogamy. Exclusivity."

"Probably. Did you want to be something else when you were younger?"

He smiled. "I certainly never went around saying, 'when I'm grown, I want to be a whore'."

I blushed, unsure if he was offended by my question.

"I wanted to make women happy. That was all I knew."

"That's an interesting thing for a boy to realize."

"You would have had to have my mother to understand. She was a very cold woman. To me, at least. I'm sure a psychiatrist would have plenty to say about that. But I suspect that's some part of why I'm here, doing what it is I do."

"Do you enjoy it?"

Didier nodded. "Very much."

"A friend of mine said your father's Spanish."

He shook his head. "Portuguese."

"Oh, sorry. Does he live in France now?"

"No, he never lived here. I used to visit him in the summers, when I was a child, but not for years and years now. My parents never married. Though I don't think my mother ever stopped loving him. I think he's the only man, maybe the only person, she ever loved, aside from her own mother. But I do not think he ever loved her back."

It was interesting to me, how freely Didier spoke of such things. Then again, surely no part of him is off-limits, not his anatomy or his past, his views on sex and love. I was reminded then how differently Europeans—and in particular the French—view love compared to Americans. When I first moved here I found it bleak, borderline nihilistic, but I can understand now how our version must seem to them— delusional and sloppy and grasping. As I sat staring at Didier's near-naked body, I ached to learn how to be blasé about the whole affair, how to be *French* about it. I ached to be a woman who, when viciously dumped or informed her boyfriend was cheating, could merely curse and spit at the ground and shake her delicate fist, then move on.

Though if I were really so unaffected, I'd surely have gotten laid long ago. So no, I'm no more fluent in France's romantic pragmatism than I am its language. Though perhaps in time, with practice.

"I'd like to watch you," I said quietly.

Didier offered me a subtle, genuine smile. "I would like for you to watch. Where? Right here?"

"Where do you usually…"

"On my bed."

His bed. Shiver. "Is that okay?"

"That's perfectly okay. Come." He stood and lifted the table from behind the couch, carrying it, lit candles and all, to the far end of the flat. I followed, fear and curiosity tightening my belly, eyes torn between his ass and shoulders and the black threshold of his room.

His bedroom is dark, even more so than the rest of the apartment, its lone window obscured by a curtain. He set the candles by the wall so they illuminated the head of his bed. It's a fascinating piece of furniture, and I bet it's been in this flat for decades, too cumbersome to bother removing. Dark wood, with a canopy—curling, carved posts draped with the same red chiffony fabric as the curtain. Sensual without being feminine, antique without stodginess. His bedspread is black and I hope one day to be able to report on the color of his sheets. Beside the bed is a small side table displaying a half-dozen bottles with glass stoppers, massage oil or lube or both, I could only assume.

He waited patiently while I took in the room, as I imagined him fucking on that bed to the noise and flash of a thunderstorm, rain hammering the window. Note—I did not say I imagined him fucking *me* on that bed. I really need to get better at participating in my own fantasies.

"It's a lovely room," I told him.

"Thank you."

"It's very…relaxing. I was worried before I got here that there was no chance I'd be able to relax."

He pulled a chair from the corner to the center of the room for me and took a seat on the bed. "You have a lot of worries about all this."

"I have a lot of worries about most things," I admitted with a sheepish smile. "Though hardly anything's ever as bad I let myself expect."

"And me? I'm not as bad as you feared?"

I grinned down at my hands. "No, not at all. You're very disarming."

"I'm glad."

Seeing him nearly naked on his bed had me coursing with heat all over again. This was where he lay when he touched himself for real, without an audience.

"Are you ready?" he asked.

"I think so. I've never watched a man before. In person."

"Does it intimidate you, to feel like a voyeur?"

"Kind of."

"That's fine. Here is what we do." He stood and got the setup going. A dark wicker changing screen from the corner of the room was arranged between the bed and the chair, all of the light on the bed's side. I took a seat and could see him quite clearly through the gaps in the weave, sitting on the edge of the mattress. He could surely see only firelit lattice.

"This is better?" he asked.

"Yes, this is perfect."

He grabbed a silk scarf from a side table and handed it to me. "This is all at your pace. When and if you're ready for me to finish, just drape that over the screen."

Didier is a genius.

As he sat once more, his expression changed as though he'd convinced himself I wasn't there. His eyes half closed and he cast them downward, looking meditative. He ran a slow hand across his throat, down his chest, circling his living sculpture of an abdomen before finally cupping himself. My pulse rocketed, arousal so potent I held in a gasp.

His hand slid up and down, up and down, over his hidden cock, glacially slow and volcanically hot.

He looked up and addressed the screen. "Is it all right if I make noises?"

"Yes, that's fine."

He braced his other arm behind him on the bed and leaned back. His right hand rubbed lower, fondling his balls, stroking deep between his thighs.

"I'd like to see," I murmured.

I knew he heard me, but he didn't take the order right away. I might have been in charge, but Didier's not entirely obedient, I was discovering. He slid his hand inside the front of his shorts with a low, shallow moan. It was the most exquisite torture, watching the flex of his arm and the shape of his stroking hand, but being denied the view.

"Does it feel good?" I barely realized it was me talking. I felt high and disembodied.

"Feels wonderful. You want to see?" As if he didn't know the answer.

"Yes."

Still, he made me wait.

Let me be clear. I'm nearly thirty and a virgin, but in my head, I'm not a prude. Between me and my hand—and occasionally my vibrator, when I'm lazy—I'm no stranger to arousal or orgasm. I know what it's like to be worked up beyond belief, and right then, watching Didier, I can honestly say I've *never* been that wound up before. My entire body was tight and fevery and impatient to the brink of madness.

At long last, when I thought I'd go crazy from the lust, he let me see. Easing the waistband over the tip of his cock, he drew his shorts down, revealing each thick inch with slow precision.

And all at once, I was in the same room with a naked man. An aroused, naked man, and the best-looking one I've ever seen.

It's almost unfair, that he gets this body and this face and voice, all these gifts, and that his dick should also exceed expectations. Not so huge that it intimidates me, though. It was then that I knew I'd made the right decision, coming to him, and waiting for all these years to have these experiences with a man so extraordinary. I might be ruining myself, setting the bar this high.

Fuck it.

I watched not only his hand and cock, but the tensing of his stomach as he breathed, and the shift of his hips. For a minute he concentrated his strokes just below the head until a clear bead appeared at his tip, then more. With a soft moan, he crested his palm over his crown and slicked it down his shaft, skin glinting in the warm light.

"I'm so ready," he murmured. There was no pressure in the statement. No request. The thought that my presence was linked to this man's arousal felt like a miracle. And the idea that I could have him, if I wanted...

"Come closer," I said.

He stood from the bed and stepped forward a pace, keeping just far enough away that our eyes couldn't meet above the screen. He dropped his shorts and kicked them aside. As he pleasured his cock, his other hand caressed his belly and chest, all the places I longed to touch myself.

"I'd like to watch you bathe sometime," I told him. Warm, soapy water dripping down his abdomen, between his legs...

"You can have anything you want."

What I wanted right then surprised me. I wanted to be close to him.

"Go back to the bed, please."

173

He did as I asked and I watched him for another minute or two. A strong, hard, pantingly horny man is a marvelous creature, everything the gender ought to be…yet so frequently isn't, in this day and age. This was how Didier looked when he was by himself. Who did he think of, when he did this?

His groans grew harsher, driving the bad thought away and drawing my attention back where it should be.

I stood and skirted the shade, intending simply to move it aside. But my fear was gone so I let my body lead me, and it led me to sit right next to him on the edge of the bed and watch from close up. His lids looked leaden as he turned his face to me. I could have kissed him, I'm sure. I even leaned in, but when we made contact it was forehead to forehead. Yet it felt more personal than any kiss I'd ever experienced, more explicit by miles. His skin was hot and damp, breath sweet from the wine and scratchy with arousal. The moment was nothing like I'd feared. It was nervous but somehow natural. Sweet. I nestled against his shoulder and watched his hand, wondering what his cock must feel like…surely as hot as the cheek pressed to mine. But I wasn't ready for the tease to end and real exploration to begin.

The smell of his sex was something I hadn't anticipated. Heady and dark as rum, dark as his eyes and brows and the tidily trimmed hair between his legs.

He pulled away an inch to whisper, "What do you want from me?"

"Keep going. Until you absolutely have to…"

He nodded, and even in the candlelight I could see how pink his lips and ears and cheeks were. His cock was flushed as well, his shaft dark against his stroking hand. It was a revelation to know his arousal was so real, when I'd imagined his experience must have turned him into a cold machine, going through the motions.

I thought, *I could kiss this man, so easily.*

Just as easily, I could discover all the things I've denied myself. I could find out what a hard cock feels like against my palm, what it tastes like, how it feels to have a man in my mouth. What it's like to have Didier above me, sliding inside me. What it feels like, the first time. If you're really turned-on, it's not supposed to hurt very much. No problem there. What would it be like, to feel his cock rushing in and out? And how would I feel to him? Does it actually feel different with a virgin?

"Have you ever done this... Has a woman come to you, I mean, who's a virgin?"

He nodded, lost in his own pleasure or the struggle to keep from losing it.

"Does it feel different?"

"Every woman feels different."

"Oh." Another good answer.

"I know if you decided you wanted me," he said, "you would feel amazing."

Fuck, that melted me. If I decided *I* wanted *him*. As if his wanting me were beyond speculation. Maybe it was even true. Maybe I was one of his prettier and younger clients. Maybe he'd even have smiled at me, had we met in line at a café and not under these strange circumstances.

I tried to imagine what other women might come here to do... To have a beautiful man kneel between their legs, take them roughly on this stately old bed, or ride his hard cock until they got their fill. He'd said nothing was off-limits. I imagined him tied down, or doing the tying. Getting spanked or doling out that punishment. He was whatever that evening's client wanted, and right now, he was exactly mine, intuitively guiding my experience. I wondered what else he'd know I wanted, before I knew it myself.

"I'm imagining you," he whispered.

My heart stopped, tangled in what he'd said. "What are you thinking about?"

"Imagining what you might have me do to you. Maybe undress you here on this bed. Taste your mouth and neck, and your breasts. Your sex."

"I don't know what I want yet."

"I can't wait to help you find out."

Oh, but he could wait, surely. I bet no one can delay gratification like Didier Pedra.

"Do you like being watched?" I asked.

"I like pleasing a woman, so yes. I like the way you watch me." His eyes were nearly closed, voice shallow and strained. "You still want this?"

"Yes." So badly I prayed it would never end. "Would you stand? In front of me?"

Didier got to his feet and it felt precisely how I'd hoped with his body looming, just the slightest streak of intimidation warming me. I glanced at the little bottles beside his bed.

"Do you ever use any of those?" I asked, pointing.

"I do. Would you like that now?"

"Please."

He reached for the largest bottle and lifted the sphere from its top, drawing out a glass wand and dripping a measure of clear liquid onto his palm. I recognized the smell—mineral oil.

"Slowly," I said, surprised again by this new ability to make demands.

He obeyed, running his cupped hand along the underside of his shaft with perfect control. Next he smoothed the oil over the base, drawing his fist halfway up, then back down. With each stroke he came closer to the head, until his entire length shone in the dancing light.

"Does it feel good?"

"Yes, wonderful." His hips joined the motion of his hand, thrusting his cock into his grip. Arousal obliterated a dam inside me, flooding me with heat and urgency.

I rose to stand at his side and study him from every angle. He seemed to understand what I wanted from this show, intensifying the movements. With his free hand he reached up and clasped the canopy rail, leaning forward to emphasize everything that had me so mesmerized. He held his fist still, fucking it with his cock and letting loose a deep groan. The sound sucked the breath from my lungs. I circled to the back, imagining this vision—the undulations of these strong hips and ass and shoulders—was how he'd look, taking me.

With a shallow, fearful inhalation, I reached out and touched him, trailing my fingertips down his spine. He moaned from the contact and I pulled away, but only for a moment. When I touched him again, I let myself linger. His skin was hot, as though he'd been standing in front of a fire, and damp with the finest sheen of perspiration. I traced the crests of his jutting shoulder blades, then down his back to his hip. Beneath my palm I felt the strength in his muscle and I marveled simply to be touching a man this way. To be touching a man this flawless. It was a glorious crime, like breaching security to stroke my palm over *Starry Night* and memorize its luscious brushstrokes.

As I rounded him, I dragged my palm across his lower back. I admired the flex of his arm, with my eyes as well as my touch. How extraordinary, that this was actually happening to me, that I was allowed to enjoy the most beautiful man I'd ever seen and he couldn't break my heart.

I went back to the bed, kneeling on the mattress in front of him. As he fucked his fist, I mustered the nerve to touch his face. His gaze, half-mast though it was, felt too intense.

"Close your eyes."

He did.

I memorized his cheekbones and the rasp of his stubble, the shapes of his ears and nose. I held his jaw, awed by how real he was. How he could look this astonishing yet still be flesh and blood. I rose enough to graze my closed lips against his lower one, not quite a kiss.

"I'm close," he whispered. The words brushed our lips together, the most potent and personal caress I believe I've ever felt.

"I don't want it to end yet."

He nodded.

"Can you stop now, or are you too close?"

"I can stop." And he did. He straightened, chest and belly rising and falling with each harsh breath.

"Could I watch you bathe?"

"Of course."

"When you're ready, I mean."

He smiled at that. "Thank you." He ran his hands through his hair and gulped a few inhalations, until his composure returned.

"That was… That was exactly what I wanted," I told him.

"Good."

I felt myself blushing but continued anyway. "Does it make any difference, that it's me here with you when you were doing that?"

"Of course." He met my gaze and as intense as it was, I welcomed it. "Everything I did was for you. Every thought that ran through my mind was of you. And it thrills me to be the only man you've watched, that way."

The blush raged to a full-blown fire. "Oh."

"Whatever you desire tonight, I want to be the one who gives it to you."

I felt too many things, at that moment—lust and awe, and a romantic thrill quickly eclipsed as my traitorous, annoying brain reminded me we were only together because I was paying him. But the illusion felt too good for the ugly thoughts to win. That's the magic of Didier—he lets you believe this romance is real. Because for the six hours you've reserved with him, it is.

"You want to watch me bathe now?"

I nodded.

"Come."

I followed him to an adjacent, tiny bathroom, lit by the clear bulbs framing the cabinet mirror. This is a garret, I'll remind you, so don't imagine he has an actual tub, merely a shower cubicle. But it's an elegant little nook, tiled in teal and turquoise and indigo, with antique copper fixtures. I took a seat on the wooden lid of his toilet and marveled at how close his naked body was. He got the water running, leaving the glass door wide open.

For whatever reason, this seemed more intimate than sitting beside him on his bed. There was his shampoo bottle, a brand I'd seen in the drugstore a hundred times. On the sink, the razor he shaved with—however infrequently—his toothbrush, his comb. All of these things felt more explicit than his bare cock, perhaps because they negated the illusion. He's an actual man, and I'd been invited into this, his actual home.

"How hot do you want the water?" he asked me.

I balked a moment, worried he thought I wanted to join him.

"Choose for me," he elaborated.

"Oh." It felt like an odd request, but when I rose and put my hand under the flow, it made perfect sense. Did I want him to be warm and comfortable? Cold and tense? Scalded to within a gasp of fainting? I opted for the temperature I like myself, hot but not too hot. I took my seat.

"Thank you," he said, and stepped inside.

I don't know what it is about a man in the shower... His eyes shut and his dark hair turned black as the water cascaded over his face and shoulders, down his chest and stomach and legs, slipping from his oiled cock. My pulse sped as he took a bar of soap from a tray, turning it around and around. He taunted me until the lather was thick and dripping from his hands. His eyes opened, holding me hostage.

He slicked a palm across his throat, his shoulder, down his arm. As he stroked his chest, the suds slid down the crests of his abdomen and between his legs. He broke eye contact to turn, letting me watch as he soaped his hair and his elegant back. He slicked lather between his ass cheeks with a slow, explicit sensuality. The caress unleashed strange, taboo possibilities in my head, ones that had never held much interest for me before that precise moment.

He turned to face me again, leaning back against the tile with his feet braced at shoulder-width. For what felt like ages he soaped his chest and neck and stomach, before he finally slid his hands lower. Those dangerous eyes closed as he cupped his balls, fondling and lingering, the filthiest act of ablution I've ever seen.

After a few more slippery turns of the bar in his hands, he lathered his cock.

"Good," I murmured.

He didn't touch himself as he had on the bed. This was for me, first and foremost, not merely a voyeuristic glimpse at private acts. He gave himself long, lazy strokes, as if he knew exactly what I wanted—to savor every wet, glistening square inch of his bare body.

"Tell me what you think I want," I said. "Not just tonight. But eventually."

Eyes still closed, he paused before he spoke. "I think you want me to take you."

"How?"

I could have sworn his fist gripped tighter, his strokes no longer a show meant only for me, but pleasure for himself. "Slow," he said. "Slow at first."

"Where?"

"In my bed. You want me on top."

My throat and pussy tightened.

"You want to be taken, your first time," he went on. "You need to be passive before you can feel ready to take for yourself. When you trust my body, then you'll explore."

"Explore how?"

"Find out what it feels like, to have a man in your mouth."

"That usually comes first, doesn't it? Before the actual sex?"

He smiled to himself. "That *is* actual sex. And yes, it does often come first, but I don't think it should."

"No?"

"No. I think that act is more explicit that mere fucking."

I shivered, wondering if maybe I shared this view.

"To trust someone when you can barely see their eyes," he murmured. "To give up your own comfort and control and take pleasure in their commands, their experience. And for the one who receives, the vulnerability of being seen so close up, smelled and tasted."

"I never thought about it like that. It always seemed like...like the thing you do between fooling around and going all the way."

"It can be, if you like. But it isn't to me." His brown eyes finally opened. "When sexual pleasure loses its mutuality, that's when the fear and the trust emerge. That's real intimacy. To me."

I was being offered lessons on real intimacy from a man who fucks for money, yet I was inclined to subscribe. Then again, with that deep and nasty-sexy accent, Didier could tell me how to strip wallpaper or press flowers and I'd still be riding on the brink of orgasm.

"I like that," I told him. "Your views about it all."

"This is just what I've learned from the women I've been with. When you leave here, I'll have learned something from you as well, I'm sure."

I found that hard to believe...I'm the least sexually experienced woman I know. But the way he said it had me *wanting* to believe it, which was enough.

"You'll teach me what it's like to get a private woman to open up, perhaps."

"I hope so. I'd like to learn that, myself."

"What else would you like to learn?"

"Well, how to be with a man, I guess."

He gave me a strange, crooked smile. "You want me to teach you how to be a good lover?"

"Maybe. Well, no. Not really. I just want to know all the things I should by now...what it's like to touch a man, what everything feels like."

"I can only teach you what it will be like between you and I."

You and I. I could've sighed aloud at that concept, the two of us encapsulated as a couple. "Then that's what I'd like to learn. At my own pace."

"At your pace," he agreed.

Didier's own pace had me hypnotized—the slippery, gliding pulls that had his cock looking so hot and thick. How would I want it to be, when I touched him for the first time? Who would be above whom, or how could it be made equitable? I thought perhaps I'd like to touch him as we kissed...or did I want both our pairs of eyes on my hand, his cock? I was already trapped in the worries of what would come, wasting the magic of the present.

"Are you enjoying this?" he asked me.

"I am. But I'm making myself anxious, thinking about whatever's going to happen next."

"Did you think when you first arrived that we'd come this far?"

"No, I didn't," I said.

"What happens will happen, exactly the way it's meant to."

As I nodded, I truly believed him.

"All you need to do is be honest with yourself and with me about what you want. You've done that perfectly so far."

"Thanks."

"What are you wanting?" he asked. "Right now?"

"I think I want to touch you. But not here. Maybe on your couch."

He released his cock and set the soap aside. As he rinsed his magnificent body, he said, "Then we will go to the couch and find out if that is meant to be."

I preceded him to the living room, turning on a dim reading lamp and refilling our glasses while Didier dressed. He joined me on the couch in his pants, his shirt unbuttoned, to my great delight. He accepted his glass and took a deep drink, staring at me over the rim.

"So," I said.

"So. You are pleased with how this is going?"

"Very. You've made me way more comfortable than I'd guessed was possible."

"Good."

I leaned a bit closer, addressing his chest. "You're very intuitive. What else do you think I want, tonight?"

"I think you want to control when I come. You want to feel some control, but also feel safe. Passive."

"I think you're right."

"You've seen that before, I'm sure. A man pleasuring himself? Coming?"

"Yeah."

"Do you enjoy watching? Videos? Or looking at pictures?"

I shook my head. "I've been curious enough to check them out, but I don't really enjoy it for more than a minute or two. I'm never attracted to the men, and I don't want to see the other women, in case I catch myself comparing myself to them."

"I think you're possessive, maybe?"

"I think I'm too fussy. And I think I've spent too much time in my own head, imagining things I'll never be able to have, and no one in real life could ever live up to my ideas."

"You can have those things with me."

"I hope so. But once I leave…I'll never really be able to have you, a man like you. But I want to experience it anyhow. Like a wonderful feast I'll never be served again."

Didier's face turned thoughtful and he sat up, drawing a knee to his chest and wrapping his arms around it, obscuring my view. "What do you mean, a man like me? Why can't you have whatever you want?"

"I'm not pretty enough," I mumbled. "And even if I could land a man as perfect-looking as I want, I don't think I could ever relax, I'd be so worried he'd leave me."

"Do you think maybe that's not what you're afraid of at all?"

I *did* think that, sometimes, but I just shrugged.

"Maybe," Didier said, "you're more afraid of being left by a man you see as your equal. So you tell yourself you'll only ever be satisfied with one you think is better than you are, and you give yourself permission to not bother."

"But I don't want to settle. I don't want to spend my life pretending the man I'm with turns me on when he really doesn't."

"What turns you on, aside from the perfect face and body?"

I blinked. "I'm not sure. Charisma, maybe."

"Wit? Kindness? Talent?"

"I guess."

"You like the way I look, yes?"

I nodded. "Very much."

"Say we fell in love, got married."

"Okay." I shifted in my chair, unnerved by the impossibility of such a notion.

"All of this," he said, circling his face, "will become mundane. What if you do not like anything beyond what's on the outside?"

"You make me sound like a man, after a trophy wife."

"And if we are together forty years, for maybe ten of those I might still be the object you crave. What then?"

"Are you trying to make me feel bad?"

He smiled. "No. I'm trying to understand why you've constructed these rules for yourself. Why you seem to want permission to opt out of love."

"It's scary."

"Of course it is. That's what makes it so exciting."

"Maybe."

"On your end," he said, pointing at me, "you fear the rejection of a man you deem too attractive to ever want you. On my end, I might fear that what I have on the inside will only disappoint you, once my looks are gone. Put out on the pavement like a once-loved chair, after the cushions are stained and worn."

I frowned, a potent pang of sadness twisting my insides. "I don't think about men that way. Really."

"I'm not suggesting I understand you," he said in a kind tone. "But I'd like to. That's why I'm asking all these questions. You're a very extraordinary client. You interest me very much."

I blushed at that. "You must think I'm a sociopath. Or some female chauvinist."

"I don't. I think you're just scared. I want to know what you're scared of."

"Of being left, I guess. Of not being good enough."

"Did that happen to you, when you were young?"

I laughed, partly uncomfortable, partly amused. "You *are* a prostitute, right? Not a shrink?"

"If I'm prying too much, tell me so."

"No, I don't really mind. And I wasn't ever really left as a kid. Both my parents were around until I was in high school, and when my mother moved out it was actually a relief. But I was a really awkward kid. I know, all children are at some point, but I was like, properly homely. I didn't really get it together until I was out of high school."

"And your classmates were cruel to you?"

"Yeah, but not just because I was weird-looking. I was mean, too. Bossy and rude when I thought I was smarter than other kids." Why was I telling all this to the sexiest man I'd ever met, sitting open-shirted and wet-haired mere feet from me? And why precisely did it feel so good?

"A bully?" he asked.

"No, not quite. I didn't go after anyone, wanting to hurt their feelings. I was just clueless and reactionary. I didn't know how to hold back whatever I was feeling. I couldn't separate emotions from reality, my dad used to say. Everything hit me on this intense, visceral level, and if I was angry or insulted, I couldn't step back and calm myself down before I reacted."

"I could see how that would be alienating."

"My mother was the same way, sometimes. But she's severely bipolar. I'm not, but I learned how to interact with people from her. It wasn't until she left and I went to college that I really realized how not-normal it was, living that way. I'd grown up seeing that my dad always caved in the face of her mood swings, until the day he filed for divorce. So my kid brain thought, hey, that's how you get your way."

"Usually it is the parents who teach the child that tantrums are not the way to get what you want."

I nodded. I felt odd, woozy from having told this stranger so much. Much more than I'd ever shared with anyone since moving to France.

"It's nice," Didier said, "getting to hear about you."

I laughed. "Really? I must sound like such a mess."

"Everyone is a mess. If you and I are meant to make love, I wouldn't want to do that without trying to understand you first."

"I thought this would be way different."

"That I'd be some object?" he asked.

"Kind of. Just that it'd be all about appearances. I mean, I figured the women who come to see you are looking for the fantasy, the illusion. Like a place where they don't have to worry about sharing anything personal."

"I suppose some whores offer that."

It gave me pause, hearing him use that word. An ugly, blunt word, though his heavy accent made it less a cinderblock than a strong shot of liquor.

"For me," he went on, "I think the experience is better for everyone when there is a connection. And you cannot connect to someone if you know nothing about them aside from their body. A woman could have a scar across her throat, and I cannot help it—I want to know, was that from an assault? A surgery? A cycling accident? I'm curious. Every woman goes beyond a body and a collection of kinks, even a personality. Each woman is like a landscape to me, and I want know the history, not just the placement of the rocks and trees."

"That's rather poetic."

Didier grinned, that smile that makes my middle melt.

"Would you like to kiss?" he asked.

My stomach gave a flip. I hadn't expected him to initiate anything, but he must know as well as I do, I need coaxing if I'm ever to get anywhere. "I'd like to try that."

He lowered his leg and turned onto his hip, leaning one arm on the back of the couch. I scooted closer and did the same, pulse speeding.

"Do you like to kiss, or be kissed?" he asked.

"Somewhere in the middle."

"I will kiss you first. As I would if we were coming to the end of a very good first date."

"That sounds nice."

Annoying worries clustered in my brain—I would hate the way he kissed and my attraction would die, tossed into the mass grave alongside so many others.

"Close your eyes," he said, pushing aside all the buzzing thoughts.

I did. I held my breath as his large palm cupped my jaw. He spoke and his words warmed my lips. "I want this very much."

"So do I."

His lips brushed mine, and suddenly, this *was* a date. This was my fantasy, one I rarely let myself indulge, a scenario that actually included me. I'd had a date with the best-looking man I'd ever seen, and he wanted me as much as I wanted him. And it occurred to me then…I'd kissed perhaps a dozen guys in my life. But I'd never before this moment kissed a *man*.

And I'd never before felt like a woman, doing this. Always a girl.

Another graze of his lips, the faintest drag of skin. Tight, urgent heat spread from my mouth down my neck, through my chest and belly and down between my thighs. Eyes still closed, I found his throat with my palm. The skin I'd watched him bathe felt as clean as it smelled from his olive oil soap. He took my lower lip between his, then the top. I slid my hand back to feel his damp hair, the heat of his neck. He cocked his head, the kiss still closed-mouth but promising more, soon.

I let myself imagine the acts he'd mentioned doing with others, and though they'd thrilled me before, now I couldn't picture such things. In this moment he was my cautious first date, my maybe-a-boyfriend. He was no other woman's, and he'd never kissed any girl and made her feel this way before. His body was far from innocent, but I fantasized that his heart was as untouched and virginal as mine.

As with everything else about Didier, he did not kiss as I'd expected. There was no showing off, though I'm sure his skills are untouchable. I realized in those moments that he might be the most intuitive human being I'd ever met. Part psychiatrist, part psychic, part prostitute.

I pulled away millimeters to whisper, "Kiss me deeper."

"You want to go further?"

"I think so."

"Do you want to watch me as we kiss?"

My pussy ached at such a thought. "Yeah, I'd like that."

Didier kissed me again, more insistent than before. Heat shot through me as his tongue penetrated, our mouths locked, his chin scratching mine. For only a moment did I freeze up from his forwardness. I gave in to the fear, to his maleness and his lead. His palm left my neck and I could sense it as he opened his pants. I broke away to watch. He slid his hand under his shorts, the flex of his forearm taunting me for a minute or more. I could see his erection growing, framed in his open fly.

"You are always welcome to touch," he whispered.

"I know. But not yet. Not tonight."

He nodded. A deep shiver ran through me as he eased his waistband down to expose his cock.

"You're big," I mumbled.

"I suppose I am."

"I hoped you might be."

That earned me a mischievous smirk. "Then I'm glad I've pleased you." The arm draped behind my shoulders shifted and he held my head gently as he began to masturbate. Putting his lips to my temple, he kissed me there, then down to my ear. His warm mouth took my earlobe, breath so close and ragged I shut my eyes, overwhelmed.

His whispered words tore through me. "You're going to make me come."

I opened my eyes and cast my gaze at his pumping hand. "I'm not doing anything."

"You're here. You're watching. You're letting me show you all this, things no other man has been allowed to."

I felt near to fainting, my breathing as labored as Didier's. "Let's go to your bed."

He stood at once, erection tucked behind his shorts. He held his pants by the belt and took my hand in his free one, leading me back to his room, where the candles still burned.

I sat on the edge of the mattress and watched the shirt drop from his broad shoulders, watched as he stripped naked. I moved to the far end of his bed and patted the space next to me.

He sat. "How are we doing so far?"

I laughed. "You're doing just fine...not sure about myself. I haven't kissed many guys. And I haven't kissed those few guys very, um, extensively."

"I could not tell."

"Really?"

A fond smile. "Really. I like the way you kiss. You kiss as though you are nervous about it, but curious. It's very sexy."

I reached for his face and he did the same to me, cupping my neck. It felt so intimate, his palm on my pulse point as explicit as fingers on my clit. We kissed deeply and I gave as much as I took, tasting his mouth then welcoming his tongue, like a dance. We must have made out for ten minutes or more, until I felt woozy and nuts and ravenous, ready for more.

I broke my mouth from his, lips and chin tender. "Touch yourself. Please."

We paused as he adjusted his legs, spreading his thighs and fisting his neglected cock. I watched with utter fascination as he grew, as his skin went from tan to deep pink, as his erection lengthened and his foreskin receded to expose his smooth head.

This was the closest I'd ever been to a bare cock, and the experience was nothing like I'd feared. He didn't look silly or scary. Everything about him was right. Everything about him made my body ache the way it was designed to, and I felt normal and functional, boring adjectives that are nothing less than magical to me. "Lie down."

He reclined, head on a pair of pillows, clasping his cock. I lay on my side, propped on my elbow, thrilled all over by how close we were, close enough for me to feel the damp heat of his freshly bathed skin and hair. I breathed in the scent of his covers and pillows, the old wood and the candles and his sex.

I brought my mouth to his ear, speaking softly. "Tell me how you think it might be, if you took me." It would be right here, I thought, in this bed. We were so close. All it would take was his strong, slow hands stripping my clothes away, the shifting of his body to cover mine.

He ran his hand lightly along the underside of his shaft. "We would do nothing, until you were ready. Wet and trembling for it. Then I'd go slow, sinking inside you, holding back each inch until you asked for more."

I swallowed. "You're on top?"

"Yes."

Good. That was how I'd imagined it, too.

"Then when you told me to, I'd start moving. Still slow. Until you were right there with me, wanting it."

I watched Didier's powerful arm, the elegant twitch of his tendons as he stroked.

"Do you touch yourself?" he asked. "When you're alone?"

"Yeah."

"I would have you do that, while I made love to you. It would feel so amazing, your body tensing around me as you took pleasure from both of us. Not just to be the one who had you first, but to know you enjoyed it. That's what I want. To give you the satisfying experience so few actually get their first time."

"Does it turn you on, being my first?"

"Yes, it does." His hand seemed to speed at the thought.

"I'm afraid it might ruin me, to have someone as beautiful as you. I'm not sure how I'd be able to date anyone, even after I got my first experience out of the way. I don't think anyone could ever measure up."

"I'm only a man."

Oh, but he's so much more than that.

"And you said, getting this experience 'out of the way'. If it were up to me, that's not how it would be. I would want you to feel that all this waiting was the right decision. Utterly worth it."

"It will be. But I am eager to finally, you know. Join the club, I guess."

Didier smiled, an odd tweak of his lips. His hand paused and he looked right into my eyes. "You make it sound so ordinary."

"No, if it really were just ordinary to me, I'd have done it years ago. But you know. I'm nearly thirty. I want to have a lover, like everyone else seems to."

His smile deepened. "And you chose me?"

I nodded, feeling shy. I looked back to his hand and he resumed the show.

Didier's voice softened and his eyes shut. "I want to spoil you, if you decide you want me. Anything you wish to do with me, you only have to ask."

"Your other clients..." I thought it would hurt, to remember that so many women had had this man and his extraordinary body, but it only filled me with hot, antsy curiosity.

"Yes?"

"What sorts of things do they like to do with you? Do they want romance, like being seduced? Or are they aggressive?"

"Every woman has different needs and desires and secret curiosities. Some want it to feel like a date, and to be seduced, yes. Others want to be in complete control."

"Do you ever get tied down or anything?"

"Yes, I've done that. I will do nearly anything. Anything but physically hurt a woman, or be hurt myself—enough to scar. But I've been tied. I've been spanked, and done that for others. I've had clients who want me to get them drunk and take them to bed against their seeming wishes, so they can imagine letting a man take advantage of them. So they won't feel guilt over having desires. And I have clients who like to treat me as their slave, order me around and demean me."

"And you don't mind?"

Another mysterious smile. "I love indulging a woman's fantasies. No matter what they are."

"Even being demeaned? What do they do to you that's degrading?"

"Well, it's not degrading, because it's all an act. But sometimes they talk down to me, call me a whore, reduce me to a hard cock, a servant. I love to be whatever a woman wants, so it turns me on. Some want the opposite, to be the one who's ordered. But I've done many things. I've been bound and gagged and sodomized."

"Oh. Whoa." I tried to picture such a thing but stopped, not enjoying the image. Didier to me is masterful, not overbearing but certainly not made to kneel in silence and submit to anything, least of all penetration.

"Whatever a woman's fantasy is, that is what I want to become. That is what gets me hard."

"When a woman wants to be the one who's degraded, what do they want you to make them do?"

"Suck my cock, perhaps. Or have me take them, rough and selfish."

I imagined trying all of those things, sampling a dozen other women's desires for this gorgeous man.

"Whatever you decide you want," Didier said, "I'll love that too. What I'm doing for you right now..." He looked to his hand, drawing my attention there as well. "My cock is aching, I want this so much. You want to watch and so I want to show you everything." He sat up and I did the same, letting him bring our faces close. "Do you wish to touch me?"

"I'm not sure. Not yet." I didn't know which of us I wanted to taunt with the anticipation, I only knew it felt right, waiting.

For a minute we both watched, and I sensed his gaze darting all over in my periphery.

"Does my body please you?"

I nodded.

"I'm glad."

Disbelief gave me a second's pause as I realized anew that the most beautiful man on the face of the earth was close enough to kiss and smell and touch, and that he wanted to make me happy.

"I hope that whatever you've waited to find with a man, you can find with me," he said.

"If it's not here, it doesn't exist."

I brought my lips close and he took the hint, kissing me. A couple of innocent nips, then back into the deep, rousing caresses that had steam filling my head, clouding my doubts. I let myself wonder about the other things his tongue might be able to make me feel, and imagined surrendering to such things. As the kissing grew more explicit I felt his strokes turn aggressive, until his mouth faltered and our rhythm broke down. I stole a glance at his arm, his fist, his dick.

"Say my name," he murmured. "I like how it sounds, in your accent."

I smiled at the astonishing notion that he might find me in any way exotic. "Didier."

He replied with a soft moan and his hand sped. "Carolyn."

"Caro-*ly*. *Oh, el, egrec,*" I said, impressed to realize I could spell in French without thought, even lightheaded from arousal.

"Apologies. Caroly."

"Didier."

"I'm close," he muttered. "I need to stop, if you're not ready for that."

"I'm ready." How long had I waited for proof that I was capable of reducing a man to this state of desperate need? "I want to see."

"How?"

I watched him, thinking. "On your back, I think."

He lay back against the pillows. I shuffled to kneel between his calves. I've never felt a rush quite like that, the strangest kind of equality. Strong, handsome man on his back, uncertain guest looming above. He spread his thighs wide, gripping his cock, other hand stroking his stomach. I reached down to touch his shins and calves. I realized this was how he might be when he takes me, this hard and needy. The excitement of the thought had my body buzzing, and I slid my palms up his thighs, recording his firm contours, his soft hair.

As he stroked, the muscles of chest and abdomen and arm stood out.

"Is this how you normally are, when you..." I trailed off.

"On my back? Yes."

"What do you think about?"

"About women I know. Experiences I've had, or would like to."

I wondered what those things might be...the things he wants but can't demand of a client. "Like what?"

"I imagine a woman I've been with, and the things I know she would never ask me for. I imagine the moment she lets me take her to those places."

"What kind of places?"

His hand slowed. "It depends on the woman. I have known women who think themselves above pleasuring a man with their mouths. I imagine how it might be if they gave in and asked me for that. If I know a woman who only demands rough sex in the dark, I fantasize about taking her slowly in the daylight, face-to-face. It's not my job to challenge my clients, only to obey. But I imagine what could be, if they let me push them just beyond their boundaries."

I wondered what my own boundaries were. Anal, certainly. Anything that reeked of lad mags and thongs and the tacky *Girls Gone Wild* culture of woman-as-porn-star.

"What are you imagining now?" I asked.

"I don't need to. You're right here, already testing your limits. I love that I'm showing you these new things."

"What things do you think I'd be afraid to do with you?"

"It is too soon to tell. And there are too many things you want but have denied yourself. I want those, first. What does it mean to you, to watch me now?"

"I guess... I've never seen this in person. I never thought I might have anything to do with a man being this excited. It makes me feel sort of...full of myself."

Didier smiled. "I like that. I want you to feel that way. When I come, I want you to know that it's from you, only."

"Show me."

He nodded and looked to his hand, drawing my attention down with his.

"You're so big."

"I haven't felt this way in ages, this hard. You've kept me so close, for so long. It hurts, I want to come so much."

My chest swelled with pride, to imagine this was true.

"Do you like that you've done this to me?" he asked.

"Yeah."

"I wish you could feel how hard you've made me." His strain was audible, the uttered words harsh and hoarse. "Fuck."

I squeezed his broad legs and slid my palms higher, mere inches from his cock. I gasped as his free hand covered one of mine, holding it tight against his warm, damp thigh.

All at once, he lost control. I could see the unraveling of him, in his jerking arm and twitching hand, his clenching muscles and wild eyes.

"Caroly." His breathy voice matched his disbelieving face.

I shuffled closer, my arm brushing his as I reached out to touch his stomach, to feel that most coveted landscape of male beauty.

"You're so strong."

"No," he groaned. "I'm helpless." The hand covering mine clasped my fingers, the muscles beneath my other palm clenching. His perfection ripped apart at its seams, mouth trapped in a silent gasp, gorgeous face flushed and contorted. He let go a final moan, and his hips bucked as he gave in. I took my hand away as the come streaked his belly, white against his flushed skin, more with each body-quaking spasm. I wished he might draw my trapped hand up to touch it, but his intuition was long gone with his composure. His body went slack, arched back relaxing against the covers.

He let my hand go and reached for a cloth on the side table, wiping himself clean. He folded it neatly and set it aside, closing his eyes. For a minute our breathing was the only noise.

"Thank you," I finally said.

He swallowed, blinking hazily. "And thank you. For asking me to be the first man who showed you that."

"You're very different when you're like that. All worked up."

"I'm sure."

"It's fascinating. You're so... I don't know, graceful, I guess. I liked watching you come apart."

"Just as I like fantasizing about a woman, aroused by the things she most denies herself. So much of taboo is in the contradictions."

I smiled at him. "That's very philosophical."

Didier laced his fingers together atop his ribs, gazing up at the canopy.

"I'd like to stay a little longer," I said quietly. "Unless that's awkward now."

"Not at all. I'm yours until the dawn. Just give me a moment to collect myself."

"No rush."

No rush indeed. I reclined a few inches to his side and we lay in companionable silence for a half-hour or longer. Eventually he dressed and we returned to the living room, along with the candles. We finished the wine and chatted for another hour, until I knew I had to catch the Metro before the real weirdos emerged from their holes.

As Didier bade me goodnight, my nerves returned. I opened the door to the hall, but more than I feared being spotted in a known prostitute's threshold, I was enlivened merely to be associated with this man.

"I'd like to see you again," I managed to say.

He smiled. "I would like that too. How is Sunday for you?"

Sunday was awful, as I had a staff meeting first thing the next day. But I also knew I'd be high as hell from whatever would come of that evening, and nothing would be able to touch me come Monday morning. "Sunday is fine. Seven?"

"Perfect. I will cook you dinner, if you like. And if you bring the wine."

I laughed. "I'm a bit terrified to pick wine for a Frenchman."

"And I'm a bit delighted to force you to be brave, so I insist."

"Okay, fine."

"You know the way out?" he asked.

I nodded.

"You have a safe trip home. It was a pleasure to meet you."

I was prepared to shake his hand, but Didier clasped my shoulder and bent to exchange kisses on each cheek. I waved lamely and headed down the hall for the stairs, not hearing the gentle click of his door until I was well out of sight.

Sunday
The Second Visit

ʕ

The wine was chosen at the urging of the pushy man who runs the liquor store near my flat, a dry red that cost slightly too much for my comfort. But I'm a simpleton when it comes to wine. The higher the price, the more adamantly I'll convince myself I like it.

Gone were my work clothes, for my second date with Didier. I wore a dress this evening, a patterned boat-neck that's more quirky than elegant, and forgives my broad shoulders and flatters my long neck and gangly arms. I felt positive, if not confident, as I walked up Rue des Toits Rouges. Excited if not prepared.

I rang Didier's bell ten minutes early, no longer ashamed of appearing eager. He buzzed me in and my nerves felt different as I mounted the steps. On Thursday they'd had me edgy and dry-mouthed, but this second night I was giddy, even bubbly, blood gone from my veins and replaced with champagne.

His door swung open at my knock and Didier was as tall as I'd remembered, even more handsome in his familiarity. "Good evening, Caroly."

"Good evening." I handed him the wine and followed him to the threshold of his kitchen, watching as he slid my offering from its twisted bag to examine the label.

"Very nice. You spoil me."

"I asked for a Portuguese one, and that's what the man at the store suggested."

"This is very fine, I've had it."

"Oh good."

"I have not started dinner, so I hope you're not starving."

I shook my head. "No rush."

"Have a seat." Didier beckoned me inside his small kitchen, pulling up a stool to the butcher-block-topped cabinet that serves as a center island. He set a glass before me as I sat, and uncorked the wine. I breathed it in, that dry, warm aroma, and studied him as he filled his own glass. He was dressed in his understated but stylish way; a crisp, cream-colored shirt rolled up to his elbows and unbuttoned to mid-chest.

"Did you ever live in Portugal?" I asked.

"No, but I visited when I was younger. Quite young, perhaps eight or nine."

"Which part?"

"On the coast, not far from Cascais. Very pretty. Very different after only having known Paris."

"You didn't leave the city much?"

He shook his head. "My mother detested the countryside, even the suburbs. She was very much addicted to Paris, all the noise and excitement and crowds and attention of it. Cheers."

I joined him in clinking our glasses and tasting my offering. "Oh, that is nice."

He nodded. "A very good choice. I only hope my cooking does it justice."

"You cook a lot?"

"Oh yes, though nothing too fancy. Is there anything you do not eat?"

"I'll try anything."

"I was going to make pasta. A friend came by with sausage from a Sicilian butcher this afternoon, the best I've ever had. That with tomatoes and basil and bread."

"That sounds wonderful."

Didier prepped ingredients and sautéed onion and garlic and the meat in a pan, then gathered flour and other things, setting a metal, cranked contraption on the island.

"You make your own pasta?"

He nodded, eyeballing measurements. "It's not so hard. I enjoy cooking. It's the hobby I indulge the most these days."

"What else do you like to do?"

"I read a lot. Sometimes I take things apart and put them back together. Watches, clocks. My hobbies are quite simple."

I nodded, sipping my wine, watching this fascinating creature at work. "What did you want to be, when you were younger?"

"I always thought I might be a writer, but no matter how often I try, it never gives me the joy I expect it to. It never feels quite so romantic as it seems it should."

"That's too bad. I bet your memoirs would be very eye-opening."

He drove his fingers into the dough, flour puffing up to settle on his forearms. "What about you? What did you want to be?"

"I wanted to be an artist, but I never got very far beyond imitating other people's work. When I went to college I fell in love with art history, and that's what led me to curating."

"Who is your favorite artist?"

"I couldn't pick any one favorite. But I probably love Klee and Miro best."

He nodded. "Miro was fascinating. I heard he was an accountant, and that he suffered a nervous breakdown and that is how he came to art. Is that true?"

"I believe so."

"You must know the Louvre inside-out, after two years in Paris."

I nodded. "That's not where I work, though. I work at the smaller museum, just a couple blocks east. But I was lucky enough to get a summer internship at the Louvre when I was twenty. It was heaven, seeing all the works I knew from books in person."

"Yes, it's much different." He fed dough into the pasta maker and turned the crank, a nest of noodles gathering on the floury wood.

"In a book you can't move around, see the way the light hits the brushstrokes from all the different angles," I said.

"Or smell the wood or stone or paper."

"Exactly. It changed my life, that summer." I sipped my wine as Didier cooked, studying him in the cool dusk light, my very own work of art for the evening.

"What's it like, seeing yourself as other people's art in galleries?" I asked.

"It's humbling."

I smiled, unseen, liking his answer.

"It does not feel like me, in their photographs. Just some man I resemble. Though I've always been poor at reducing people to their outsides."

I pondered that, wondering if it was the willful habit of a man sick to death of being objectified, or perhaps one merely enamored with minds.

"Have you heard of that disease where a person cannot recognize faces?" he asked.

"Sure. That disorder Oliver Sacks has." I frowned. "Do you have that?"

"No, but I understand it. I've always been terrible with faces and names, even worse with places and buildings. I get lost very easily."

I smiled at that notion, at the visual of Didier's perplexed expression as he stared at a street sign, a dozen arrows pointing every which way.

"As a child," he said, "I only remembered how to get to places by counting the blocks. Three blocks straight, one block left, two blocks right. That was school."

"You couldn't just look at, I don't know, a fountain or something, and remember where you were?"

"It's odd, I know. If I passed the fountain I would ask myself, do I see that on the way to school? Or was that somewhere I went on the weekend with my mother, the post office, perhaps?"

"Weird."

"Indeed. I got better, if only at memorizing street names and writing notes to myself. And later I grew quite fond of taxis, letting directions be someone else's burden."

Didier switched on the lights as the daylight died, and before I knew it he was dragging over a second chair, clearing the island and setting dinner before me.

This was a date. A meal, drinks, the promise of foreplay if not sex. I didn't let myself diminish it, knowing I was paying for his company as surely as I'd purchased the wine we were enjoying. He's extraordinary, that way. He doesn't trick you into believing this is something other than what it is. He merely makes what it is a thing of substance. I'm buying Didier as I might a gourmet meal or an evening of live music, a fleeting indulgence. Does it really matter that I paid for any of them, that I didn't prepare the food or compose the music; that others could enjoy the pleasures if they too were willing to pay for them? Was it really all some New World hang-up, the demand for permanence and ownership and exclusivity? I hope so. My parents were such a cautionary tale against two people staying together, it's no wonder I've never pined for commitment.

Didier spoke after a long silence. "You look rather thoughtful."

"I feel rather thoughtful."

"You are not sad, I hope."

I shook my head. "Not at all. I'm having a lovely evening. Everything is delicious. Thank you."

He lifted his glass. "And thank you, for sharing it." Didier is as smooth as I'd expected a Frenchman to be, but not in the cloying, coercive way I'd feared. His seduction puts you at ease, like a slowly sipped cocktail or a hot bath.

Didier is a fine cook, and the bite of the tomatoes brought out the tang of the grated cheese, the sweetness of the onions, the tartness of the wine. I will never be able to eat linguine again without thinking of him, his hands and mouth and voice.

"What else would you like to do tonight?" he asked.

"I hadn't thought too much about it. Just drink and talk, like Thursday. See where that goes."

"That sounds perfect. And if you are interested...if you enjoy music and you grow weary of my voice..."

Fat chance.

"I have a phonograph and some records. I know that's old-fashioned..."

"No, that's cool."

He smiled. "Good. I love old things. Typewriters, gas lamps. Those things that are trapped between history and the present. What we used to call technology, now antiques."

"That's interesting. What other sorts of things?"

"Toys fascinate me, like wind-up tin animals, miniature railroads, slot cars, music boxes. When I was a child I would get lost for hours in my grandparents' attic. My grandfather had nearly all of the toys he'd grown up with, board games too, and so many photographs."

"Wow."

"Yes. I would fantasize about living in that time, between the wars. I have a cabinet full of things I've collected, if you'd like to see, after dinner."

"I would."

I watched Didier as he ate, marveling again at him. Surely no one is perfect, and yet he seems so. A large man, big enough to seem exceptional but not so big that he feels inaccessible or overbearing. I adore him from every angle, his jaw, his strong nose, the dark, graceful arch of his eyelashes when his face is cast down. I remembered this face as it had looked on Thursday evening, seconds before he came. An entirely different strain of perfection.

When we'd cleaned our plates he took them to the sink and refreshed our glasses.

"May I see your cabinet?" I asked.

"Oh yes. Come."

We went through to the main room and set our wine on the coffee table. He turned on a lamp and I followed him to a corner, to an old china hutch I'd not noticed before. It contained no dishes, but a multitude of treasures. Beyond the glass stood tin toys, clocks, brass scales, metronomes. He opened a drawer to reveal a carefully spaced selection of watch faces. From behind them he withdrew a tied leather bag and unrolled it, taking out tiny tools to show me—a set of magnifying lenses, minuscule screwdrivers and the finest-point tweezers I'd ever seen.

"Wow."

"Thank you. It's not so astounding as art, merely taking apart others' inventions."

"It's still really neat." He'd taken out a jeweler's monocle and I put it to my eye, examining my fingernail. "You're quite the mad scientist."

"Not so mad. Just curious. Many of these things came to me broken. It's very satisfying to understand them enough to make them work again."

I pointed to a pocket watch in the drawer. "May I?"

"Please."

I opened its face and peered at its insides through the monocle. Didier took it from me, just long enough to wind it so

I could watch all its miniscule parts tick and snap and whir, like the X-ray of a marvelous little brass animal. "I can see how you might get lost in this."

"Yes. I find it very interesting, these tiny spaces, like little rooms. Microscopic factories full of gears and springs. I find the human mind very interesting as well, but these... I feel I can understand these."

I set the monocle down. "I think you understand people's brains just fine."

"Perhaps."

Didier put away his tools and I strolled to the couch. I watched his back as he adjusted his collection, fussy but not obsessive. When he joined me I asked, "Have you ever owned an ant farm?"

"I haven't, but I always wanted one. Have you?"

I shook my head. "I wasn't allowed any pets." Actually it was my mother who oughtn't be trusted with the care of an animal, but I didn't elaborate.

"We always had fish when I was growing up," Didier said. "They were the only pets my mother stood any chance of maintaining, she was out so much. Eventually I did all that, feeding and cleaning."

"Flushing."

He smiled grimly. "Indeed. I remember when the very first fish died, how I found it and agonized over telling her. Then she came home and I said, 'Mother, I have terrible news. The fish has died.' And she blinked at me and pulled a franc from her purse and told me to go and get a new one."

I laughed.

"I was devastated, but to her it was as if a light bulb had burned out."

"Did you get a new one?"

"Oh yes, we must have had twenty of them, at least, one at a time, one after the other. It did not upset me so badly after the first one died, because I loved the pet store. I would loiter there for an hour or more before selecting a fish, and then I would be so gentle and full of pride as I carried it home six blocks in its bag."

"Six very carefully memorized blocks."

"Indeed. If the latest fish died in the winter, I would keep the new one inside my coat, wrapped in my scarf as I walked home. I gave myself a cold once, doing that."

"That's sweet."

Didier's smile faltered. "They are nice memories, the fish. Until the last one."

"Oh. Why?"

"The last time I was given a franc to buy a fish, when I was perhaps thirteen, it was taken from me."

"Taken?"

He nodded, eyes cast down at the glass in his hand. "Older boys from my neighborhood, mean boys, pushed me down and took the bag."

"What did they do?"

"I do not know. But it was one of the worst days of my life, as dramatic as that sounds. That stupid little creature was in my care, and I thought I was rescuing it from the pet store. But I didn't keep it safe and who knows what became of it. Stepped on or tortured or who knows what. I felt very weak, very worthless for weeks."

"And you never got another fish?"

"No. I tried to go back to the pet store, but the guilt hurt so badly, I was sick."

"Oh my."

"That was the first time I truly understood how unsafe the world can be. And how unfair it is for the gentler creatures in this world of bullies."

I wondered if Didier meant the fish or his thirteen-year-old self. "That's very sad." I surprised myself, setting my hand on his forearm. He smiled at me, most of his melancholy seeming to lift.

"Would you ever get a fish again?"

"No, I don't think so."

"I'm pretty sure no one would try to take it from you now." I pictured Didier's bare body, wondering if he knew how to exploit that physique for violence as well as art.

"I think my time for fish has passed. I would enjoy its company, but I would always think, what kind of a life is this, living in a tiny bowl with no other fish, your only purpose in life to be a living trinket for some other animal, in exchange for food?"

I shifted in my seat, knowing too well that, to some, this man must boil down to nothing more than a six-foot-something trinket.

"I am too sensitive now for the pet shop," Didier concluded. He smiled suddenly. "And I am too depressing a date this evening. Forgive me."

"I don't mind. Everyone's allowed to feel sad now and then."

"I am carrying on about goldfish when you are here for romance. So come, let's leave all that behind us." He took my hand and put it to his lips, a gesture I'd imagined before but always skeptically, always as a stereotype of the cheesiest ilk. But in reality, I liked it.

He stared at my fingers and squeezed them gently, one by one. "Have you any idea what you would like from me, this evening?"

"No. I'd like to kiss you again, but beyond that, I'm not sure."

"Whatever you wish."

I looked to him nervously and he got the hint. He took the glass from me and set it aside. His hands were warm as he cupped my neck, his mouth bold, lips tart from the wine I'd purchased with exactly this in mind. Just as his kisses grew deep and my head grew cloudy, he pulled away.

"May I tell you something?"

"Sure."

"I thought of you, Friday afternoon. I touched myself and I imagined it was you, pleasuring me."

Every inch of me tightened and released, heat dropping over me like a sheet. Our eyes darted, his dark ones mesmerizing in the warm light of the lamp.

"Really?"

"Yes. I bathed and I remembered how it felt to have you watch, and before I knew it my hand was wrapped around my cock. Your hand, in my mind."

I conjured the scene, thick lather dripping from his fist. "I've thought about you as well." But strangely enough, I hadn't come since meeting Didier on Thursday. I'd been wound up beyond reason, but each time I thought I might touch myself, misgivings gave me pause. Had I known he'd still thought of me after I disappeared down his stairs—that he'd *come*, thinking about me—I'd have given myself permission to indulge in my own memories. But as it was, I'd been afraid as always that my lust was laughably one-sided.

Yet for some incredible reason, despite that fact that he's the finest man I've ever seen and miles out of my league...I believed him, just then. And I realized something I never had before. Deep down, I want to be seen as an object too. I want to be coveted and sought after. I want to be taken apart and understood, reassembled, filed away in Didier's cabinet. I don't even need to be pretty to have this. I only have to allow him to open me up.

After more kissing I said, "I know you've said that what women want from you is different, depending on who they are."

"Of course." I loved how rough his voice sounded then, and knowing it was partly my doing.

"Well, what do *you* like? If the woman had no preference and it was all up to you, what do you like best?"

"I cannot divorce the two that easily. Even in my own head, by myself, what I imagine has everything to do with the woman in my thoughts."

"Even if she was just a totally neutral, up-for-anything woman?"

He smiled. "As much as I love clockwork, I would never want to fuck a woman as soulless and without preference as a robot."

I sighed, pretending to be outrageously exasperated.

Didier laughed, a glorious noise. "Do you really want me to have some singular need? Do you want some secret key to pleasing me? Because you don't need one. You're doing just fine, right now. What excites you excites me."

"I just want to know who you are, I guess. By yourself."

"I can't give you some simple answer. It all depends on the company. I love wine," he said, "but I won't drink it with ice cream. I love coffee but I do not want it with mussels, you see? I may adore two things, coffee and mussels, a certain sex act and a particular woman, but all are ruined when they don't go together."

"Fine, I submit to your logic. What am I then? What would you pair with me?"

Didier offered me a mysterious smirk and laced his fingers between mine, a gesture that triggered a rush I cannot adequately describe. "I do not know all of your flavors just yet."

I squeezed his hand. "Guess, then."

"Because you're cautious, I think I should keep everything equal, no one the aggressor or the passive one. Slow explorations, to start. And when I get a better feel for you, I'll know what beyond that to offer." Another smirk. "But I suspect you are like shellfish, meant to be coaxed open and savored. I would pair you with a dry white wine. Something sharp, not dark."

It may not be the most likely poetry, comparing a woman to shellfish, but I felt warmth burst in my cheeks and chest, outrageously flattered to be reduced to food and drink to this man. Something to be consumed.

"But again," he said, "I have so much yet to learn about you."

I gazed down at his fingers twined with mine. I had much to learn too, but perhaps that evening I'd find another lesson or two to check off my list.

A finger crooked under my chin, brought my face up, a tender bit of pushiness I adored. I let Didier kiss me and what had felt romantic before turned carnal, deep and insistent. I let his hand go to stroke his neck, his shoulder. I felt his hard arm through his shirt, touched the bare skin and soft hair at his open collar. He didn't touch me back beyond my face and neck, and I wasn't yet sure if this was a relief or a disappointment. But my own hands were bold, running down and over his front to feel his abdomen. As I traced the waist of his pants with my fingertips, he freed his mouth to sigh.

I leaned close to open his buttons, one, two, three, until I spread his shirt open and feasted my eyes on his body.

He slid his fingers from my hair, bringing them lower not to touch me, but himself. As I roamed his chest and stomach, he cupped a hand between his legs.

"Are you hard?"

"Yes." He traced his erection with his thumb and forefinger, pulling the fabric tighter to show me. I know if he'd asked me to touch him, I'd have clammed up. He didn't. He made no requests, only fondled himself, illustrating what I was missing out on, what I could have.

"I want to touch you," I whispered.

"You can do whatever you like with me."

"I know. I'm just afraid I'll be lousy at it."

"You've never done this to a man, no?"

I shook my head.

"Caroly." My name on his breath short-circuited my brain. "Tonight, with you... Your cautious hands on me, unsure what they are doing, will be more exciting than the touch of the most masterful woman on earth. I don't need to be served, only explored."

"Oh," was all I could think to say.

"I want mine to be the first cock you ever know."

His words hit me hard, making my light head lighter, my pussy hot. "I want that too."

"Here." Gently, impossibly slowly, he took my hand, sliding it from his belly and over his belt to cover his erection. He held it there for a long time before guiding me, coaxing my palm up and down, a faint graze over his hard, hidden arousal.

"That is not so bad?"

"No," I mumbled. "That's very nice."

His hand abandoned mine to its clumsy devices. I measured him with light caresses, loving how tense the rest of his body had grown.

"You feel harder than I expected."

"This is how I felt when I thought of you the other night. Thinking of you made me hard then, just as your touch does so now." He was quiet for several strokes, save his labored breaths. "Do you like it?"

"Yeah." Bolder, I wrapped my hand around him as much as possible through his slacks, squeezing to discover how thick he was. He moaned and I felt different, as I never had before—powerful and beautiful and wild.

"I'm the first," he murmured.

The idea that he was fetishizing this experience gave me permission to do the same. I'd already grown quite fond of Didier—surely fonder than was rational, given our perhaps six cumulative hours of acquaintance—but reducing him to a stiff, suffering cock was electrifying. I'd always loathed this idea, openly lavishing a beautiful man with my admiration. As if such a fortunate specimen deserves more validation. But of course it felt nothing like that with Didier. I adored this glimpse into another side of him, a darker, cockier version of the man I was just coming to know.

"Kiss me," I said.

He did. He turned and kissed me as no one ever had before, urgent and demanding. I ached for his hand on top of mine again, dictating—perhaps even *forcing*—the friction. But I was in charge. I imagined teasing him this way until he begged to be taken out and given release. I imagined denying such a request, degrading him with my refusal until he lost control, quaking and pleading and erupting beneath my hand, inside his clothes, perspiration shining on his forehead.

But of course I wasn't ready for that. Indulging the idea was breakthrough enough. Having a hard cock against my palm and Didier's mouth on mine, the sensations feeling so natural… That was enough.

Everything was different now. More real. He was as horny as he had been controlled our first night together. And here I was, pursuing his body instead of having it offered. The fact that he was still dressed was a change in itself. Wicked fantasies aside, he felt alarmingly like my boyfriend, and the idea turned me on far more than it should have.

"What do you want?" I asked. I realized how backward the question was as it came out.

Didier surprised me with his answer. Our first evening he'd have turned it back on me, asked what I wanted, but this evening…

"Want to touch you."

I'd been nervous about such a thing, but far more potent than my anxiety was the pleasure of being at the heart of Didier's desperation.

"Okay."

His eyes met mine, and the neediness fogging them was the sexiest thing I'd ever seen. "Show me what I can have," he murmured.

I shifted, still stroking his hard cock through his soft pants. I took his wrist with my other hand and placed his palm on my collarbone. His skin was warm, and though he'd touched my face and neck before when we kissed, this felt very intimate, only a few inches lower.

"Touch where you want to," I whispered. "If it's too much, I'll stop you."

He kneaded my shoulder and stroked my upper arm, raising goose bumps. I could sense the tension in him as he held back. I gripped his shaft tightly and he repaid me with a sharp grunt.

"You're different tonight," I told him.

"Is it too much?"

"No, I like it."

"The way you're touching me… You feel different as well. It finally feels as if you own me. That you know you can take, instead of requesting."

"Do you like that? Feeling owned?"

"I do. Especially with a woman who comes to me so unsure."

I imagined pushing him back against the arm of the couch, opening his pants and taking him with my mouth. How he'd moan and pant, and the weight of his strong hands on my head or shoulders. Then I recalled what he'd said, about oral being more intimate to him than intercourse.

But if I couldn't rush that act, I'd at least taunt him with it.

"I keep wondering what it would be like to taste you."

His hand clasped my arm tighter and he made a noise, as though a gasp had gotten lodged behind his tongue.

I let his erection go to free his belt buckle. His hand slid to where my shoulder met my neck, and the pressure was exquisite, a taste of plaintive aggression that lit me up. I freed the clasp of his slacks and lowered his zipper, his thick cock already straining at his shorts as I spread his fly open. It was *my* cock tonight. Mine to take, not his to offer.

"I love this," I said, stroking him. It was far more explicit now, one thin layer of silk between us. I could feel his skin sliding, feel his heat and the contour of his shaft and head. A damp spot darkened the fabric and all I could think was, *I did this to him.*

He whimpered. "Anything you want from me, you can have."

"I want you to be the first man I ever take inside me."

I gasped as his hand covered mine, squeezing his cock through the silk. It would have scared me only a few nights ago, but it felt amazing now. This polite, poised man, driven to bossiness by what I could make him feel.

He put his mouth to my throat, nearly kissing but not quite. His breaths were heavy and hot, as fast and rough as the strokes he made me pleasure him with. After half a minute he released my hand and pulled away.

Through a gasp he said, "Forgive me."

"No, I liked it."

"I did not mean to be so rough."

"It's good, really. I love that I've managed to make you that...worked up."

"You have. I feel crazy, I want you so badly."

"What do you want, when I touch you that way?" *So often, we're asking one another what we want...*

"Everything. I want to feel like the biggest, hardest cock you've ever had. Ever *will* have. I want you on top, using me. I want you on your knees before me, possessing me with your hands and eyes and your mouth. I want to hear you beg for me to take you, to come for you. Everything."

I shivered to realize again how in tune with me he was. I wanted such a messy mix of things too. To be both aggressive and passive, cruel and helpless. Everything, indeed. I've always kept myself so separate from men, now that I've found one I'm willing to be close to, I want to be so close to him that everything jumbles, our roles mashed and swapped and switched, two bodies twisted in a frantic heap of sweat and mangled, modified kinks. I want his weight on me, his voice in my ears, his cock inside me. Behind me, above me, beneath me, even beside me, once the sex has had its way with us.

I like who Didier is turning me into. I like who I am with my armor stripped away. Stronger in my defenselessness.

I felt so thankful and energized, I wanted to spoil him. Without a trace of fear, I pulled his waistband down to free him. His cock looked new again in the lamp's weak glow, bigger now that it was bare. He watched me, watching him. As I traced a finger along the ridge his flesh twitched, as though pleading for more. For *me.*

He slid his thumb under his waistband, holding it down for me. Something about this, about him presenting himself, exposing himself… His other hand palmed my shoulder. As I wrapped my fingers around him, his touch slid lower, lower, until he glanced my breast. The touch made me buck and he took his hand away.

"It's okay," I said. "You're fine. It's just intense, having someone do that."

He cupped me softly and my racing pulse slowed.

I glanced down at my hand, his cock. "I'm not quite sure how to touch you. Beyond just exploring. How do you do it, when you're…you know."

"Here." He wrapped my fingers around him, just below his head. I clasped him tightly as he directed, easing my fist up and down, up and down, at a steady, sensual pace.

"Then when I am close, I go faster. Harder." He squeezed my fingers tighter and sped my pulls, rougher than I'd have ever done, taking my own liberties. He took us back to the slower caresses.

"Is that the same as when you're inside a woman?" I asked. "Slow, then more frantic at the end?"

"Typically, yes. You tease me for long enough and my body grows impatient and greedy."

A greedy Didier intrigues me greatly. For a long time I stroked him, liking the heat of his palm on my breast. I didn't want to feel *fiddled with*, and I didn't. I felt comforted. As my confidence with touching him grew, my mind wandered to what else I might do with this cock. What might bring him to that greedy, frantic state…

"I know you said oral sex is more intimate than intercourse."

"You do not agree?"

I laughed. "I'm not one to ask. But I've never had a man before, either way. And actually losing my virginity feels like a bigger deal. I mean, I might still be intact, down there."

His brows rose, curious. "You think so?"

"Maybe. Possibly." The science behind hymen preservation had always struck me as murky. Tampons, sure. Horseback riding, minimal and non-vigorous. Could I have made it to thirty, my seal unbroken? The curious look on Didier's face made me hope so. Such an old-fashioned notion of purity and ruin seemed fitting in this old-fashioned place, with its old-fashioned objects. Didier and his timeless, classical beauty.

"You do not use any toys by yourself?" he asked.

"Not inside me. I always thought I should save that. Since it's been so long already."

"Well."

I nodded. "So that kind of feels like, I don't know. The grand finale."

"I understand."

"But you do... You like going down on women, right?"

He grinned and released my breast, propping an elbow against the back of the couch and leaning back. "Very much. Perhaps that is why I save it for last."

Heat trickled down my neck through my chest and belly to my cunt. I'd happily be Didier's dessert, if that was how he felt about the act.

"You're blushing."

"Yes, I am."

"Was I too bold?" he asked.

"No, I like what you said."

"If I can make you blush just talking about this, I cannot wait to know what the actual caress will do to you."

"I'd like to find out. Some night."

"Some night?"

"Yeah. Maybe tonight... I'm not sure." All my clothes were still on and I wasn't sure if I was ready to go to the same base Didier had allowed me to take him. But I was here to find out.

"Could we go to your room?"

"Of course."

I let him go and he stood to refasten his pants.

"Candles?" he asked.

"Please."

The card table was in its place behind the couch and he carried it with us to his room. I sat and watched him light the many wicks, his exquisite face golden in the multiplying glow.

He turned to me as he shook the match. "More kissing?"

I nodded. "And could you maybe take your clothes off? Except your underwear."

He slid his open shirt from his shoulders and dropped his slacks. He was still hard from what I'd done to him, erection curved to one side behind the silk. More of that sticky, self-satisfied pleasure filled me, banishing the nerves.

"Could you sit here?" I patted the center of the mattress.

Didier did as I asked, facing the head of the bed, and I arranged his long legs as I wanted them, in a V. Mindful of my dress, I scooted close, also in a V, with my legs draped over his. Mirrored this way, I felt vulnerable but equal. I edged even closer, enough that my hem gathered against his straining cock, our crotches still two or three inches apart.

Didier ran his palms over my calves and knees, smiling. "I like this. Feeling your body against mine."

I liked it too, my smooth legs pressed to his manly ones. I imagined more, both of us naked. I kept the idea in mind as I touched his face and his mouth lowered to mine.

Every time we kiss, it feels different. New, exciting, dangerous, sweet, and now fond. I'd never before felt mastery over any of the men I've kissed, the sort of confidence that practice and familiarity breed. With Didier I was beginning to. He dominates just enough for you to kiss him back, but to also feel without a doubt that *you. Are. Getting. Kissed.*

I hope it's exactly how he fucks.

I fumbled our rhythm to scoot even closer, finally near enough for my dress to ride up and for his erection to press the crease where my thigh meets my hip. It was harder to kiss now, because he's tall and we were so close, but the fascination of having my thighs against his waist and my chest brushing his... Further than I'd meant to go, but so exactly where I wanted to be.

Strong hands slid down my arms to my lower back, kneading. Punctuating the gesture were tiny movements from his hips, the faintest thrust of his cock against my bare skin.

I needed more, but I wasn't sure what. Against his neck I whispered, "I want to go further."

"You want me to take you there?"

I nodded.

"Everything now is fine? You just want more?"

"Yes."

With no further preamble, Didier took hold of me beneath each thigh and pulled me against him, my legs wrapping around his waist. All at once, a hard cock was pressed to my pussy, where no man's hand had even ventured. Our mouths were level once more and I'd found paradise, our bodies so perfectly enmeshed. He reached between us to center his shaft against my lips.

"Good?" he asked, our noses touching.

"Yes."

"Nice for me as well." He stroked my back and waist, my butt. I hadn't expected that area to be so loaded with nerve endings, but the weight of his palms there took my breath away. When his hands moved to my hips, I felt the request in their gentle tugging. I wrapped my arms around his shoulders for support and adjusted my legs to kneel, and began to move.

I was awkward at first, grinding too hard. But he was patient, and before long I found my way, softly grazing his cock with my pussy. This was heaven, surely. Even better than sex, the perfect torture of anticipation. He held my ass, following the rhythm I set.

Didier's breath went from deep to shallow to heavy to harsh. I leaned back to see what I'd done to him, his brows gathered in a tight line, eyes shut, mouth open. There's no way to make that face anything less than stunning, but whatever I was making him feel, the results were ten times more handsome than any smile. I could imagine him tied down now. I couldn't yet imagine actually inflicting his pleasurable suffering, but the thought of him submitting suddenly made sense.

His eyes opened. "Feels wonderful." His hands left my butt and he braced them behind him on the bed, leaning back. It tensed his chest and arms and stomach, and gave me more freedom to explore this act. So unlike the old Caroly—who would never dare look directly at a shirtless man in the park, lest she affirm his vanity—I *stared* at Didier. His body was mine for the evening, every inch of hard muscle, the spray of dark hair trailing from his navel to his cock, all that bare skin, his scent and his face and his voice. His pleasure. He stared at me in return and I felt no judgment, only awe.

I paused to surprise myself once more, peeling my dress up and over my head.

I didn't need his hands on me; his eyes were more than enough. I wondered what gave him that look... My skin, perhaps, far paler than his. My small breasts in the laciest bra I'd ever owned, purchased with a racing heart for this exact occasion. I didn't feel like any of the adjectives I usually do, being seen in a bathing suit or suffering the harsh light of a dressing room—*gawky, pasty, bony*. His gaze turned all those words on their heads. I felt rare and graceful. Electric.

I wanted something that hadn't actually occurred to me before. I wanted to come tonight.

Before, my thoughts had been nothing more than a carnal menu of unknowns—the proximity of naked man, the feeling of his flesh against mine, the surrender of my moldering virginity...perhaps to kiss a man and actually take pleasure from it, as a bonus. But never had I bothered to wonder if I'd have an orgasm. How much of my life had I wasted, opting out of experiences? The thought sobered me and my hips slowed.

"Is everything all right?"

I hesitated before answering, long enough for emotion to take hold. Tears came, just a few. Didier sat up and wiped them from beneath my eyes.

"We can stop."

"I'm not upset, not from this. I just feel sad."

"Sad?"

"This is all really wonderful, but it makes me realize... I don't know. I wish I hadn't wasted so much time and energy, avoiding being this way with someone."

"You're here now, with me," he murmured. He kissed my cheeks, my ears, my neck.

"I am."

"So enjoy that this is all still new to you. That all this, these thrills most people can barely remember at twenty-nine, they're still ahead of you. Right in front of you."

I smiled, tears drying up. "You're a very smart man. And I am, I'm here with you, right now."

Didier smiled, something mischievous in his narrowed eyes. "You're very pretty when you cry, though."

I laughed, and Didier kissed me again, to the left of my lips.

"Better?"

I nodded.

Another kiss, on the other side.

"You're sweet," I said.

One more kiss, square on the mouth. It was a relief—a release—to allow him to lead. I welcomed him inside, the sweep of his tongue against mine. It was in that moment that I knew for certain, I'd have him. Not tonight, perhaps, but soon. I'd hoped he would feel just like this, intuitive and easy. As bold as I so often felt lost and unsure.

He spoke against my lips. "Lie back."

Excitement surged as my head found the pillows, all my sadness reduced to a figment.

Didier knelt between my legs, palms on the bed beside my ribs, bringing our centers back together. "Tell me if I'm too forward."

"I trust you."

He locked his forearms tight to my sides and the unexpected possession of the contact shifted everything. His hips began to move, the ridge of his erection teasing my clit with short, faint strokes. *Faster*, I thought. Fast enough to burn away the last scraps of our clothes.

He looked strong and solid, felt just as good as I lay my hands on his shoulders. I wondered how many women had been taken on this bed, head against these pillows… It sounds like an ugly, sabotaging thought, but weirdly enough, it only thrilled me more. I wanted to be that sort of woman, the kind who took what she wanted. I wanted to be with Didier, a man so skilled with his body that he'd made a craft of sex.

I watched his hips, fantasizing we were actually having sex. I pictured his cock surging as he fucked me, gleaming wet in the candlelight. I glanced to his bedside table as a thought tugged at me.

"Yes?" he asked.

"Do you have any water in here?"

He craned his neck and I spotted it—a pitcher and tumbler on his deep windowsill. He left me to fill the glass.

I suppose he expected me to drink it, but I sat up, pouring a bit into my cupped palm. I felt his gaze on me as I brought my hand to his abdomen, letting the liquid slip down his skin to darken his shorts. Another palmful, dripped right against his bulge, underwear going translucent. Even sexier than I'd hoped. I could see nearly everything, only the most explicit details obscured, as though behind fogged glass. The camera of my memory clicked madly and I pictured him kneeling in the ocean surf, pummeled by waves… Dirty-poetic; how I imagine a pornographer might shoot a cologne commercial. A decadent marriage of sleaze and luxury.

"I love the way you look at me," he murmured.

I drew my palm across his cock, side to side, reveling in the contrast of his hot flesh, the drag of wet silk. If I'd thought for even a second, the next words would never have fallen from my lips. "I'd like to feel you…in my mouth."

"You know you can have whatever you want."

I nodded. "I want that. And I have no idea what I'm doing."

"That's fine. That's very exciting, in fact. But do you know how you'd like to *feel*? In control?"

"Just free to…experiment, I think. Maybe you could tell me what feels good to you, give me instructions. Nothing too aggressive." I traced my thumb and finger down his shaft. "I'd like to be the one doing everything." I imagined the scenes that turn porn from exciting to *ick* for me—gagging and ears-as-fuck-handles are not my idea of *sensual*. Not that I could imagine Didier cast in any such sloppy imitation of the erotic.

"How would you like me? Lying down, or standing before the bed? Something else?"

Less intimidating on his back, but perhaps more exciting towering above me… "I'm not sure."

"I think you will feel most in control if I lie down."

I nodded. "That sounds wise."

Didier and I swapped places, and as I set the glass aside and knelt between his legs, the reality of the moment set my heart racing. He was the only man I could imagine doing this to. Beautiful beyond reason and aware of his looks, even profiting from them…but no smugness. No *getting his way*. This was my way, pure and simple. I don't care if that makes me selfish or cowardly. It feels safe. And I need *safe* to get off as surely as others merely need *horny*.

Below me, Didier cupped his cock through his wet shorts, the touch patient and seductive. I touched him myself, running my hands over his hard belly with its exceptional muscles, then his broad thighs.

"Let me see," I whispered.

He tucked a thumb inside his shorts and pushed them down.

"I'm nervous."

"And I'm just a man," he said. "I want only what you do."

I was tempted to correct him, to tell him he's more to me. He's my fantasy, maleness in its near-unattainable, ideal state. He's the one I waited for, even if my delusions of once-in-a-lifetime, breathless romance wound up mutating into the more two-dimensional courtship called prostitution.

I stared down at his bare length, needing a push, the tiniest shove past hesitation.

"It excites me to be the first," he said.

My body melted at the notion — molten, not gooey this time. Lava, not chocolate. I could smell him even before I brought my face closer. I held his thighs as I lowered, letting the scarier sensations wash over me, nothing but initial icy waves to endure en route to submersion. Submission.

"You have my word that I'm clean," he said. "But if you want a condom I'm more than happy."

I was torn... The good girl in me wanted to do everything right, but I also wanted the real deal, the taste of his skin and perhaps his come, not latex and lubricant. And God help me if it makes me a fool, but Didier's word was enough.

"I want you bare."

"Then that is how you'll have me. Get comfortable." His directive was kind, though also a touch devious if I wasn't mistaken.

Reclining on my hip, I propped my elbow beside him, sliding my hand under the small of his back. Heat seemed to roll off him, hot enough to ripple the air. Didier took my other hand and wrapped it around the base of his cock, holding it there gently. His head no more than three inches from my lips...

He waited while my dramatic pause turned to hesitance, hesitance to misgiving.

"Too much?" he asked. "Too soon?"

I met his gaze. "No, I don't think so. Just at the edge of the diving board, you know?"

"You need a push, I'm sensing?"

I laughed faintly. "Probably."

He let my hand go, smoothing a rogue curl behind my ear before resting his palm on my neck. "Taste me."

Ah, blessed nudge. I brought my mouth to him, the smooth, hot skin of his head grazing my lower lip. He smelled like sex — a scent so exactly its own, I could never have guessed it. His soap and skin, his sweat, his sheets, beeswax, the kiss of wine still lingering on my tongue. It was as unique and raw as hide or soil or grass, perfect and potent.

Warm fingers traced my jaw. "Open your mouth, Caroly."

Oh, that was it. The push, the plunge, all my stalling swallowed by the blessed deep.

I parted my lips and kissed him. The tiniest sweep of my tongue, then a bit more. A glorious noise brightened the dim room, the involuntary sigh of an excited man. *My* excited man, for the evening. Until that sigh I hadn't been sure who all this was for, but suddenly it was about more than me and my checkboxes and lessons. I wanted to pleasure him. I didn't want to know merely how to suck cock, but how to suck *his*.

"Tell me what you like," I murmured.

"Many things. Stroke me, and learn what feels right in your mouth. Learn how far is too far."

I did as he said. I gave his shaft slow, artless pulls as my mouth found its way. It was harder than I'd expected. I knew to keep my teeth covered, to suck but not too hard. I was learning to swim — the rhythm, how to breathe, how to coordinate my hand, my tongue, my lips, my lungs. It was frustrating. But high-schoolers can do this, for better or worse. Surely I can too.

"Don't be afraid to rely on your hand, if you need to rest."

I nodded. My throat felt tight from disappointment, because I had always hoped that if I found a man I deemed deserving of this, I'd discover I was a phenom.

I'm not.

And I didn't feel what I'd so hoped I would, with the right man—comfort. I felt small and fearful. I felt I was failing, and for the second time since we'd entered this room, tears were percolating. My jaw ached, as it always did when I was about to cry.

He gently drew my face away and coaxed my fingers from him, letting his underwear ride up to hide his cock.

He patted the covers beside him. "Come here."

Already crumbling, I complied. He urged me onto my side, facing the wall, and wrapped a strong arm around my middle. Kisses peppered my neck and ear, unspeakably tender.

"Sorry," I muttered.

"Nothing to be sorry about."

"Everything's been easier than I'd hoped, until just now."

"What did you feel?"

My airway was so closed up, I could hardly swallow. "I don't know. Panic. About failing."

"You thought it would feel different?"

"I thought... I hoped I'd be better at it. A natural, I guess. As dumb as that sounds."

Another sweet press of his lips, just behind my ear. "For whose benefit?"

"Yours. And for my ego, probably."

"What you can offer me is more intimate and special than discovering you are some great talent at this. There is no one else I know of, and will likely ever meet again, who can offer me your uncertainty. Your innocence, to perhaps risk patronizing you. I do not expect or want you to be perfect. So take me out of that equation, if it helps."

A huge tear rolled across the bridge of my nose, dropping onto his pillowcase. "I think it does. But I don't know... I wasn't expecting to panic. Not with you."

"I'm no magic spell," he whispered. "There's nothing about me that should make you think we're more than what we are."

His words perplexed me, *scared* me at first.

"We are two people getting to know each other," he went on, restarting my heart. "Two people who are fond of one another, attracted to one another. I like you vulnerable." I heard the smile in his deep voice. "I don't want to upset you by any means, but it touches me, to be here as you figure these things out. If you have any fear that I'm seeking perfection from you, and that you stand any chance in hell of ever disappointing me, please dismiss it. You can only be perfect in your intentions. Do not worry about the performance."

"Really?"

"Really. I may be your teacher in some ways, but trust me, there are no marks. No exam."

"No pop quiz?"

A tiny laugh. "No, no quiz. Just two people in this bed together. Two new friends, on their way to lovers. Okay?"

I nodded.

"Let's give that a rest, though, for tonight."

"Probably wise. Maybe you're on to something, saving that for last."

I felt him shrug. "Maybe. Or maybe this simply was not the night for it. When you want to try a second time, that is when we try a second time."

"Right." Bless him. If not for that lazy philosophy, I'd surely have stigmatized myself, let the act grow to looming proportions in my mind. But he's right. Some other night, that's all.

"I'd still like to...do things. I'd like to make you come," I mumbled. "Or watch, at least."

"Not because you feel you should, I trust."

"No, because I want to."

"Good. Whenever you're ready. Do you want another glass of wine, a break from this room?"

I twisted myself around to face him, our noses nearly brushing. "No, it's nice in here."

He kissed me, soft to start. It told my pulse to slow, my breaths to deepen, my mind to quiet. He reduced us to two mouths, two bodies in this tiny corner of Paris. He fit us together like gears in a pocket watch and shut its shell, hearts ticking in time, safe in the dark.

Before long, my nerves were gone. Excitement came back and just as he'd promised, my earlier shortcoming was reduced to a little slip, a case of the wrong moment. This new moment eclipsed the lousy one and my body warmed through, itchy to be nearer to him. I lay my thigh over his, thrilling as he held me close by the hip. His body felt hard and almost excruciating male against my softness — chest to chest, belly to belly.

I spoke against his lips. "You feel good."

"So do you... I'd like to touch you. If you'll let me."

The gentle request made me shiver, hot as a barked order. "We can try that."

"Turn over."

I did, settling my back against his front, only the slightest bit embarrassed to feel his erection against my butt. He palmed my breast first, filling my chest with stifling warmth and quickening my breaths. It's a peculiar erogenous zone, for me at least. It can go either way, sexy or unnerving, but I liked how his touch felt, the faint squeeze of his broad palm far nicer than pinching or tweaking or some such. The lace had gone damp with perspiration from one or both of us, and my nipple perked, exquisitely sensitive. He brushed his palm over it, soft as a whisper. The friction lit me as I hadn't known it could, connecting my breast to my pussy like an electrical impulse. It sizzled. No other word for it.

"Wow."

"Good wow?" he asked.

"Yes. Very."

For a long minute he spoiled me with the caress, until I was flushed all over, actually, literally panting.

"I would like to go further," Didier whispered.

"Go ahead." I was so fever-stricken, he could have done anything and I'd have been helpless to resist.

As his hand slid down my ribs, he kissed my ear. I'd never understood how that could be sexy to anyone, but *fuck*. I'd also never known the heaven of a man's deep breathing so close, his hot breath, the tiny noises of his lips moving as he tastes your skin.

He slid his thumb under the side of my panties, pushing them down my hip. I got them the rest of the way off and he coaxed my legs open, slipping his knee between mine. The air was cool and dry against my swollen sex. For a few moments he touched my thigh and hip, then my lower belly, my mound.

I'd been torn about the state of things down there, annoyed by the idea of waxing or shaving but not so adamant that I'd been willing to go completely natural. A trim in the privacy of my bathroom was what I'd settled for, and as his palm grazed me, the contact prickled. I muttered his name.

Two fingers slipped lower, glancing my clit. I tensed against him, from pleasure alone. Another touch, another, then lower. He traced my lips, already slick. It filled me with pride for him to find me this way.

"More?"

"Yes."

He teased my clit with a few light strokes then parted my folds. The edges of his fingers to start, then deeper. The most I've ever been penetrated, outside the doctor's office.

"No man has touched you this way before?"

All his questions…before I'd thought it was mere courtesy. But he knows the answer. He wants to hear it again. He's objectifying me the way I do him, and it's a wonderful sensation.

"No, never."

"You're so soft." He slid his finger out, then deeper, the pad of his hand rubbing my clit. I bucked, earning a happy noise at my ear. I know his cock will feel nothing like this, but I let myself imagine it. He could so easily have me, right now. Push his shorts down and slide his cock between my thighs and be my first. Tempting. I thought of his mouth, his tongue.

"Didier."

"It feels good?"

I nodded.

"I am imagining how it would be, taking you."

"Me too," I said.

"So warm." Drenched from me, his fingers slid back to my clit and I gasped. "Do you think I could make you come?" he asked.

"I think so."

"May I try?"

"Please."

"Like this?" He moved his fingertips in tight, light circles.

"A little harder."

More pressure, and in seconds I felt the blood pounding, that gorgeous, angry, desperate feeling mounting against his touch. He fidgeted behind me, erection brushing my butt.

Jesus, the things I'd do to that cock if he let me come... I pictured it from Thursday night, shining with oil, dripping with lather, erupting against his stomach.

The frenzy doubled. "Oh fuck."

His hard arm locked tight to my side, muscles tensing with his strokes. "You're close?"

I grunted a senseless, "Yuh."

"Caroly, please." Fuck, those lips on my neck. "Please."

I reached behind me, grasping for any bit of him I could get and finding his shoulder. I rubbed maniacally at his damp skin as the pleasure crescendoed, rising, rising, rising until I lost my mind. I think I kicked. I'm sure I groaned, perhaps even swore. The climax was like none I'd ever had, because I wasn't controlling it. The first orgasm I'd been *given*, and it reduced me to mush, a pile of wobbly woman trembling against his still fingers. My lungs heaved as though I'd sprinted a mile, chased by a lion.

Didier moved his talented, wonderful, miraculous fingers to my ribs, kissing my jaw. I could feel his happiness and pride, nearly as pleasurable as my orgasm.

"Thank you," I sighed.

"Thank *you*."

A wicked, selfish idea struck. "I want to watch you again."

"Of course."

"In front of me, on your knees."

I took his place against the center pillows and he did as I asked, straddling one of my calves. He pushed his shorts to his thighs, and as he gripped his stiff length, I touched my clit. His lips parted, a look of dark excitement passing over his face. He stroked himself as I rubbed my clit, and it felt like nothing I could have predicted, having his eyes on me. My pleasure rose anew, my second release nearly always a given. Plus I wasn't done hypothesizing... He'd drop forward, bracing his arms at my side. One clean, gruff push and he'd be inside me, and I'd feel... Full? Ecstatic? Drunk? Complete? I'd be the thing making him moan, not his fist, certainly no other woman, not until he was done with me. He'd hammer his body into mine until he came apart, pushed so deep we'd fuse into one sweaty, happy whole.

In the end, it was that last thought, the most romantic of the bunch, that tipped me over. I came with my eyes wide open, locked on his naked body. *He's the one,* I thought idly. I wasn't sure for what, but he was the one.

Didier's strokes had sped right alongside mine, and by the time I recovered from my climax, he seemed on the verge of his own.

"Caroly."

"You close?"

He nodded. "Where?" His gaze flickered over my thighs, belly, breasts, and I knew what he was asking.

"It's fine," I assured him. "Wherever you'd like."

"Your hand. I want your hand."

I sat up and he took my wrist. I let him cup my palm over his head, the warm, slick heat of his pre-come yet another first for me. Watching him masturbate, watching the way his arm trembled as he lost control... I was dizzy.

"Come," I said.

He answered with a gasp, his back arching. His free hand held my shoulder and I stared at his biceps, his chest, the flush in his neck. I thrilled from the way he held me—tight and frantic, possessive. I wanted that hand on my shoulder when we finally fucked, tugging me into his thrusts.

"Caroly."

Our gazes locked. I didn't look away as he came, just stared straight into his dark eyes and memorized them. Hot come filled my palm, coated his knuckles, and I felt dirty and happy and honored to be a part of this mess, with *this* man. I smiled up at him.

With a final weary groan, he released my shoulder, leaving me to grab a towel from the bedside table drawer. He handed it to me first before tidying himself.

"Well," he said as he lay beside me.

"Yes, well."

He turned to grin at me. "So many new things tonight."

"I was thinking that too."

"And the night is not over."

As he said it, I felt a yawn rising. "I think it may be over for me. That was plenty for my second evening."

"I suppose... My, look how far we have come from the other night, you watching from behind that changing screen. At the rate we're going, we'll be married by morning."

Though I laughed, his words upended me. Being teased about such a thing made me both giddy and sad. Such a wonderful but impractical, impossible scenario. This man could never be mine for keeps.

I sighed, suddenly exhausted. "I wonder what time it is."

"Not very late. Perhaps ten, maybe earlier."

Wow, not even my bedtime and look how much I'd accomplished! Being seen in sexy, matching underwear! Inaugural cock-touching! An orgasm at a man's hand! Then another, just as the thrill of watching me triggered the same in him. Fellatio, if barely. I deserved a gold star.

Didier leaned close, resting his chin on my shoulder. *Oh, melt.*

"Are you staying the night? You're always welcome to sleep here."

"I know, thank you. I hope you're not offended if I don't. Not yet, anyhow." I was already stripped bare emotionally, and I knew I'd wake up whiplashed by the memory of everything that had happened. Better to do that alone and not have the worries of my greasy morning complexion and nasty breath casting an anxious shadow on the moment. Though perhaps if one evening I did sleep over, I could convince Didier to come out for a coffee. Didier by my side, in the broad daylight...

After twenty minutes' murmured fondnesses, we dressed in easy silence and he walked me to the door.

I patted his arm. "I had a wonderful time."

"I'm so pleased. I'll see you again?"

How I fluttered, that he thought he had to ask. "You will."

"Would you like to choose a date now?" He touched my ear, a fond, teasing gesture. "Since you seem allergic to the telephone?"

I laughed, blushing. "Not allergic, just shy. And sure. What evenings are you free this week?"

"How about Tuesday? Or is that too soon?"

I nodded, liking the notion—an otherwise boring day, but oh, how I'd float through the rest of my work week... "That sounds fine. Seven?"

"Whenever you arrive. I'm always home."

"Okay, great."

I waited for the cheek-kissing, but he surprised me. A warm hand on my neck, hot lips pressed right to mine. The goodnight kiss I'd dreamed of since junior high, the one that had never hit the mark at the end of an actual date. My face burned with pleasure as he stepped back.

"Goodnight, Caroly. Have a safe journey."

"I will. See you in a couple days."

That roguish smile. "I will count the seconds."

I rolled my eyes at him and waved, heading for the stairs.

He called after me. "How come you never take the lift?"

"I'm afraid of it." Glancing over my shoulder, I saw his eyebrows rise.

"So am I."

"Great minds," I called.

"Indeed."

A final wave, and I turned the corner. I counted the steps as I descended — sixty-eight. I tapped each mailbox on its glass window, smiled at every person I passed on my walk to the Metro station through the wet, good-smelling spring air.

Everything is beautiful in Paris, when you're a young woman in lust.

Tuesday
The Third Visit

෨

I arrived at Didier's flat late, having gone home to change
after a long workday. It was blustery out and I'd stupidly gone
with a skirt, one I had to fist at my side to keep from flashing
the whole of the Latin Quarter. My bobby pins lost the war
with the gusting wind.

Yet when Didier answered my knock, my lateness and
wild hair seemed not to register. His smile was like a door shut
on a gale, calm dropping down around me, warm and easy.

"Good evening, Caroly. Come in." He took my purse and
a paper shopping bag I'd brought and set them on a table by
the door.

"Evening. How was your day?"

He shrugged as he led me into the living room. "I did not
wake until nearly two, so I could not tell you yet. Ask me
again at the end of our date. I'm sure I will say it was just
lovely."

"I, um, brought you something."

He turned. "Did you? What is it?"

I went to my bags and came back with the gift, swaddled
in striped tissue. I handed it to Didier and watched him
unwrap it, praying he couldn't tell how much of my heart was
folded inside that gauzy paper, how long I'd stood obsessing
in the antique shop, debating whether or not to buy this for
him. He set the tissue aside and to my great relief, his face lit
up.

"A clock." He turned the brass box around in his hands,
twisted its winder and opened its glass front. "This is fantastic,

thank you." He smiled right at me, a new smile I'd never seen from him before. No mystery now, only delight. My heart felt hot and swollen.

"You're welcome. I'm glad you like it."

"I do." He pressed it to his ear.

"It doesn't work."

His smile deepened. "Even better. I'm sure I'll spend many hours with my silly monocle and my tweezers, dissecting this."

I watched him examining it for a few moments longer, overwhelmed by how potent my pleasure was. The thought that he'd busy himself with the gift in my absence, perhaps even associate me with whatever fascination it brought him... It felt better than any physical touch, any carnal indulgence.

He set the clock on top of his cabinet and fussed with the angle. "Wonderful."

I was inclined to agree. "I wanted to buy you a fish, but I know you said that might depress you."

He returned to me, taking my elbows in his hands. "You're very kind." He leaned down and kissed my forehead, dissolving all my bones.

"Well, you're very welcome."

"You've spoiled me, and now I hope you will let me spoil you."

"I suspect I will." I suspected, too, that tonight was the night. The new knowledge that I wasn't a natural-born cocksucker only stung the tiniest bit, and I was ready to jump back into my education, head-first.

Er, make that sex-first. Head some other night, perhaps.

"Are you hungry?"

I nodded. "Are you cooking?" I held my breath, waiting for a no—for an invitation to go downstairs, to grab dinner at a restaurant and be seen with Didier by the world.

"I am."

A mental sigh. Not that being catered to by this fine man was anything to feel disappointed about. Plus knowing my luck, Ania or Paulette would walk by the restaurant window and spot us, and my reign as the demure, gossip-proof member of my small social circle would come to a dramatic close.

Didier made us a delicious meal and shared with me an extraordinary bottle of…cabernet? I can never tell. Some kind of hard-to-pronounce dry red. We spoke about my workday and a new exhibit that was opening next week at the museum, and when the conversation lagged in its comfortable way, my mind wandered.

Didier was wearing a thermal-type knit top with a generous neck, not quite a scoop; a look only a European male model can pull off. Though I wouldn't have minded pulling it off myself, right up over his head. The sleeves were pushed to his elbows and I studied his bare skin and his collarbone, his dark stubble. This man with all of his extraordinary nuances… He could be above me, before the night was over. I could leave here calling him my lover.

"You're very quiet," he said, tapping my forearm. "What are you thinking of?"

"About tonight."

"Me too. Come."

He says that a lot—*come*. A very interesting order. Or in the case of Sunday evening, a plea. Whatever its meaning, I'm happy to comply. I took our glasses and he grabbed the bottle and I followed him to the living room. As we sat on the settee, the wind rattled the old panes behind us.

"So you think tonight may be the night?"

I nodded. "I'd like it to be."

"I would like that too. Have you thought about how you might wish it to feel? Aggressive, gentle? Romantic?"

I think it's fair to say I'd given it a *ridiculous* amount of thought, easily a hundred hours' theorizing in the past week.

Curio

The previous evening I'd lay in bed for ages, fantasizing about Didier and running through every scenario, sweet and nasty alike, that crossed my overheated mind.

"Whenever I imagine it," I said, "I think about you. What you're doing. More than I need it to be, you know, satisfying, I want it to be *hot*. I care about that more than I care about coming, I guess is what I'm trying to say."

"You'd like a show?"

I laughed. "Sounds that way. Sorry, I'm not explaining it very well. When I fantasize about sex, it's usually just about the man. I'm not usually there in my fantasies."

"Really?"

I nodded. "That's always how my brain has worked with sex."

"You really do fear rejection."

"I really do."

"Well, we are not in your mind tonight. Before you know it we'll be in my bed. I don't know what you're picturing, but usually for two people to have sex, they both need to be present."

I rolled my eyes at the tease. "Of course."

"But I think I understand what you're saying."

"That makes one of us."

"And how do you want me?" he asked.

"Really...worked up. And aggressive, I think, but not mean. Just sort of desperate. Does that make sense?"

"Absolutely. I can be that way."

I sipped my wine. "How do most women like you to be?"

"They like many different things. Sometimes they wish to order me around. But far more often, they want to be the one who's dominated."

"And you like doing that?"

241

"As I said, I like pleasing women. I can be cruel, if that is what's desired of me."

"Does anyone ever just want to pretend you're their boyfriend?"

"Yes, sometimes. That is how many dates begin. With a meal or a drink, just as you and I have done. Talking leads to kissing, leads to bed."

"Do you… Are any of your clients married?"

He nodded. "I imagine so."

"Oh. How do you feel about that?"

"I don't."

His answer gave me pause, but he went on.

"My world is very small, and when I'm with a woman, I think it is my job to reduce that even further, to the space between her and I. It is my job to be someone's fantasy. And unless they, like you, wish to question me about reality, I give it no thought. For as long as someone is here with me, reality is just whatever happens between our two bodies."

"You aren't bothered that you might be helping a woman cheat on someone else?"

"That is not my job, to be bothered. And to be frank, that is a very American kind of guilt." He smiled at me.

"I know. I was just curious."

"It is not my job to ask questions."

"Does it bother you that I ask so many?"

He shook his head. "It's a nice change, to have someone so interested in what goes on in my head. I so often play the role of the seducer, it's flattering to think that maybe I'm interesting to you beyond all that."

"You are. Very much." A thought I'd turned around in my head the past few days popped through my lips. "Has a woman ever asked you to get her pregnant?" He's certainly the man I'd turn to if I needed some genes.

242

"That has happened."

"What did you do?"

He laughed. "I said no. How on earth could I say yes?"

"Of course. That would be complicated."

Didier took a deep breath, gaze focused on the table or our empty glasses. "I'm not capable of being any woman's husband, certainly not a child's father. Even if my presence weren't desired, I would not be able to live with the anxiety of knowing such a child were out there, and that should I one day be needed, I wouldn't be able to do what is required of me. Of a father."

"Because you're not willing to be that emotionally invested, or…?"

"It's more complicated than that."

For the first time, I could sense that Didier was not eager to answer my questions, so I let it drop. I felt torn about the idea. On the one hand, what a waste that such a passionate and beautiful man would never be some lucky woman's husband. A shame for both her and him, because I truly believe he's a good person who deserves happiness…not that happiness can't exist without marriage or family. My father could attest to the miseries marriage can reap.

On the other hand, Didier's insistence that he could never commit to someone means I can't feel jealous at the idea of him belonging to anyone else, for keeps. A prettier, smarter, warmer, worthier woman than me. I frowned as my ugly, familiar thought patterns intruded.

He leaned close, pulling me out of my head. "Have I said something wrong?"

"No, I was just thinking about things. You're fine."

My heart raced as he put his fingers to my temple and drew his thumb across my forehead. "I do not like to be the reason you wrinkle your brow this way."

I laughed. "You're not. But I suppose we're a little bit the same, the way we think about commitment. I don't think I'm cut out for it either."

He swept his lips against mine, whisper-soft. "Then it is very convenient that this is where we find ourselves, for now."

"Yes."

He kissed me, brief and tender.

"I'm ready to have sex with you," I mumbled. "Tonight."

"It will happen if it is meant to happen."

I nodded.

"Would you like to go to my bed and kiss?"

"Yes, that sounds nice."

He stood and took my hand, led me to that wondrous dark room. *Our* room, for the evening.

"Candles?" he asked as I sat on the edge of the bed.

"Please."

He came back shortly with the table and its many pillars, and lit them one by one. Each flame brought more details to the room. The texture of the bedspread I'd lose my virginity beneath or on top of, the glint of bottles, the face of the man I'd chosen for this occasion.

Once the room was aglow, Didier took a seat beside me on his bed. No more questions. He kissed me, neither timid nor forceful, with perfect confidence and ease. The simple fact that I knew how to kiss him back was thrilling beyond words.

Soon we were on our sides, legs tangled, hands grasping. I remembered the moments from Sunday when I'd had him on the brink, graceless with desire. That was my only requirement. I needed Didier half-insane with lust when he took me.

I slung my thigh over his hip, and just as I'd hoped, he was hard. I rubbed against him and the reaction I earned was unexpected—a deep moan, a fundamental shift in how he felt. He rolled me onto my back, breathing harsh, eyes wild.

Things started happening very quickly. Shirts were wrestled away, my skirt stripped, his pants kicked aside, belt buckle jangling to the floor. Socks and underwear and my jewelry were shed until it was just two panting animals atop his covers.

Awareness set in. Not panic — clarity.

I was naked. He was naked. There was a naked, gorgeous, aroused man braced above me, knees between mine, hard cock at the ready. I'd always dreamed but never quite dared to hope that such a man might be the one to do this with me for the first time. Now that it was actually happening, I felt such a potent flash of gratitude I thought I might cry.

Everything about him was right — his chest hair, the smell of his skin, the weight of him, his soft voice and hard muscle. This was how it was meant to happen. I'd waited just shy of thirty years to arrive here with this exact man, and if the tenement blew down before he took me, I'd wait another thirty for such a perfect moment.

With a warm, possessive palm on my hipbone, he swept the head of his cock along my lips, slicking wetness over my clit.

"Ready?" he asked.

"Can we go really slow?"

"As slow as you wish."

"Then I think I'm ready."

He nodded and leaned over to take a condom from the bedside table, sat back on his haunches to open it. The scent of latex was out of place in this drafty garret, with its pretty glass bottles of oil and carriage clocks and carved bedposts.

I watched him roll the condom down his thick length, slow and practiced. It was a far sexier moment than I'd guessed, less a sobering intrusion of etiquette than a gesture of affection. Respect. It didn't detract from the atmosphere at all, only made it more real.

"This is how you want me?" he asked. "Above you?"

"Yeah."

"This is how I imagined it too." He lowered again, bracing his arms tight against my sides, just as I'd fantasized.

"You've thought about it?"

He smiled. "Of course. It's exciting, being your first. This is special for me as well. But if that feels too personal, I won't make a big deal of it."

"No, I don't mind." I didn't mind at all. The only thing that could've made losing my virginity to Didier any better would've been believing the act meant something to him beyond another greedy woman in his bed, another night's work.

"Bring your legs up," he said softly.

I hugged my knees to his thighs and he reached between us to grasp his cock.

"Ready?"

"I'm ready."

The moment arrived. The head of his cock pressed at my entrance, feeling far different than his fingers. Scarier and sexier at once.

"Breathe," he whispered, backing off.

Right, yes, that. I did my best to relax, knowing it might be the key to a pleasurable first time versus a painful one. I stared at the cock intended for the task. Ambitious. I imagined him disappearing inside me and the lust grew, crowding out all nervous thoughts.

"Good." Didier's knuckles brushed my clit as he guided his crown between my lips once more.

A push. A twinge, but not the one I'd anticipated—too deep to be my hymen, and more like a cramp than anything being torn. I held Didier's arms, needed to feel grounded in him. "More."

Another inch and a strange new sensation. *Fullness* is too stupid a word. It felt like *violation*, only nicer... A lovely, thrilling intrusion. He gave me more and the pain arrived, a mean cramp and the small, unmistakable sensation of something surrendering in my body, welcoming him deeper.

My sharp "Ooh" gave him pause.

"It's okay," I said. "Just a cramp. It'll pass."

He was still and steady as I waited for the pain to fade. I watched him, the swell of his abdomen as he breathed, the patient, dark expression on his face. And his cock, half buried in me, obscured by his hand. Jesus, what a man.

"It's going," I said.

"Good. Whenever you're ready."

I stroked his arms, sinking back into the mood of this moment. "How does it feel for you? How do *I* feel?"

A grin—shy, if I wasn't mistaken. Cute. "You feel wonderful. Warm... Your body feels hesitant," he added, "just like your heart."

I smiled at that.

"More?" he asked.

"Yeah."

He withdrew first then slid back inside, infinitely easier than before. "You're very wet."

"Because I want you. And this." I aimed my gaze between our bodies.

Didier pushed again, another inch intensifying that feeling of intrusion. No cramps came and I relaxed further. The exotic slide of his body inside mine as he withdrew, the intoxicating pressure as he claimed me again...

Oh my.

I was having *sex*.

"Bring your knees up, if you can." He urged my calves higher and I raised them to his waist. When he thrust again it felt entirely different—smooth and easy. His muttered "Yes" sent a happy shiver all through my body.

He set a slow pace, taking me a little deeper with each push, until at long last our bodies met, utterly. He dropped to his elbows, burying his face against my neck and letting me wallow in him. This strong, big man momentarily weak. I combed my fingers through his hair, suddenly the reassuring one. I felt his cock...the heat of his skin against my lips, even the faint pulsing of his hard flesh inside me. Tick, tick, tick, a clock counting down to whatever was to come.

His head came up and he stared into my eyes. Something burned there. Something male and primal that made me high. Fuck feminism. I'd stay monogamous to him the rest of my life if it meant I might get to see this look again, be made to feel I was his sole possession. His territory. Whatever might make his eyes narrow at another man who wandered too close, whatever set a growl humming in his throat.

Enough with the gentle deflowering. I wanted to get *fucked*. "Take me."

He straightened his arms and edged his hips closer, spreading my thighs even wider. Still slow, he began to thrust again. For a minute or two I merely watched, recording it all in my mind, these new sights and scents and feelings. I hesitated before sliding a hand between us. I didn't want this to be about me coming, or to stress myself out by trying too hard to make it happen. But what if I *could*? And not just for my own pleasure, but for his... How smug could I make this man?

I circled my clit with the pads of two fingers, and it was extraordinary. Far different with Didier inside me. Everything felt taut and intensified. I glanced to his table.

"Yes? Do you need something?"

"Just a little of the oil."

"Not with the condom. Here." He pulled out, leaving my body cold and hungry as he grabbed a smaller bottle. I put my hand out and he dripped slippery liquid onto my fingertips.

I waited until he'd replaced the bottle before touching myself. As he slid deep, I teased my clit with the lube.

His dark eyes took it all in.

"Caroly." Brows drawn, cheeks flushed, a vein rising along his neck. Didier is even more perfect when he's a mess. "Do you think you could...?"

"Come? I'm not sure, but I'll try."

He nodded.

"You feel wonderful," I said. "It doesn't hurt at all. Feel free to take me however you want."

His lips parted with words that never came. If he felt as I did, he held those thoughts back because they were too loaded, too tender for people in our complex position to share. I ached to tell him any number of inappropriately earnest things. Our bodies would have to express the feelings too risky to utter aloud.

He took me faster. Not rough, not yet, but the speed was enough to tell me I'd like that...a forceful man. I abandoned my clit to wrap my thumb and finger around his cock, at my lips. I measured him, objectified his heat and stiffness. As I went back to touching myself, his thrusts grew harsher.

"Didier."

"Okay?"

"Yes, very."

He sat back on his haunches, candles drenching his torso in warm, wavering light. He held my hips as he pumped and the vision was...*gah*. Those tight, hard muscles are gorgeous at rest, but *fuck*. Surely this was exactly what God had in mind when designing the male body.

As I watched him, he watched me. His tongue wet his parted lips, his nostrils flared, his throat twitched with a deep swallow.

"Let me," he muttered. My fingers were pushed aside as his larger, rougher ones took over.

So much of sexual pleasure comes from the spasms of the brain, not the flesh. His fingers worked wonders but it was watching him that brought flares of pounding heat to my clit. His touch merely stoked the fire, kept it glowing. A glance at his eyes, his chest or hips, a moan in his deep voice…those bits of evidence were what had me tight and antsy.

"Do you like it," he asked, "my being rough?"

"Yeah."

Again, his lips taunted me with words they wouldn't share.

"What?"

"I want… I'd like to take you from behind. If you're willing to try."

How about that? I'd driven Mr. Whatever-You-Wish to dirty requests. "Sure, I'll try. I'll miss the view though," I teased.

"Would you like a mirror?"

"Oh." I blinked. "If you have one."

"I do." He left me to cross the room to his tall mahogany wardrobe. He opened one side to reveal neatly hung shirts and a full-length mirror on the inside of the door. He angled it, glancing at me.

I got to my knees. "There," I said, when the bed was centered in the reflection. Studying his naked body as he returned to me, I was suddenly beyond intrigued by the idea.

"The way you look at me," he said, climbing onto the bed, "made me think you would like to watch."

To watch *him*, yes. My only fear was that my own reflection would distract me, that I'd not like how I looked paired with a man so breathtaking. Too much reality, too much chatter from my brain…

I needn't have worried. I dropped to my hands and knees, facing the headboard, our bodies reflected in profile, but all I truly saw in the mirror was Didier. The shape of his hip, the curve of his ass. The shadows playing on his arm and back, his handsome face. And the way he *looked* at me, looked *down* at me. Hungry but patient. A predator.

And heck, a nervous glance told me I didn't look too shabby myself. Pale gold in the candles' glow. We made a rather pretty portrait of hunter and prey, I decided.

The weight of Didier's hand on my hip took my attention off our reflection and back to our reality, here on this bed. He edged forward on his knees until the fronts of his thighs touched the backs of mine. His thick, hot cock slid between my legs—not taking me, but brushing my lips and clit. My eyes shut, not opening until I felt his head at my entrance. I looked to the mirror and the sight of his face cast down, hand guiding his dick, muscles flexed.

"Didier."

He sank deep, the angle smooth and natural. As his hips met my butt, the contact electrified me. I reveled in this helpless feeling. He took me again, again, and the force that accompanied each thrust was honest-to-Christ the hottest thing I'd ever felt.

Before long he was fucking me as fast as before, and I was high.

In the mirror I watched my fantasy come to life in his pumping, greedy body. His moans started low and shallow, growing deeper and harsher by the minute. He became more than the man I'd paid for, more than the one I'd honored with this privilege. He was hot and strong and selfish, all things male, personified.

"You're wet." I loved the way he said it, as if he were accusing me of something. "I want to feel you come on my cock."

I gasped as he stooped to wrap an arm around my waist, fingers on my clit. His touch matched his driving shaft, fast and masterful. After a dizzying minute, he stopped.

"Forward." He nudged me with his legs and I shuffled closer to the top of the bed. "Up," he said. I braced myself on the headboard. The view of the mirror was ruined but something better took its place. Didier leaned into me, damp chest and belly against my back, free arm curled around my ribs. I felt everything a woman should—owned, spoiled, protected, exploited. I didn't need to see him. The most gorgeous man on the planet he may be, but I had everything I needed from Didier in this union.

His fingers knew exactly how to tease me and it wasn't long before a miraculous realization dawned on me. I was going to come. I was having sex and I was going to have an orgasm—be given an orgasm—by Didier. The world's biggest sexual fusspot was getting laid and, how do you fucking like that, it was hot.

"Didier."

His arm tightened around my waist, thrusts short and rapid. "Are you going to come for me?"

"Yeah. Just keep doing exactly what you are."

"Yes. Please." Oh, when he begs...surely no drug feels that good. "Come," he whispered. "Come for me." He said it over and over, plea morphing to a command as I began to shake. My sweaty palms slipped along the headboard, arms trembling.

"Make me come."

"I will. I will."

And he did.

No crashing waves, no ripples of ecstasy. Violent pleasure tore through me, a whiplash at my clit that bloomed and radiated through my belly and chest, down my arms and legs to my fingers and toes. I felt possessed. I felt like *his*. And goddamn, I felt like a woman.

He'd slowed everything when I came, and as the mania faded I heard him. Heard his crazy breathing, smelled his sweat and the sex we'd created. I craned my neck to see what my climax had done to his face. One glimpse at his wild eyes was all I got before he kissed me.

As we broke away, I knew what I wanted.

"Sit back."

He let me go and did as I asked, and I shuffled around to face him.

He'd made me feel a million things, and being dominated by him physically had taught me what had been missing the previous time I'd tried to suck him. We'd made it too much to do with my comfort, and now I knew that wasn't what the act was about. It was about service, and I wanted my second chance, my "some other night". He'd shown me the commanding, merciless man he was, and I wanted to worship him.

I settled between his legs, and after some slippery fumbling he intervened and took the condom off for me. He didn't ask if I was sure, if I was ready. He just held his cock as I put my mouth to his head, groaned as I slid my lips down his shaft.

It wasn't a beautiful show, I'm sure, but my enthusiasm couldn't be faulted. I took him, embracing everything inelegant about it—the acrid taste left by the latex, the ache in my jaw, the stilted breathing. I felt a little demeaned, a little helpless, a little used when he gathered my hair, smoothing it away from my face for a better view. But those things were so much nicer than *comfortable*.

"That's good," he whispered.

Keep talking, please keep talking.

"Suck me. Suck the cock you waited so long for."

Perfect, filthy words. I sucked him as hard as I could, welcoming the bump of his fist on my chin as he stroked himself.

"Oh, Caroly."

I hoped he was watching us in the mirror. I hoped he was memorizing all of this and that five years from now he'd still remember me, doing this to him. Wherever each of us was, I hoped he'd wonder what had become of the weird American woman who'd come to him to be corrupted and got exactly what she was after.

"Fuck. Yes." Barely words, soon lost to gasping grunts. His strokes turned rough as his hips begged for me to take him deeper. I granted the wish as best I could, and that strong man unraveled to a frantic, quaking animal from what I was doing to him. The hand in my hair became a fist, his other palm pressed to my neck, trembling.

He went still as stone as he came. A hot spurt, a gasp, another taste. After three spasms his hold went slack and he slid his cock from my lips. I swallowed what he'd given me and stared at the beautiful wreck I'd reduced him to.

I wanted to dance around the room and sing, "I did it, I did it, I did it!" but instead I watched him recover with a silly grin on my face. After a short while he dragged me down to lie with him, cupping my head to his chest and planting kisses on my hair. I listened to his heart and willed mine to beat at the same pace. It worked.

No one said anything for a very long time, not until my body grew cool and sleepy against his.

He cleared his throat.

"Well," I said.

"Well. We never finished our wine."

I laughed. "No, we didn't. Guess we got distracted."

He pushed onto his elbow to stare down at me. "You did not bring an overnight bag."

"No."

"If you won't stay the night, after all this, at least stay and help me finish the bottle."

"Sure."

We dressed, and everything I felt was right. Shy, relieved, energized, proud. Even sore. The tenderness in my sex was welcome, because it was Didier who'd given it to me. He carried the candles back to the living room and I fetched the wine, then settled against the arm of the settee, my bare feet on his thigh. I turned my glass around in my hands, so completely, simply happy.

"You have a very mysterious smile right now," he said. "Like a certain Italian woman who lives in the Louvre."

I pursed my lips but they soon blossomed to a grin. "I'm very content, that's all."

"Oh?"

I nodded.

"So it was what you'd hoped?"

"It was fantastic. And it's just nice to... I don't know. Not 'have it over with'..."

"To be part of the club?"

"I guess. Or just to feel like, yes, I'm a woman now. I'm okay. I used to worry and wonder, will it ever happen? And if it did, would it be because I'd get desperate and settle for someone I don't really like?"

"That would be a shame. It's sad what a burden some people make of their virginity these days, a defect. They are so eager to have it done with they'll sleep with whoever's willing, far too young. Sex is not as sacred as I would wish."

So says the man-whore...but of course, he has every right to say such a thing. I'd expected someone in his position couldn't help but be jaded about sex, yet this man speaks of it with the reverence of a monk.

"How old were you, when you lost yours?" I asked.

"I was young, sixteen I think."

"Was it with a girlfriend?"

Didier nodded. "It was love...or what passes for love, at such a stupid age." He smiled faintly.

"Since you, you know...came into your profession. Have you had any relationships? Or do the two just not mix?"

"I have." He nodded slowly, eyes unfocused, as if a videotape were playing in his head. "It's not easy."

"I'll bet. She'd have to be like, jealousy-proof."

"You have to be careful, that's true. I have dated two women since I became a prostitute, two very different women. The most important thing is to establish primacy, I think. When I've dated I cut down on how many clients I saw, and how often. I wanted to make sure my girlfriends got more time with me than my clients. I did my best to prove they came first."

"Did it work?"

"One relationship did not work so well. No matter what we tried, she could not get over what happened when she was not with me. We had a no-speaking policy about it, pretending it was not happening, and of course that failed. We had two hopeful months and another very painful one, then we went our separate ways."

"What about the other one?"

He smiled in a fond way and bit his lip. "The opposite. She asked to hear about the other women. It excited her. I respect my clients' experiences and I like to keep them private, aside from the most general details, which frustrated her, I think. She mistook my confidence for secrecy. But overall, that went quite well."

"Why did you break up?" My heart froze. *Had* they broken up? Yes, yes, of course they had. Past tense. *Calm down, Caroly.*

"We broke up after perhaps six months, when she became interested in a colleague of hers."

"Were you sad?"

"I was. But I had seen it coming. She was wonderful in some ways, very free and exciting, but also I knew no single man could keep her attention forever."

"Did either of them ever ask you to stop, you know..."

"Only the first woman, the jealous one. She offered to help pay for my flat and expenses, if I gave it up."

"But you wouldn't?"

He sighed. "It's hard to explain why I wouldn't. Why I still won't. Part is pride. I'm not willing to be a kept man. But more so—and I fear it sounds like a lie—but this work is important to me. It sounds as if I am trying to elevate it, pretend it's more than the thrill of sleeping with a lot of women and getting paid for it. But I really think what I do is noble, in its seedy way."

"I believe you."

"I also do not know what else I might do, for money. Modeling is nice, but the wages aren't comparable."

"No, I'm sure they aren't. But could you see things ever changing? Like you meet a woman you want to marry and all that? Someone who changes your priorities? Sorry, I'm not saying you should—"

"No no, I did not think you were." Another sigh, and his forehead wrinkled in frustration or bewilderment. "I do not think that will happen. Not the way things are now. I have not organized my life in such a way that there is any room for a wife. I can't offer that."

"Can't or won't?"

He met my eyes, smiling an apology. "That depends on whom you ask, I suspect."

I nodded, ready to abandon my interrogation. I could sense I was putting him on edge. Like earlier in the evening when I'd asked him about fatherhood, a wall rose between us.

"I should get going pretty soon," I said, swirling the last swallow of wine in my glass.

"That is a shame. Will I be seeing you again?"

"Yes, I hope so. Maybe Friday?" I held my breath, wondering if Fridays and Saturdays were, I don't know, *reserved*. For premier clients.

"Friday is fine."

"Oh good. I was thinking…and forgive me, I don't know if you have policies about dates or anything. But would you ever be interested in maybe meeting for a meal or a drink somewhere? On me, obviously."

His smile faded and my heart sank.

"Sorry. Are public things against how you…operate?"

"It's not quite that. And trust me, I would be happy to be seen with you at a restaurant or a bar, on a date."

"Oh."

Didier's lips quirked in the tightest, saddest smile. "My hesitation has nothing to do with you."

"You don't have to explain yourself. I was just curious."

"No, I owe you an explanation, for that question and others. And please believe me, I'd very much like to go out with you somewhere for one of our dates, but I can't."

"Okay."

Didier swallowed and met my gaze squarely. "I haven't left this flat in nearly three years, you see."

I stared at him for I don't know how long, struggling to make sense of what he'd said.

"I've lived in Paris for two years…" I trailed off.

"Then I was already a year into my exile by the time you arrived."

How on earth was that possible? The time since I'd moved here had been the most vibrant and exciting of my entire life. All those months and more, and he'd not set foot outside this apartment? I pictured him here, snow falling past the windows in the dark winter, sun beating the panes at the height of summer. Generations of pigeons marching past and Didier never leaving these walls.

"Really?"

He nodded.

Curio

I remembered what he'd told me about the pet shop and the fish. What was he really, aside from an isolated, pretty distraction, anyone's to possess for the right price? Was this flat just Didier's ocean, reduced to a tiny tank, his meals bestowed by kind acquaintances? Did he fear he'd die here, some routine inconvenience for whomever was in charge of handling such unpleasant inevitabilities?

"You look upset," he said.

"I'm... I'm surprised. Okay, and upset. It's a very sad thing to hear."

"Apologies."

"What set it off? Or was it gradual?"

"Gradual, throughout my life, but then all at once I couldn't leave at all. The last time I left, something terrible happened." He emptied the last of the bottle into his glass. "I was waiting to cross the street, a half a block from here, and so was a woman and her small child. Before the light came on to tell us to walk, a friend passed by and I started talking to her. And when the woman and her son crossed the street, they were struck and killed by a car that didn't stop for the red light."

"Oh my God."

"Yes. It was very...graphic."

"I'm sorry. That's horrible."

He spoke to his glass. "It was also barely a week after my mother passed away, and for a long time, checking on her had been one of a very few things that got me out of the flat. I've always been anxious about being outside, in big spaces, with traffic and busy sidewalks, in the Metro... The accident took everything I feared and avoided, and multiplied it so greatly, I simply haven't been able to leave. Even talking about it now..." He held up his free hand and I could see it trembling.

"How do you get the things you need?"

"I have friends and clients who pick up groceries and other things for me, and take my laundry out, go to the bank.

On a good day, I can make it downstairs to collect my own mail. Every other day, perhaps."

"What if you need to go to the doctor?"

"I pay a steep surcharge to have my doctor come to me."

"No offense, but that's no way to live."

He met my gaze. "No, it's not. But if you don't have that fear, it's impossible to understand it."

I considered that, and my own fears. "I sort of understand. I mean, I've got social problems. With men, obviously."

"But you're braver than I am. You're trying to change." He smiled. "Perhaps that makes me your therapy."

"Actually, yeah. That is how I've thought about it."

We were quiet for a minute then Didier asked, "Do you pity me?"

I stared right into his eyes. "No. Well, maybe. I'm not sure. But is this what you want, to never leave these four rooms?"

"No, of course not. All the time, I try to leave. I make it halfway down the hall, maybe even to the front door, my hand shaking on the knob…then an idea comes into my head, of seeing someone robbed, a car crash, an animal being hurt, simple rudeness. All these injustices and disasters, things I have no control of. Though of course at the time, I think nothing so rational. I feel as frozen and terrified as I might with a train speeding toward me. But I don't even fear for myself, really. I don't fear death. I fear helplessness, of being in the midst of a bad situation, and being unable to do anything about it."

"And it doesn't make you feel helpless, not being able to leave?"

"Of course it does. But it's far worse feeling helpless in the face of other people's cruelty or carelessness."

I know what he means. Every balanced, empathetic human knows that frustration and shame and anger, witnessing assholery. The shame of not challenging it, or the powerlessness of knowing your actions won't change anything fundamentally. I tried to imagine multiplying that nauseating, worthless sensation by ten or fifty or a hundred, and having to endure it. I'd hide in my flat too. Probably under the covers. With a bottle of gin.

"Do you feel like the bad people are what keep you in here?"

He shook his head. "I know it's only me. It is my fear of experiencing those ugly feelings that keep me here. It's a terrible, suffocating fear that maybe I'm right. Maybe the world is as senseless as it feels, and if I go outside, I'll find proof of that. I fear the potential of what *could* happen, if I left."

"Oh."

"But of course, locking myself in this flat proves nothing. But I cannot explain it any better than I have."

"You don't need to." My goodness, how did he stay in such fantastic shape? Sit-ups? There was a rack of iron weights in the corner of the living room, but sex wasn't enough cardio for a man in his thirties, was it? So many questions... "Were either of your parents that way? Agoraphobic, or whatever it is?"

"It did not occur to me until recently that my mother likely was, but not the way I am. Like me, she hates the unknown. But the space she called familiar and safe was all of Paris, whereas mine is merely these few rooms. But yes, take her away from the streets she knew and loved, and she got very mean, very edgy and snappy. When I was growing up, I thought she was just spoiled and demanding. Selfish for not taking me traveling. Now I know better. And she always loved men from other countries. That must have been the only tourism she knew how to indulge in. Men and books and films, and her foreign language tapes."

I nodded.

"But I don't blame her for the way I turned out. This is just how I am. Who I am. I've always liked going inside, more than out, to explore. Inside objects. Inside people, in whatever manner you wish to take that—emotionally, sexually." He sipped his wine. "It feels safer inside."

"I'm sure."

"This flat is almost like my body now. The idea of leaving...it would feel like walking around without any skin holding me together."

"Yikes."

"Being exposed, outdoors... It's always done something to me. Made me so poor with direction, because I can't focus outside. When I am out there, there is just *so. Much.* It is like being barricaded in a room with fifty televisions turned on, all loud, all on different programs."

I remembered my first visit to New York City and the anxiety attack the crowds in Times Square had given me. I'd wanted to run back to the Met and spend the rest of the trip hiding in the relative quiet of the galleries, where the frames and plinths and soothing-voiced docents herd you, guide you, instill order.

"I think I understand. It's an awful shame though. You're really quite an extraordinary man. It's sad so few people get a chance to know you."

Didier's nostrils flared with a tight, harsh breath, his gaze darting around the floor and our legs.

I leaned forward to touch his knee, offering a kind smile. "I'm glad to be one of the lucky few though."

"I'm glad you are too." He looked up, glancing around as though just realizing where he was. "Well, here we are again. On a date that I've dampened with my stupid rain clouds."

I laughed. "Not at all. You're far better company when you're imperfect. And much less intimidating."

"No one should be intimidated by me," he said with a crooked grin. "I am just some strange, broken man born with my mother's good genes. And her bad ones. I'm one of those watches, fine on the outside, but my gears…"

"Someone put you back together wrong?" I offered.

Didier covered my hand with his and gave it a squeeze. "Yes, I think they did."

"It's okay. That's how my mother was too. How she is, I mean."

"She's still alive? The way you spoke about her before, I thought she was not."

"She is. But we rarely talk. On Christmas, basically. For a while she was doing well, living at a residence. But she left and went off her medications, and she's back to how she was when I was a teenager. She's living alone in New Hampshire, probably raising hell for her neighbors." I drained my glass.

"That's very sad."

"It is. I have an older brother who lives two towns away, where I grew up. If he wasn't keeping an eye on her, I'd be worried. But he's always been good with her. Plus he's a *gigantic* guy. He can handle her when she's in one of her really dangerous moods."

"You haven't talked about your brother."

"No, we were never super-close. He's twelve years older than me and moved out when he was sixteen, so I don't remember ever living with him. He's a good guy, but I don't think we'll ever have that bond. What about you? Any siblings?"

"Three half-siblings. Two sisters and a brother, who all grew up in Portugal, with my father."

"Younger than you?"

Didier pursed his lips.

"No?"

"Older," he confirmed. "I suppose you might say that my mother was my father's mistress for a summer, though I do not think she knew he had a family back home."

"Oh my."

"When she got pregnant, he told her everything. I do not know exactly why she had me... To spite him or perhaps to try to keep him, because I do believe he's the only man she ever loved. It's easy to forget sometimes, that our parents were ever as young as us, younger. She was even younger than you, when I was born. But needless to say, I was not welcomed warmly by my stepfamily those few times I went to visit. I did not even understand who they were. I thought this must be my aunt and my cousins."

"God."

He nodded. "It was all very confusing. But my father was a good man. I'm sure it was not his choice for me to be born, but he didn't keep me a secret. He did his best to make things right, though there was really no right to be found, in that situation."

"Well, my parents did everything the way you're supposed to. High-school sweethearts, engaged while my dad was in college, married, bought a house, had my brother. They checked every box in the right order, and it still fell apart."

"But they raised you, and you're successful."

"I guess I'm on my way. But the first twenty years of my life I was a real train wreck. If I hadn't fallen in love with art, who knows what I'd have gotten into."

"Well, I'm so glad you did. It's brought you here, to Paris. And here," he added, waving a hand to mean the flat.

I blushed. "I'm glad too. Everybody dreams of having some amazing love affair in this city. I did too. Then I started to think it'd never happen. But now it sort of has, just not quite in the way I'd imagined."

He held his glass out and I clinked it with my empty one.

"What's it like," I asked, "being with someone as inexperienced as me? Do you feel any different about it than you would a woman who's already had lovers?"

"Of course I do."

"How so?"

"Well, I feel a bit possessive of you, I suppose."

My body roused at the notion.

"And I do feel... What's the right phrase? Full of myself."

I laughed.

"I won't pretend it's not a thrill, knowing you waited so long, and that you picked me. And that I'm the only man you've known. I think that is engrained in a man, to wish his was the only cock a beautiful woman would ever want or ever feel."

"You really think I'm beautiful?"

"I do. You do not?"

"No, I don't. I'm less of a freak than I used to be, but I don't think I'll ever look in a mirror and see what's there now. Only what I grew up seeing."

"Well, I think you're very beautiful. You have very soft hair." He draped his arm along the back of the couch to smooth a curl behind my ear. "And this." He traced my jaw and cheekbones with his finger.

"I hated that when I was little. I was always mistaken for a little boy, even when I had long hair."

"In the art and fashion worlds, interesting faces are treasured. Androgyny too. Are people surprised to find you're American?"

"Yeah."

He nodded. "I was too. Surprised to see you at my door, after your postcard said you're from the States. You look...I'm not sure. Dutch, perhaps. Pale and haunted."

I laughed.

"Americans are so robust, we think. Soft and pink-faced and smiling and loud. You are none of those things. Although I do occasionally see the pink in here." He leaned in and held my face, running his thumbs across my cheeks.

"That's your fault."

"Oh yes, such a scandalous man I am." He let me go to sip his wine.

"Can I ask how you started...you know. It started with modeling, I imagine."

He nodded. "It did. It always held much appeal, any money I could make at home. Even before the incident."

"Of course."

"It began as a favor of sorts. The line between posing for a photo for someone you're attracted to, someone you might sleep with anyway... They blended together. A woman who paid me to model for her drawings came here every week, and things evolved, as they do. But some sessions, we did not get around to the drawing." He bit his lip, his shyness charming me. "But she still paid me, those days. That's how it happened. And once such a thing happens a few times with a few different women, those women become clients, and word gets around. And I won't lie, I enjoyed the attention. Whether I'm wanted for a photo or a painting or in someone's bed, the excitement to me is the same."

"I see."

"I want to be whatever people wish of me. Perhaps because I'm so broken in other ways. And actually, you... You're the first client I've had in a very long time where I do not feel as if I'm playing a part. Maybe that first night, but even then..."

"Well, I have no idea what I want. That probably helps."

He smirked. "And here I thought perhaps you just wanted me, exactly how I am."

Never has a sentence filled me simultaneously with such sadness and delight. My lips trembled as I returned his smile. "Perhaps I do."

"I've gotten so used to modifying who I am for women, I lost myself a little. Being with you feels very nice. I feel very pleasantly naked, like a costume has been removed."

"I'm glad." I wanted to tell him so many things—how not only did I feel I've rediscovered who I am, in this flat, but that maybe I never even knew who I really was until I met him. I was like one of his projects, busted and hollow until I arrived here, opened up and cleaned and put back together the right way, reanimated.

For a long time we sat in thoughtful silence, until Didier finished his wine and a deep yawn overtook me.

"It's time?" he asked.

"I think so."

I got my shoes on and he walked me to the door, as always. To the edge of his aquarium, as far as he could go without risking asphyxiation.

Didier took my hand. "Much has been said since we spoke about seeing one another on Friday. Do you need time to rethink anything?"

I felt my eyes widen. "What? No." I laughed. "I don't feel any different, knowing all that. Well, I do, but I certainly don't think any less of you."

"No?"

I shook my head. "I think you're lovely. I'd like to see you on Friday. Is there… Do you need me to bring anything? Wine, or anything else?" Anything, anything at all.

"Would you like to bring an appetizer, perhaps? It's supposed to be cold and rainy, I heard on the radio. I could make us soup, if you'd bring something as well."

"Perfect."

"Not so perfect as this evening." Didier stooped to kiss me, light and fond.

It occurred to me anew—I'd just lost my virginity. "Indeed. Thank you, again."

Another kiss and we bade one another goodnight, sweet dreams.

After I turned the corner to the stairs and heard his door close, I doubled back. For a minute or longer I stood staring at the iron panel beside the elevator, before I finally pushed the call button. The car rattled and clanged, every terrible noise a promise of my violent, plummeting demise.

At least I wouldn't perish a virgin.

But when the death-cage squealed to the fifth floor, I hauled the folding gate aside and stepped in. My heart hammered all the way to the foyer, yet when I wobbled down the steps and into the cold breeze, I felt lighter. Slightly nauseous, very shaky, but dizzy with delight as well as adrenaline.

I passed couples on my way to the subway, and though my chest ached to know I'd never enjoy even the illusion of such a thing with the man I adored, I couldn't feel poorly. I'd had sex tonight, and ridden in an elevator. I may not ever hold hands in the streetlight with a handsome man, but I would be okay. Every day, I was more okay.

And every day, I felt more and more like the woman I've always wanted people to think I am. The woman I want to be.

Friday
The Fourth Visit

℘

I spent thirty-five euros at the deli up the street from my museum, on cheese and fruit and salty meats and fancy crackers. That's fifty dollars' worth. Easily enough money to feed me for an entire week, but the pretty packaging seduced me, as always.

I felt a bit inadequate, not having had time to make something impressive from scratch, arranged just so on in a pretty dish. But in the end, showing up with a plastic sack full of self-contained deliciousness was best, as the rain Didier's radio had predicted touched down as something closer to a monsoon.

I arrived nervous and excited as always, if perhaps wetter than usual. We kissed and he asked me about my day. I felt strange when I asked him the same, knowing he'd been here, only here.

"It was a quiet day, until the storm arrived," he said, taking my dripping umbrella. "You look nice."

I laughed, looking down at the leggings plastered to my thighs, the puddle forming beneath me. "Thanks. You too."

Didier looked far better than *nice*, of course. And that night he was wearing jeans, which appealed to me far more than I'd have guessed. Such an any-guy piece of clothing, when I'd grown so accustomed to this exceptional man verging on formal. But goddamn, he looked good. Cozy.

Which was perfect for what I had planned. I pictured my pajamas, folded in my overnight bag. Cozy, cozy, cozy.

"Wine?" he asked.

"Sure. And I have to get my half of dinner put together, if you've got a platter and a cheese knife."

He set me up at the butcher block and uncorked a bottle. The kitchen already smelled fantastic from whatever soup was in the pot on the stove.

"Wow," he said, watching me unloading the various goodies on the wood.

"I went a little crazy in the shop."

"And I was worried I would not have enough to feed us both. Here." He handed me a glass.

"Thanks. Cheers." We clinked. "I have a favor to ask you tonight."

He sipped his wine and set it aside. "Anything."

"Tonight…" I took a breath, petrified to utter my wishes. "I was hoping I could pretend you're my boyfriend."

Didier smiled in that way that exploded inside my chest, my heart a water balloon full of warm, squishy pleasure, bursting. "Of course."

"But I mean, I guess… Just be how you'd be, with a woman you've just started sleeping with. I trust you, sensing what my boundaries are. You seem to know what they are even before I do sometimes."

"Okay."

"So no asking me permission before we do anything we haven't before. Anything you want to initiate, please just do."

"Very organic."

"Exactly. I don't want to be reminded that I'm calling all the shots, you know?" And I didn't want to be reminded that I was paying to get whatever I wanted.

Didier didn't nod, didn't utter an agreement. Instead he skirted the island and took my jaw in his hands and kissed me, brief but forceful. He licked his lips as he stepped back.

"That was exactly what I wanted," he said.

Heat rose, flooding my cheeks. "Good."

"May I be frank?"

I nodded.

"I'm very attracted to you."

The blush burned hotter. "Oh?"

"And you're asking me to treat and approach you as if this was not all under your direction, everything done with your permission already tendered."

"Right."

"So please tell me, honestly, if it's too much. If I come on too strong. What you and I have done before... Nothing is an act with me. I'm a passionate man."

"I know. I just want to know what it feels like, hanging out with the man I—" I stopped, knowing the word I'd nearly used was *faaaar* too loaded. "The man I'm sleeping with. I don't want to drive, is what I'm trying to say."

"Very well. But don't hesitate to change your mind, if I am too fast for you. I would hate to sour our time together, just being myself."

I laughed as I spoke. "It would take a lot to undo the good you've done, but thanks for your concern. I'll tell you if it's too much, I promise." I turned my attention to the cheese.

"Right. That is all I will say about it for the rest of the evening. From this moment, unless or until you change your mind, I am just your lover."

My lover. I pursed my lips, a shiver giving me goose bumps despite the warmth of the room.

Didier clapped once. "But enough of this. You are my girlfriend. Let us worry about dinner first, before I make a panting fool of myself, yes?"

I nodded officiously. "Yes."

He started toward the stove then stopped short, turning to grin at me.

"What?"

"So you are my girlfriend tonight?"

"I am."

"And does this mean you are finally sleeping over?"

Oh, swoon. "I guess I could. I mean yes, I am. I brought pajamas and bathroom stuff."

His grin deepened. "Pajamas. That's adorable. Do you have little slippers with rabbits on them as well?"

I blushed. Of course this man must sleep nude. I made my tone snotty. "They're very nice pajamas. Very sophisticated. And if you tease me like that you won't get to see them." Oh my crap, was I actually *flirting* with someone?

"Understood." He circled and came up behind me, wrapping his arms around my middle. I felt a kiss at the crown of my head, my temple, my neck.

"You're very good at taking liberties," I said.

More kisses, then gentle, silly gnawing at my shoulder. It seems the real Didier is far more of a goofball than I'd expected. Not a criticism. He kissed my ear, a great barrage of noisy smooches designed to annoy.

"I'm armed, you know." I sliced the cured sausage demonstrably.

He straightened behind me. "You wouldn't dare castrate me. I know what it is I can do to you."

I smiled to myself. "Perhaps."

"Plus I am your boyfriend tonight. And that would make you a very lousy girlfriend." With a final peck on my cheek, Didier let me go, stealing a fingerful of triple crème brie as he went to check on his half of dinner.

"What did you make?" I asked as he lifted the lid.

"Onion soup, with mushrooms."

"Yum."

Curio

"I hope so." He stirred and tasted it, added a splash of sherry and a few shakes of salt. He replaced the lid and fiddled with a knob, then came to lean on the far side of the island. I rapped his knuckles with a nearby whisk when he tried to steal a strawberry from the carton.

"Wait 'til I've got it all arranged."

"You're a very abusive girlfriend."

"You love it."

He laughed then switched on the radio while I sliced the rest of the fruit and cheese and meat. I fanned them in arches, alternated with the overpriced crackers.

"This is a feast," he said.

"Yeah, I didn't know when to stop. They kept plying me with samples and my basket got heavier and heavier. Okay, I think we're ready."

Didier doesn't have a dining area, so we pulled up stools and ate at the island. Every last thing I tasted was exquisite and I ate enough that a stranger might assume I was in my second trimester. I didn't care. Didier was my boyfriend and I was happy. I told him some war stories from the museum, about the weird things rogue patrons try to get away with. It was more satisfying than the wine or the food, hearing him laugh and knowing I'd inspired it. And as another boyfriendish liberty, he lapsed into French now and again, and I let him bear witness to my abysmal accent and any number of improperly conjugated verbs.

As the nibbling wound down, my thoughts turned to other treats. What would be different, when Didier took me later? How different would his approach be when meeting my every delicate need wasn't the order of the night?

He set his napkin aside and sighed. "That was delicious."

"It was. I need your soup recipe now. I don't even like onions, but that was amazing."

"You don't like onions? I wish I'd known. I'd have made something else."

I shook my head. "Nah. I enjoy being converted. And I enjoy the idea of not telling you what I *think* I don't like, then you surprising me, and proving maybe I do like things. I like being proven wrong."

"You are talking about more than just onions?"

I shrugged. "Maybe."

He smiled at me and narrowed his eyes. "You're different tonight. You're very... I'm not sure. Cunning."

I laughed. It was an adjective I'd never have assigned to myself in a million years. But I suppose he was right. I did feel a bit devious.

"Have you started fiddling with the clock yet?" I asked.

He nodded. "It needs a new part, I'm afraid. I will look through my catalogues and see if I can find a replacement. But otherwise it is in very good shape. Very interesting construction. Like you, it is somewhat simple on the outside, and an intriguing, complicated mess when you open it up."

I tried to fake offense but was smiling too much to pull it off.

"But I'll soon understand you both, every tiny spring and wheel and pin."

"I'm afraid it'll probably take more than a replacement part for me to ever make any sense, but good luck to you."

He bumped my knee with his then stood. "Let me put away the leftovers."

I helped him with the food and the dishes. I will say this about Didier—he's quite handsy. Any chance that arose as we puttered, he had a palm on my ass. Again, not a complaint. With any other man it surely would be, but with Didier it only reminded me how it might feel to be pulled hard against him as his cock sank deep inside me. Anything that tricks me into thinking I'm his, for real.

"You're very frisky tonight."

He smiled, hanging up a dish towel. "Apologies. I assumed I was meant to be your boyfriend of four dates, not thirty years. But if not, we can brush our teeth and fall asleep reading by nine o'clock…"

"No no, frisky is nice."

He backed me up against the sink and kissed me. "Oh good." More kissing, more handsy. He backed off at length to say, "Your clothes are still damp."

"I know. I better change before that hot soup wears off."

"Do you need something to wear?"

As unreasonably sexy as the thought of flouncing about in one of Didier's oversized shirts was, I declined. I'm not a flouncy girl. Maybe someday, but not quite yet. "No, thanks. I think I'll deem you worthy of seeing my pajamas."

I grabbed my bag and changed in the bathroom, into the new PJs whose price would give my father heart failure, considering it's basically a camisole and drawstring shorts. But come on, Turkish silk satin! And my exact favorite color, greenish-grayish blue — just like in Paul Klee's *Blick Der Stille* — and with tiny embroidered white-and-orange fish scattered all over. I know that sounds weird, but trust me, they're awesome. And since I bought them before Didier told me about his goldfish, it all felt rather serendipitous. So worth having to eat cheap pasta every night for the foreseeable future.

Thank goodness I don't have any credit cards, lest my penchants for artisan cheese and Turkish silk and Parisian men tempt me away from reason. Which, sadly, they are on the verge of doing. I needed to talk to Didier about that, but not just then. Perhaps in the morning.

I found him in the living room, cuing up a record on his gramophone. He angled the old-timey brass horn and noticed me behind him.

"Oh. Those *are* adorable."

"They've got goldfish on them."

He smiled and approached to inspect my ensemble. "*Il te rehausse les yeux.*" *It brings out your eyes.* He rubbed a thumb over the shiny satin and one of its little fish. "You'll be cold, though. Do you want a blanket, or shall I turn the radiator up?"

"A blanket's fine."

And that's how the evening went. We sat on the couch, sipping wine, chatting and listening to the croony old records Didier had inherited from his mother. I pictured her as a French, brunette version of Marlene Dietrich, though that assumption was likely the fault of the music. Still, in my head she spent endless hours perched before her vanity, smoking and brushing her hair, lamenting the failure of a recent love affair, all in grainy black and white.

After an hour or so of lazy flirtation, Didier found us a deck of cards and taught me to play *piquet*. I did terribly, but he kept kissing me so I don't think my poor performance was strictly my fault.

Didier is very…playful. Off the clock, as it were. He's also very convincing, which would probably have worried me if the pleasure it inspired hadn't been so potent.

Rarely while I'm with Didier—but often after I've left, perhaps the following day—will it occur to me exactly what he is. I'll catch myself thinking of him fondly, then an ugly part of my brain will pop in with, "Don't be an idiot. You aren't actually dating him. Plus think about it. You saw him Thursday, Sunday and Tuesday. Who was he with those other days?" I would wonder, "Does he like them more? Are they prettier or more exciting than me?"

But funnily enough, the thoughts always slip, like an egg off a greasy pan. For the first time in my life, I'm not jealous of the other women in a fantastically handsome man's bed.

As we sat playing cards, I put my finger on the crux—Didier's body isn't sacred to me.

When all this had begun, that was all he'd been—a body, one I'd been prepared to suffer a less-than-stellar personality in order to enjoy. That he's kind and likeable was merely a bonus. But it took shockingly little time for his body to become incidental, and the thing I anticipate now goes far beyond his physique or face or even his skills in bed. It's how he makes me feel...like a woman worthy of his extraordinary company. And the glow from that lasts far longer than any post-orgasm haze.

It's scary, because I never expected any feelings I might develop for him to go beyond the sexual. I assumed the sheer fact that he's a whore would erect a wall and keep my heart safely on one side.

No such luck.

When yet another hand of *piquet* dissolved into a make-out session, he took our cards and tossed them on the coffee table. I was hauled onto his lap, back to his chest. Didier in boyfriend mode moves quite a bit faster than his professional self. His cock was hard from the kissing, feeling impatient against my backside.

He put his mouth right behind my ear, breath hot against my skin. "I want you."

"I want you," I murmured.

His hand glided up my slippery top to cup my breast.

I fumbled and turned around, straddling his thighs.

He fondled me as we kissed. I felt one tiny strap slide over my shoulder, then the other. Satin slipped away, replaced by his palms.

His lips left mine to find my ear. "I want to taste you."

"Okay."

A happy, cocky noise heated my skin.

I thought I could guess which words would come next—*where, how, in my bed?* Silly me. I'd forgotten who I was with tonight.

Didier leaned over to grab a throw pillow from the chair, tossing it to the far end of the couch. He ousted me from his lap. My heart beat fast as I leaned against the cushion, nerves and excitement stirred together, capped and shaken. Exactly as I'd longed to know how he looked naked, how he kissed and tasted and sounded in person, now I wanted to know how he'd feel, taking me simply as himself.

Just as I got my camisole hoisted back up, he was slipping free the bow of my drawstring. I lifted my butt and let him slip my shorts down my legs. He pushed the coffee table away, kneeling before the settee. A week ago I'd have been afraid of how I looked or smelled or tasted, but not tonight. Not seeing that gleam in his eye, that expression that told me I was far more exquisite a delicacy than any you could sample at the cheese shop.

I ran my fingers through his hair as he brought his face close. His nose glanced my clit, then his lips, his tongue. It felt nothing like I'd imagined. The opposite of sloppy. He indulged me with caresses, soft and teasing, deep and decadent, hungry and insistent. I felt imperious with this man on his knees before me. Utterly spoiled.

Spoiled felt wonderful...for ten minutes or more. Then my attention was drawn beyond his face to this room, the flat; his private world, where I'd learned far more than the mere mechanics of lust. As good as his mouth made me feel, I wanted more of him. At a gentle push on his shoulder, he let me go with a final deep lap.

"Stand up."

He got to his feet.

"Take your shirt off." As he did, I freed his buckle, brushing his hard cock as I opened his fly. When his jeans were kicked away, I clasped his erection through his underwear and gazed up at him. Marvelous. I've never before met anyone whose outside so matched their soul. You could drill clean through Didier and find nothing but layer upon layer of beauty, dark and strange and kind and prurient, but all of it perfectly, utterly pure.

I stroked him for the sheer pleasure of feeling his weight and heat in my hands, until his breathing grew labored and he spoke.

"I need to fuck."

"Good."

He pulled me to standing, pressing our bodies tight together, that bossy palm on my rear. "*À mon lit. Maintenant.*"

As ordered, I headed for his bedroom, his energy right behind me, tangible as echoing footsteps. No candles tonight. No patience. We tumbled across the sheets and my camisole went missing, followed swiftly by his briefs. Being trounced was as lovely as being seduced, perhaps even lovelier after so many nights of caution and gentle firsts. At moments I felt we were nearly wrestling, fighting to be the one touching, kissing, stroking. Kneeling, he pulled me onto his lap, his cock pinned against my pussy. His hands issued orders, drawing my wet lips along his shaft, friction so hot I scraped my nails down his back in retaliation and bit his ear.

He groaned and pushed me onto my back, leaning over me to open the bedside table drawer. With a smooth stroke he was sheathed, half a breath and he was at my entrance.

"Didier."

He sank deep, claiming my cunt with the smooth, sure thrust of a lover who'd known me for ages. No pause for reverence. He took me fast, not quite rough, until I was dizzy and frantic and high.

"Fuck me," he said.

One forceful flip and I was on top of him, no time to worry about my performance. No need. All I needed was to feel this hard, thick cock moving inside me. I gave my body everything it wanted from his, shutting my eyes and letting his moans and murmurs fill my ears. His fingertips grazed my thighs, my belly, my ribs, finally my breasts. The brush of his palms over my nipples set my whole body on fire. My clit was rubbing his base with each motion, and though I wasn't practiced enough to make myself come from it, just knowing maybe someday I *could*, that someday I *would*, filled me with giddiness.

"I want you like the last time," I said.

"On your knees?"

"Yeah." On my knees, with a rough, selfish man taking me from behind.

The moment his cock slid from me, I wanted it back. But first I got his hands on my hips and ass as I was turned over, his thighs nudging mine wider. When he took me again I sighed from the sheer, dirty completeness I felt.

"Make me come."

That voice, low and dark. "I will."

The sex was hot and fast and noisy, a flurry of slapping skin, his moans, my whimpers. I hadn't known I was capable of sex like that. Animal sex. There were a thousand things I hadn't thought I was capable of, not until I'd found the one key that fit my lock. I came hard against his taunting fingertips, the deepest, scariest orgasm I've ever experienced. When I recovered, he urged me onto my back.

"*Regardez-moi.*"

I did as he ordered, eyes on his laboring muscles in the dim light leaking from the living room. I watched the only man who'd gotten to know my body this way, watched him grow frenzied with lust until he couldn't hold on, then watched him succumb. He ground our bodies together as he came, so hard my hip may bruise. If it does, I'll miss the mark when it fades.

He tumbled from me in a sweaty heap, stripped the condom and grabbed me around the middle. Powerful arms held me close, possessive and familiar, and after a few wordless minutes Didier whispered, "Spend the night."

"I will."

He sighed and released me, rolling onto his back. "Oh good."

"You knew that already. I brought my pajamas."

"Yes, but it's nice to hear it again. Perhaps I should hide all of your clothes and your shoes, in case you change your mind..."

I propped myself on my elbow and smiled at him. "You really care that much about my sleeping over?"

"Very much. I want to make you coffee. And see you with your wonderful curls, all wild against my pillows."

My grin deepened.

"I want to see you with your hair wet from the shower, and the morning light in your eyes when you wake."

I hope everything he says is true. I hope he's not just lonely. Or that my company only feels so good because he's forgotten what it's like having friendships and romances, out in the real world. Then again, this flat is real. I've had some of the most genuine and eye-opening experiences of my life inside these walls. And damn it, *I'm* real, this night more than ever. Maybe I *was* alluring. Maybe I ought to quit letting my decades-old insecurities dilute every wonderful thing he says and just fucking believe the man.

I used the bathroom and put my pajamas back on. As I joined him in bed, the world felt lovely. He wrapped his naked body around my satin-clad one, and he was my boyfriend. I'd dreamed of sleeping with a man exactly this way for half my life, and here I finally was.

It really had been worth the wait.

* * * * *

I woke as the sun broke through the curtains, and I felt so much. Cool silk on my skin, Didier's warm arm cradling mine, a sweet soreness between my legs once more. I rolled over and stroked his chest until his eyes opened.

"Good morning."

"Hi. This is your chance to see me with my hair a mess, before I take a shower."

He tousled it, gaze taking me in. "Very nice. Thank you." He squinted at the window. "My goodness, I don't know when I was last awake at daybreak. Or indeed asleep by midnight."

"Keep sleeping if you want. Do you want me to go down to the baker's and get us breakfast?"

"That would be very nice, if you don't mind. Let me know when you're leaving, and I'll bathe and make us coffee."

I nodded and left him in bed, stealing a long look before I exited. This was exactly how Didier ought to be styled — stripped to the waist in the morning light, sage-green sheets wrapped around his legs. Click, click, click went my mental camera.

It was nine by the time we'd showered and dressed and pastries and coffee were served in the living room. I picked at my croissant. Worry had caught up with me at the bakery, right as I'd handed my money to the clerk.

"I need to talk to you about something," I said.

Didier set down his mug. "Oh?"

I shifted in my seat, addressing the hands fidgeting in my lap. "I won't be able to come by as often as I have. It has nothing to do with wanting to. Or from getting to know you better, or the sex, or any of that."

His forehead wrinkled. "All right…"

I laughed sadly. "I just can't afford to." My throat was tight, heart hurting to admit aloud what we are, what's brought us together. I'd let it become so much more in my mind. Even in my gut. But it had always been just checks slipped in his mailbox, hadn't it?

"I'm very sorry to hear that."

I nodded. I wasn't foolish enough to expect to be told I needn't pay, or that I merited some discount. I didn't want to hear anything that underscored what a transaction this entire arrangement was, behind the glittering veneer of romance.

"I would always welcome your visit, no matter how infrequent," he said.

"Thank you. I'd still like to come by, just not this often."

"Of course. And that's very normal. Usually when I meet a new client, we see each other several times very swiftly. Then soon enough it slows, one, two, three times a month."

It made me inexpressibly sad to be told I was typical. A typical *client*. I felt my heart retreat, like a little crab scuttling back inside its shell.

"Though I won't lie," Didier went on. "I've become rather attached to your company."

I looked in his eyes. "I think I've learned more about myself in the past week than I'd gotten figured out in almost thirty years, so thank you. I'm a better person for having met you."

A look of great melancholy transformed his handsome face. "This sounds very much like a goodbye."

Was it? Did he know what I ought to? That the time for deluding myself was over? "I don't know."

"Perhaps you're ready to go out and find a real man."

"You're real." I said it loudly, too loudly, panic hijacking my voice.

A weak smile. "You don't need to protect my feelings. You deserve a man who is capable of taking you out. Literally *out*. You come here and all I can give you is a few hours of make-believe. I can't walk you out that door and take you to dinner, see where you live and work. You deserve far more than what I can offer."

I was near to tears, because of course Didier *is* what I want, in enough ways to let me overlook anything he may lack, for better or worse. Plus he's the only man I know how to be with, and I'm not sure those skills are transferrable.

"But I do love your company," he said again. "And you're always welcome here."

I nodded, confused. Was this a breakup? Was Didier giving me the diplomatic brush-off with this talk of his inadequacies, our collective impossibility? He could probably sense how attached I'd grown. The notion that perhaps I ought not come back to this flat felt likely, and terribly heavy. I suppose he was only ever my training wheels, an illusion of capability. Out in the real world, how badly might I fall and mangle myself, attempting an actual romance with an actual, available man?

I stood. "I guess I'd better head home soon."

"Would you like me to wrap the pastries up for you, or any of the cheese?"

"No, you keep them. Thank you for the coffee."

As I turned to begin gathering my stuff, he got to his feet and grabbed my wrist. "It feels as if everything changed just now. Did I say something wrong?"

I stared at his collar, afraid of his eyes. "No, you're perfect. I'm sorry. I'm just sad that I can't come as often as I have been. It probably sounds pathetic, but this has been the highlight of my life the last week or so, my visits here."

"I hope that is not pathetic, as they've been my best days as well. Though if it is, we'll be pathetic together."

Didier always knows what to say, but at that moment, nothing could neutralize the pain I was feeling. The grief.

"I, um…"

He rubbed my arm, waiting as I swallowed my fear and assembled words. "I've had a wonderful time with you. More wonderful than is probably wise."

"What do you mean?"

"I like you, a lot. Enough that I probably need to step back for a while and remind myself, you know… About what we really are, I guess. Not to freak you out or anything, but if I keep seeing you this much, I'm going to fall in love with you."

A lie—I was already in love with him. Jesus Christ, give the frigid girl four nights with a French prostitute and what happens? Like I never drank a drop, then one pub crawl and I wake up with cirrhosis. "I'm losing perspective, the more I see you."

"I understand." Surely it's happened before, with any number of his clients. Didier gave my arm a final rub and let me go to collect my things.

Neither of us quite knew what to say when we met at the front door, but he kissed me, soft and slow, fingers tangling in my damp hair. It morphed into a hug, and he whispered, "Goodbye, Caroly."

"Goodbye."

Wednesday
Any Other Normal Day, Yet Not

ℬ

Things sucked for a few days.

Once I left Didier's flat on Saturday morning, I felt lost. I felt unsure of who it was I'd said goodbye to, and unsure if I might see him again.

He'd cut me loose—I just knew it. I'd heard it in his voice. He'd cut me loose and I couldn't help but wonder which of us he thought it aided.

The second I left him, the emptiness arrived. I missed Didier in a way I hadn't known it was possible to miss anyone, short of them dying. And I missed more than his body or company or the anticipation or the sex—I missed how I simply felt around him. How I felt about myself, and the new person I'd begun blossoming into. I mourned her loss too.

Plus I'd made such a full-time hobby of fantasizing about him and replaying our time together, I was at a complete and utter loose end and nothing felt fun. Nothing sounded like the thing I ought to be doing. Nothing tasted or smelled or sounded very good anymore. My soul had the flu.

The arrival of the work week was a relief. And by the time I woke this morning, my symptoms had eased. My heart had quit actively hemorrhaging, but it still hurt. It simply hurt more quietly.

I share an office with the head curator but she was busy elsewhere that day, so I had the cave mercifully to myself, free to mope without witnesses. Normally I grab lunch from down the street and eat with Ania and Paulette next door, but I wasn't feeling up to their energy just yet. There were plenty of pending emails to fill an hour and keep my thoughts from wandering into the dark, dreary corners of my head. I'd use them as an excuse for staying in, should my friends catch me walking by the gallery on my way back from the deli—

My phone rang.

"Caroly Evardt."

It was one of the girls from the front desk. "*Quelqu'un vous attend à l'entrée.*"

A visitor? Ania, likely, with gossip that couldn't wait another moment.

I thanked the girl. I picked up my purse then put it back, lest my friend try to talk me into a so-called quick coffee.

But when I reached the lobby, my heart froze.

Didier.

Didier, in shoes. In the sunlight and the vastness of the building.

As I approached the front doors, he smiled and raised a hand.

I felt I could only half recognize him here. He looked like a photograph of himself, those brown eyes Photoshopped brighter in the daylight. As though he were a painting finally restored, a million long-lost details emerging to dazzle the viewer.

"Hi," I said.

"Hello." He bent to kiss my cheeks. I could tell he was nervous. That normally warm smile was tight and twitchy, jaw set.

I goggled at him a moment. "You left. You left your flat."

He nodded. The lobby is huge and was especially chaotic this afternoon, guests streaming in for the opening of a controversial new exhibit. I wondered if I ought to bring him somewhere smaller and safer, my office or the archives.

"Is everything okay?" I asked.

"It is. Is it okay that I've come here? I know some of your friends know what it is I do. You can tell them we know one another from a gallery event, if you—"

"No, I don't care about that. What's going on?"

He cleared his throat and stood a little taller. "I came to see what you're doing for lunch. If you're free to eat with me." He lifted a handled paper bag. "I made sandwiches. I did not think I was ready for a restaurant yet, but maybe the park...?"

This wasn't easy for him. All his typical ease was gone, his posture rigid, eyes alert, bag and hand shaking faintly.

"That's what got you to leave your place? To ask me to lunch?"

Another smile, slow and nervous. "Yes. So I hope you'll say yes."

"Is it a date?"

"That is my wish."

I felt... I felt like a pomegranate sliced open, all my ruby-red capsules spilling out, sweetness leaking everywhere. I felt like a beautiful, delicious, sticky mess.

"Like a regular old...date?"

Didier nodded.

"I'd like that. I'd like that very much. Let me get my purse."

I went back to the offices and I swear I was floating, walking two inches above the tile and wood and carpet. And there he was when I returned, right where I'd left him. How about that.

"Ready?" I asked.

He crooked his arm and I linked it with mine, and we strode through the automatic doors.

"How do you feel?"

His gaze panned the veranda and sidewalk, the intersection. "I feel better than when I first left the flat. But nervous now, letting you see me this way."

"I can tell you're nervous. But I don't mind."

The park was just across the street, and I watched his face as we reached the curb and waited for the walk sign. His gaze was trained hard on something in front of us, expression simultaneously blank and intense.

"You're doing great." I gave his arm a fortifying squeeze and to my great relief, he looked down at me and smiled.

Parisians are kamikaze street-crossers, and businessmen streamed past us on both sides, happy to take their chances with the lunch-hour traffic. Our light came on and I was mindful to look both ways. I took Didier's hand, feeling a bit like a guide dog. But he's led me to so many new and scary places, it felt nice to return the favor and be the confident one for him.

People talk about hearts fluttering, as soon as we stepped onto the opposite sidewalk, danger officially over, mine did. It absolutely did. I felt the opposite of that stupid, stubborn grudge that keeps me from making eye contact with handsome men. I was giddy, knowing I was so obviously *with* Didier. Lovers, hand-in-hand. Even if my lover was pallid and wide-eyed and trembling at the threshold of a panic attack.

We found a nice spot on the grass in the shade, sitting hip to hip, facing the fountain. The pigeons spotted us. They must live for that noise—the rustle of a paper bag. Beggars flapped and landed, watching us from a pushy, patently European distance.

Didier eyed our stalkers. "Oh dear."

"It's okay. I don't mind them. They remind me of your little nosy neighbors, on your roof."

"I worried so much about the people, I forgot about the animals."

"I'll protect you." I grabbed a stick and waved it at the birds, scattering them, if temporarily. "I'd hate for you to leave the house for the first time in three years and get some weird pigeon disease."

He grinned at me. "It'd be worth it."

I laughed, blushing. "That's very romantic. I think."

We unwrapped the picnic he'd prepared, and I didn't press him for more insight about his feelings, not just yet. We ate in silence, watching the children and shooing the birds.

I finished the first half of my sandwich and licked garlicky mayonnaise from my fingers. "This is delicious, thank you."

He laughed. "I made this lunch three times."

"How do you mean?"

"I made it on Monday and Tuesday, and again today. Today was merely the day I managed to get past the front steps when the taxi began honking for me."

He'd wanted to see me this way as early as Monday? Two days after we'd said goodbye? "And today you just…could?"

He smiled at me, eyes crinkling. "This morning I just realized it hurt more, missing you. More than it hurt to deal with the fear."

"You missed me?"

His grin deepened. "You look surprised."

"I am."

"I did miss you. Very much. More than I'm used to missing people, especially those I've known such a brief time."

"Oh."

He pursed his lips and squinted thoughtfully before going on. "I like the way you treat me. And the way you look at me. Like you're looking *into* me, not merely at me. I'm sorry, that does not make much sense."

"No, I think it does. I like that...and I do think that's how I see you. I mean, I came to you because of how you look, obviously. But I like the rest of you even more."

"The man who cannot leave his house?" he teased.

I raised my arms, gesturing at the vast blue sky. "But you did. Here you are."

He nodded and looked away, seeming shy. "Here I am. Two weeks and you've gotten me to do what no one's managed in three years. Without even asking me, or pressuring me. Begging me. I don't know how. It astounds me. Thank you, Caroly."

I mumbled an inadequate, "You're welcome," my cheeks hot with pride and pleasure.

We didn't speak again for several minutes, Didier taking in the action around us. "I forgot how it smells outside. When I first left the flat, it was the petrol. But here, the grass, the air...I gave all this up for so long. I forgot how a real breeze felt."

"Now you get to appreciate it more than anyone else in the whole city." *Like a parolee*, I thought.

"Perhaps. That is a nice way to look at it. I like the way you look at all kinds of things," he said. "You must gaze all around you, putting frames around different people and places."

I smiled. "Maybe subconsciously."

"Cataloguing beauty," he mused, watching me with a mysterious gleam in his eye. He sighed. "I wish we could go down to the river."

"We could."

"Maybe. But not today."

"Something to work toward."

"Perhaps this weekend," he said. "If you would like to spend the night on Friday or Saturday—as just, you know. Not as we have been. More as we are today?"

I nodded. "Sure."

"And then maybe you could help pry my hands from the front door so I may leave again."

"I'll bring a crowbar."

As he laughed, I read deeper into what he'd said. Did he not have clients to see on Friday or Saturday? And if not, was that incidental or because of me?

"I would like to see your flat sometime," he said.

"You're welcome to. Though I'll warn you now, it's tiny and stuffy and my bed's not really designed with guests in mind. But I live above a bakery, so at least it smells nice."

"Charming. I'd like also to see you again, this way. Out like this, though hopefully when I'm not so..."

"Shaky?"

He nodded.

"I'd like that too."

Didier opened a glass bottle of lemonade, took a deep drink then passed it to me. He seemed to hesitate before saying, "What I am is not so secret, in your crowd."

"No, especially not to my friend Ania from the gallery. She's got a whole fan-girl binder full of prints, just of you."

"I did not know I had fans."

"She's quite rabid. And she doesn't know I've been seeing you. I better have a talk with her, if it seems like we're all destined to cross paths."

"Are you sure you're comfortable with this? With us being so public?"

"Yes, it's fine."

"Really?"

"I don't care what people think. Do you?"

He shook his head.

"I'd only mind if you felt badly about it. I'd like you to be who you are. It doesn't matter what others think."

"It matters to me, what you think."

"Well, you're fine then. I like who you are. And I'm not going to waste my time worrying how I might feel about it in the future. In fact, at the risk of sounding shallow, I'm proud to be seen with you. You're the best-looking man I've ever met." I rubbed his back. "And I've spent so much of my life being boring, it might be fun to be part of a scandal."

Didier stared at the sky for a long moment.

"How are you feeling?"

"I'm...I'm breathing." He looked back at me. "I haven't slept very much since Saturday morning. It's beginning to catch up with me."

"Maybe once you get home you'll be able to relax, with this behind you."

He nodded. "I haven't been to my mother's grave since her funeral, and I thought after I saw you, I would try to do that. Then I suspect I'll take a taxi home and have a nervous breakdown. And after that, maybe sleep for a day or two." He smiled sheepishly.

"That sounds like a good plan. I wish I could come up with some excuse and get the afternoon off, but I have to help host a cocktail party for some of our donors. A new exhibit opened today."

"Yes, you said."

"You're more than welcome to come, of course."

Another smile, deeper and more reminiscent of the man I've come to know. "You're kind, but I'm not there yet."

"I didn't think so. Just wanted to show you off."

He laughed.

"I'll settle for a coffee this weekend. Maybe the river. Whatever you're up for."

Didier tossed his crust to the pigeons and stowed our wax paper and bottle. "Lie down with me."

We reclined side by side on the grass and he laced his fingers with mine. I stared up at the sky. I was holding hands with the most beautiful man alive, watching the clouds drift past miles above Paris.

In a few days he'll greet me at his door, take me to bed…maybe to breakfast. Perhaps in a couple weeks' time I'll arrive and find him waiting for me on his stoop. At a bistro down the block. On my own doorstep.

We lay there for an hour at least, until I knew I was really pushing it. I squeezed his hand and sat up.

"Back to work?" he asked.

"Sadly."

We stood and brushed the grass from each other's backs.

"Are you taking a cab to see your mother?" I asked.

"I was going to, but now I think maybe I'll try to walk. It's not far." Didier dug a map from the bag and consulted it, murmuring street names to himself. The cemetery he traced a route to wasn't far at all. I was tempted to offer to escort him, but he must have felt naked enough already. After three years, he deserved to revisit his grief in private.

I walked him to the far end of the park.

As we reached the curb, he smiled down at me. "Here I go."

"You'll be fine. Three blocks straight, two blocks left. Three blocks straight, two blocks left." I repeated it a few times, making up a cheesy little tune and pumping my fists as if I were marching in a musical.

He laughed. "You tease, but I will use that."

I picked a stray blade of grass from his collar. "There's a florist's on the next corner. For your mom."

A slow, thoughtful nod. "That's a nice idea."

For a long moment we both stalled, then I took hold of Didier's shoulders and turned him toward the crosswalk. "Well, off you go."

"Off I go. I'll see you this weekend? Friday?"

I nodded. "You will. Thank you so much for lunch. You know, and for coming out to see me. It means an awful lot. Way more than I can say." And if I tried any harder to explain it, I'd surely start crying.

"Thank you for making me willing to. Really..." He trailed off. I could tell he wanted to say more as well, but it was too much on top of whatever crazy adrenaline high or anxiety attack he must have been mired in.

I stood on my tiptoes and kissed his cheek, stepping away as a large group of tourists began to cross en masse. With my gentle push, he merged into the safety of the throng.

He stopped and waved from the far sidewalk. I waved back. I watched him turn away. I watched him walk all the way down the block, until his sweater was just a dot of gray in the crowd. The most extraordinary man in a city of two million. In all of Europe or the rest of the wide world.

I hoped he'd stop at the flower shop, maybe do as I always do and spend far too long there, sniffing all the blossoms. All those scents and colors he'd left behind until today. I hoped they'd feel new to him all over again, as new as the excitement swelling in my middle.

A beautiful young clerk might flirt with him as he browsed, but she'd never see what I did. She'd see only his shiny shell, snapped shut to hide a jumble of secondhand parts, ticking not quite as they should, but ticking nonetheless. A bit rusty. A bit erratic, like my heartbeat in the moments before I press his buzzer.

As I aimed myself back toward the museum, I pondered what I'd wear on Friday. What I might bring as an offering, for our date.

I wished I didn't have to go to the party that afternoon. I wanted the workday to be done so I could walk to the shops and get lost, browsing the aisles for treats. Something fancy and overpriced from far away, that Didier would never have tried before. Something to remind him of the places that lay beyond the bricks that made up sixteen Rue des Toits Rouges. He'd opened me up inside those walls, and now I prayed I might do him the favor of helping knock them down.

The sun was hot on my hair, bright in my eyes. The breeze was cool with no promise of rain. The sky was blue as hydrangea, wide and high and limitless, and all of Paris belonged to me.

Also by Cara McKenna
ഔ

eBooks:
Backwoods

Brazen

Curio

Dirty Thirty

Don't Call Her Angel

Getaway

Ruin Me

Shivaree

Skin Game

Willing Victim

Print Books:
Off Limits *(anthology)*

Stray Hearts *(anthology)*

About the Author

෨

Cara McKenna writes smart erotic: a little dark, a little funny, definitely sexy, and always emotional. She lives north of Boston with her extremely good-natured and permissive husband. When she's not trapped inside her own head, Cara can usually be found in the kitchen, the coffee shop, or the nearest duck-filled pond.

෨

The author welcomes comments from readers. You can find her website and email address on her author bio page at www.ellorascave.com.

Tell Us What You Think

We appreciate hearing reader opinions about our books. You can email us at Comments@EllorasCave.com.

Why an electronic book?

We live in the Information Age—an exciting time in the history of human civilization, in which technology rules supreme and continues to progress in leaps and bounds every minute of every day. For a multitude of reasons, more and more avid literary fans are opting to purchase e-books instead of paper books. The question from those not yet initiated into the world of electronic reading is simply: *Why?*

1. *Price.* An electronic title at Ellora's Cave Publishing runs anywhere from 40% to 75% less than the cover price of the exact same title in paperback format. Why? Basic mathematics and cost. It is less expensive to publish an e-book (no paper and printing, no warehousing and shipping) than it is to publish a paperback, so the savings are passed along to the consumer.

2. *Space.* Running out of room in your house for your books? That is one worry you will never have with electronic books. For a low one-time cost, you can purchase a handheld device specifically designed for e-reading. Many e-readers have large, convenient screens for viewing. Better yet, hundreds of titles can be stored within your new library—on a single microchip. There are a variety of e-readers from different manufacturers. You can also read e-books on your PC or laptop computer. (Please note that Ellora's Cave does not endorse any specific brands.

You can check our website at www.ellorascave.com for information we make available to new consumers.)

3. *Mobility.* Because your new e-library consists of only a microchip within a small, easily transportable e-reader, your entire cache of books can be taken with you wherever you go.

4. *Personal Viewing Preferences.* Are the words you are currently reading too small? Too large? Too... ANNOYING? Paperback books cannot be modified according to personal preferences, but e-books can.

5. *Instant Gratification.* Is it the middle of the night and all the bookstores near you are closed? Are you tired of waiting days, sometimes weeks, for bookstores to ship the novels you bought? Ellora's Cave Publishing sells instantaneous downloads twenty-four hours a day, seven days a week, every day of the year. Our webstore is never closed. Our e-book delivery system is 100% automated, meaning your order is filled as soon as you pay for it.

Those are a few of the top reasons why electronic books are replacing paperbacks for many avid readers.

As always, Ellora's Cave welcomes your questions and comments. We invite you to email us at Comments@ellorascave.com or write to us directly at Ellora's Cave Publishing Inc., 1056 Home Avenue, Akron, OH 44310-3502.

ELLORA'8 CAVE

Romanticon

Annual convention
for women who
refuse to behave

Discover for yourself why readers can't get enough
of the multiple award-winning publisher
Ellora's Cave.

Whether you prefer e-books or paperbacks,

be sure to visit EC on the web at
www.ellorascave.com

for an erotic reading experience that will leave you
breathless.

CPSIA information can be obtained at www.ICGtesting.com
Printed in the USA
BVOW010625281111

277048BV00001B/8/P